THE

CRYPTO

TRAP

BOOK FOUR OF THE GEOPOLITICAL TECHNO-THRILLER SERIES

ANDREW B. LOUIS

Several unlikely allies get together to bring down "CryptNotes" to "punish" terrorist organizations and their sponsors.

Copyright © 2022 by Andrew B. Louis

For information regarding permission, please write to:
info@barringerpublishing.com
Barringer Publishing, Naples, Florida
www.barringerpublishing.com

Cover, graphics, and layout by Linda S. Duider
Cape Coral, Florida

ISBN: 978-1-954396-33-3
Library of Congress Cataloging-in-Publication Data
The Crypto Trap / Andrew B. Louis

Printed in U.S.A.

DEDICATION

*To all authors who have built fictional thrillers
based on real current events.*

OTHER BOOKS BY THE AUTHOR

Other novels by Andrew B. Louis include:

 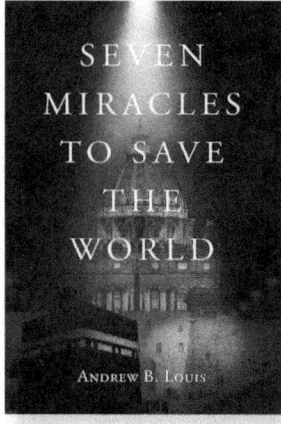 

Operation Kovesh, The Shadow Experts, Below the Surface, Glitter and Smoke (Coming 2023), *Seven Miracles to Save the World* and *A Crooked Few* available at Amazon.com.

www.AndrewBLouis.com

ACKNOWLEDGMENTS

Though all the writing and errors are solely my own doing, a number of people contributed to the creation of the text. I would like to thank the numerous friends and family members who were kind enough to comment on various drafts and led me to make material changes for the better. A special mention is reserved for my wife who labored through so many versions that I am sure she has lost count.

SYNOPSIS

A *Mossad* warning communicated through Countess Renate, the Founder and Head of the Shadow Experts, effectively saves the life of the Saudi Crown Prince. The discovery of Iranian markings on the missile that was used to bring the airplane down leads the Saudi Royal Family to conclude that they can no longer tolerate the attacks of Iran and their regional proxies. They decide that they need to hit as hard as they can, and recognizing the limitations of their military capabilities, elect to engage in a series of counter-terrorist activities, taking the totally out-of-character step of hiring Shadow Experts and *Mossad* to help.

Using high technology tools, a couple of which are created for the specific mission, the Saudis and their anonymous partners act on multiple fronts, a few involving almost traditional military-like actions, and several others dealing with unrelated fields, such as crypto-currencies. If undertaken individually, their actions might have led to a major global confrontation—World War III anyone? However, because these actions do not appear connected or to form a pattern, they do not bring the world to the brink of war. Will terrorist sponsors figure out the plot? Could this be the one strategy which had not been attempted earlier, often because conservatives do not frequently condone activities which involve terrorism or seem outside of a loosely understood global legal framework? Is this but the latest example, on a grander scale, of the role of the secret division of *Mossad* known internally as "Disruption?"

Preface: All the parties to this story are totally fictitious and if there was some resemblance with individuals or institutions, it would be purely coincidental.

PROLOGUE

TEL AVIV, ISRAEL, RIYADH, SAUDI ARABIA
AND SOMEWHERE IN THE AUSTRIAN ALPS

Saudi Arabia's Chief of Security, Abdul el Wahabi, was quietly sipping tea in his large office located on King Saud Street in Riyadh. The day was ending, the sun was already low in the horizon, and the outside temperatures had started to fall, making the air that much less oppressive. In fact, he was breathing a sigh of relief as the next several days were anticipated to be relatively calm. The Crown Prince, nominally in charge of the agency, was expected to leave the Kingdom for a short trip to Dubai, with some of his usual entourage. Of course, Abdul would still have to worry about the security of the entire Royal Family; the Prince's absence did not thus mean that the Chief of Security would enjoy a sort of holiday. Yet, the Crown Prince was the individual who was simultaneously probably the most active, the most visible, and the most controversial, thus the one of the few top members of the Royal Family who required the most assistance from Abdul's services. The Crown Prince, the seventh son of King Salman bin Abdulaziz, was young by local and regional royalty standards and probably even by normal standards; he was clearly slated to succeed his father, and he was prepared to shake a few of the old principles or rules which were in most direct conflict with evolving societal norms pretty much everywhere, except maybe, in the countries that were ruled under some form of theocracy.

Suddenly General Abdul el Wahabi was shaken back into the hard reality of his office when the phone on his desk rang:

"Colonel Abdul? Simon Rabinowitz, here."

■ ■ ■ ■ ■

Simon would not have needed to introduce himself. A previous joint-effort[1] during which he had already helped Colonel Abdul would still have been present in Abdul's mind. Abdul had in fact recognized Simon's voice right away; how could he forget someone who had allowed him to frustrate a deadly-virus-related attempt to blackmail the Kingdom? Colonel Simon Rabinowitz worked for *Mossad*, the Israeli Secret Services. He had recently been named Deputy Director of *Mossad*, while retaining his earlier responsibilities as head of a group which was responsible for the most secretive activities within the already quite discrete Israeli Secret Service. Internally, the group was known as **disruption**, though it did not appear on any organization chart that anyone could procure. Simon reported directly to Ariel Landau, the head of the agency. Simon relied on his own Deputy, David Heller, to help him in his disruption duties, as he took over broader agency management responsibilities. In fact, he had recently been named head of the agency, when General Ariel Landau had indicated that he would be retiring; with that appointment, came the promotion from colonel to general. However, upon the decision by General Landau to postpone his retirement by a few years, after his wife suddenly died, Simon had immediately agreed to have both promotions postponed. His first loyalty was always to the agency and to Ariel, his mentor.

---

[1] See "The Shadow Experts" from the same author, Barringer Publishing, 2021

■ ■ ■ ■ ■

"Colonel Rabinowitz, it's good to hear your voice. What can I do for you? You know the limitations under which I can cooperate, don't you?"

"I do, Colonel, I do."

Simon paused briefly and added:

"However, this time, I'm not calling to ask for help . . ."

Simon could almost hear the relief, which Abdul expressed in a sigh. Yet, that relief morphed into near panic when Simon added:

"I am calling you with an ominous warning. We have solid intelligence that terrorists are planning to shoot down the plane expected to be taken by His Royal Highness the Crown Prince on his upcoming trip, to Dubai I believe . . ."

Abdul was speechless for an instant. How could *Mossad* even know both the specifics of a trip by the Prince and its intended destination? He would have liked to come back more forcefully, but in the end he could only simply mutter:

"What? The Crown Prince? Can't be. How do you know? How **would** you know?"

Simon let go of a short laugh and added:

"Can't say I don't understand your surprise. I'm sure you'd surprise me, too, if you told me what you know about us."

He paused for a second or two and continued:

"Anyway, back to the point. You know I can't disclose my sources . . . at least not yet. But to help you take the warning seriously, let's simply say that we intercepted communications between people who aren't our friends; and seemingly not yours either. It made it plain who the target was and what they were planning to do."

He paused again, if only to see if Abdul would react. In fact, Abdul remained silent. So, he concluded:

"This is serious. We understand that a missile or more will be fired at his plane after it takes off from Riyadh. Most likely, they'll do it while the plane is over the Persian Gulf, but that much is very unclear, for now . . . The terrorists know there will be the usual, twin, air force jet escort, and that is why they're thinking of using missiles."

Abdul was totally confused. For a minute, he simply did not know what to say. Maybe, he did not even know what to think. One could imagine it was somewhat surprising for a man in his position to react in such a way. Yet, many people would argue the other side—he was in a state of shock, mixed with panic. Isn't that a normal human reaction? A successful attack on the life of the Crown Prince almost guaranteed Abdul that he would be the main attraction in a public beheading. In short, he was afraid for his life, not really confused. He would likely recover his spirits and his drive shortly, yet, at present, he only managed to ask with an almost meek voice:

"What d'you suggest I should do?"

Simon understood Abdul's quandary though he had never, himself, had to deal with a comparable situation. He gave him his best advice:

"I'd tell the Prince the truth, though you may not want to mention your own source quite yet. I don't mind. After all, you can also intercept other people's communications . . ."

Abdul grunted his agreement. Simon continued:

"I think the best thing would be to ask him to postpone his trip. Maybe, you could organize something that would make believe he is on the plane while he will in fact be safely on the ground. I can provide you with chapter and verse, but the priority must be to make sure His Highness is not on the plane."

Simon could feel that Abdul was still stuck in some disbelief. He added:

"By the way, I wouldn't worry about how this affects you. It's exactly your job to have friends who give you warnings. Just, maybe, a bit odd for that friend to be in *Mossad*."

Though Simon could surely not see it, Abdul still managed a meek smile before thanking him and hanging up.

■ ■ ■ ■ ■

Abdul had had the opportunity to deal almost directly with Simon, in the relatively recent past, through the good offices of Countess Renate, the founder and head of The Shadow Experts. He knew for a fact that *Mossad* always seemed to have excellent sources. He also knew that Simon was someone he had been right in trusting that last time. He had initially been reluctant to deal with a branch of the Israeli government, given the regional diplomatic realities. Yet, when he finally set the reluctance aside, he had been delighted with the results which Simon and Countess Renate were able to deliver.

Knowing as he did that the Crown Prince's plane was not scheduled to take off for another couple of hours, he still decided not to trust Simon fully yet. Rather, he called Countess Renate to get her advice. She picked up his call at the first ring:

"Countess Renate, here . . ."

"Countess, Colonel Abdul el Wahabi . . ."

"Abdul, what a pleasure. Anything I can do for you?"

Abdul gave her a rundown of the phone call with Simon, and then asked:

"What do you think I should do?"

"I wouldn't hesitate for a split second. I'd heed Simon's advice."

"How? I can't tell the Crown Prince not to fly to Dubai . . ."

"What makes you say that? You're the head of security. You've uncovered a plot against him? What else is there? Is this official business?"

"No."

"Then I suspect it can be delayed, can't it?"

"Well . . . I guess so."

Countess Renate paused for a few seconds after Abdul's response. Mischievously, she added:

"If His Highness really wants to go to Dubai, there may be a solution . . ."

Abdul interrupted, probably a bit too early:

"Ah! Wonderful."

"Hold it right there. There may be a solution, but it would take a few days to a couple of weeks to engineer if you want us to get involved."

Without waiting, for Abdul to react, she asked:

"Which plane will His Highness use?"

"Well, it varies. The Royal Fleet has eight aircraft, ranging from the smallest, a converted Airbus A318, to larger planes, you know, four Boeing 747, two Boeing 757 and one Airbus A340-200. All of them have certain defensive equipment, but that does not include error-proof missile defense; nothing like the kind of systems El Al has on its commercial aircraft, for instance. The plane is usually escorted, at least for a while, by a couple of fighter jets."

"Wow . . . Which one is he likely to use?"

"For short hauls such as a trip to Dubai, he would usually use the converted A318 . . . But wait a minute, why are you asking all these questions, Countess?"

"Simply to help you, my friend. If you want us to get involved, tell the Prince that a security issue has cropped up. Ask him to postpone his trip by a week or two and leave the rest up to me."

CHAPTER.01

SINGAPORE, BANGALORE, INDIA, TOULOUSE, FRANCE, AND SOMEWHERE IN THE AUSTRIAN ALPS

Countess Renata, aka Princess Alexandra, the orphan who had founded the Shadow Experts, had called a Zoom meeting with three of her Shadow Experts: Wong Hai Chock, otherwise known as a former professor and researcher at the National University of Singapore and now mostly a consultant, was her ultimate go-to resource whenever software or cyber security issues were a part of either the problem or its solution. Raj Agarwal, who lived and worked as a computer consultant in Bangalore in the state of Karnataka, South-central India, was her best specialist in computer hardware issues. The third individual, Francis Lefors, was, prior to his recent retirement, the senior aeronautical engineer at EADS—the maker of Airbus aircraft—and was now a member of the BEA (*Bureau d'Enquêtes et d'Analyses pour la Sécurité de l'aviation civile*), the French agency responsible for investigating all serious accidents involving non-military aircraft.

The point of the conference call was to discuss Countess Renate's solution to Abdul el Wahabi's problem. Indeed, just before hanging up on her prior phone conversation with Abdul, he had told her that any solution that would allow the prince to postpone rather than cancel his trip would be welcome. She wanted to know whether it was feasible to fly a commercial aircraft, more specifically an Airbus A318—the smallest aircraft in the single aisle A320 series—with remote, rather than onboard pilots. Though, on the surface, the question seemed crazy, she remembered work that had been done in Israel on something even crazier; after having developed drones as aircraft that operated without onboard human presence, Israel worked on adapting an existing drone to ferry a couple of humans, while the drones would still be controlled remotely. That was when the Sentinel RQ 170 had become the Kovesh.[2]

The choice of aircraft dictated by the Royal Saudi fleet would appear ideally suited to such a modification. Airbus pioneered the fly-by-wire approach to aircraft piloting and thus operation. Rather than relying on conventional manual and thus mechanical flight controls where a pilot's physical motion dictated a mechanical outcome, a fly-by-wire system uses an electronic interface which interprets a pilot's input as a desired outcome and computes the control surface positions and engine power required to achieve it. The system thus determines, sets, and controls the exact optimal combination of rudder, elevator, aileron, and flap positions together with the correct engine fuel flow, the latter driving engine power. While these computer systems can prove faulty, as the accidents with an early Airbus A320 or, more recently, the Boeing 737 Max demonstrated, they offer the opportunity to help focus the pilots' attention on what he or she wants to do with respect to aircraft altitude, speed and direction, sparing him or her the detailed inputs in all the variables under his or her control.

Countess Renate had always thought of the possibility of having pilotless aircraft. In the age of multiple drones, this did not seem like rocket science. Pilotless aircraft would eliminate at least one way for terrorists to interfere with air traffic: take-over the controls of a plane

---

[2] From the same author, see "Operation Kovesh," Barringer Publishing 2020

by overpowering the flight deck crew. Ostensibly, and unfortunately, there would still be ways for terrorists to place bombs in the luggage compartment of a plane, to board a plane with a bomb in their own cabin luggage, or to shoot them down. In fact, airline personnel at times argue that passengers might be more worried if the fate of the pilots controlling the aircraft was not inextricably linked to that of their passengers; in short, a valid question was: would the flying public accept travel in a remotely piloted aircraft?

■ ■ ■ ■ ■

Countess Renate started the conversation with a simple question:

"Is there a way for us to create a remote control operating system for an A318—and to do that in less than two weeks?"

All three experts' faces expressed stunned disbelief. After a few seconds which seemed to last almost an eternity, Francis Lefors was the first to opine:

"Countess, technically, it is possible, up to a point and given a reasonably limited range of required movements. Having all functionalities, including the reaction to unexpected technical failure, is still somewhat far away. For instance, I doubt that we could replicate Captain Sullenberger's famous landing in the Hudson River in 2009."

He paused for a second and added, with both eyebrows raised:

"Though, who knows?"

Continuing on his prior train of thought he said,

"However, the real question is this: I can't imagine how you would get it done **and** get operational approval in such a short time span?"

"Not a problem in this case. We're talking of a private aircraft . . ."

Francis came right back:

"Not so sure. Wouldn't you need an airworthiness certificate?"

"I see your point. Yet, leave that to me. I have a plan and that plan, if my assumptions are correct, would not require us to get a global or worldwide certificate."

"In short, you want us to assume that we won't need a certificate . . ."

"That or that getting a certificate will be a matter of routine . . ."

■ ■ ■ ■ ■

Soon after this conversation with her team, Countess Renate called Colonel Abdul el Wahabi.

"Abdul? I may have good news for you?"

"What is it?"

"Looks like the plan I briefly outlined may be feasible. At least, it hasn't been shot down yet."

"Really? Great."

Countess Renate continued:

"In fact, we're even close to locating an aircraft we can use. One thing is, I don't see any way around purchasing it, but I'm sure that this is well within the means of the Kingdom given the challenge."

"Can't believe it. Purchasing a used plane? So fast. I'll still need to get a formal OK. Can't make that decision myself."

"Can I assume that it will be but a formality? That you won't need to go into details?"

Abdul initially hesitated, but upon further prodding from Countess Renate he conceded:

"Yes."

"How about an airworthiness certificate?"

On that one, Abdul was quite a bit more forceful:

"I'll take care of that as well. Come to think of it, there may be a question of whether the aircraft would leave our airspace."

■ ■ ■ ■ ■

Back with her team, Countess Renate, who knew she had more than slightly exaggerated when it came to "almost locating an aircraft," still had to ask:

"We need an aircraft, though, don't we? And we know it must be an A318, since that's what the Prince would be using for this trip."

The team admitted right away that this was not simple, and in fact could be the real challenge. Francis argued:

"The real problem is that the plane we will buy will crash in multiple pieces within a few hours of delivery. That makes it an expensive joke . . ."

Countess waved the problem away with her hand:

"Given the client and the circumstances, that's not a problem."

She paused and ominously added:

"Yet, the question is where can we find one and fast?"

Though the team was surely not short of ideas, as there are plenty of places where old planes are stored, the question however was still unanswered when Francis almost yelled:

"Wait a minute. Wait a bloody minute. I've got it! I know that there are at least two A318s in the vicinity of the Airbus plant in France, in Toulouse. I am not sure whether they are in Toulouse proper or stored at the airport of Tarbes-Lourdes-Pyrénées, less than an hour's flight away from Toulouse."

He paused and excitedly resumed:

"In fact, it would be better if we could carry out the modifications in Lourdes. This would surely be much more discrete, away from the Toulouse plant and the Toulouse airport crowds. In Lourdes, planes that land are principally pilgrim flights and nobody there is paying much attention to aircraft. Plus, the company that operates aircraft storage and maintenance there has a capacity of up to 270 aircraft, including two other storage facilities. On average, you've got to have more than 100 aircraft parked in Lourdes, if not more. So, one more or one less . . . Who cares?"

The Tarbes-Lourdes-Pyrénées airport is in the foothills of the Pyrénées, the major mountain chain which separates France and Spain. The city of Lourdes itself was indeed a very small town until it became popular because of apparitions of the Virgin Mary to a fourteen-year-old peasant girl in 1858. Pilgrimages to the site considered holy by Roman Catholics created massive tourist inflows during the Easter to the end of October season, often complemented by skiers and other snow sport lovers in winter.

■ ■ ■ ■ ■

Francis Lefors started to work with a team of engineers and mechanics he had hired on a consulting basis from the myriad of contractors who work with Airbus. The short-term nature of the project made it easier for their usual employers to give them the time off, all the more so as the request coming from Francis Lefors almost guaranteed that they might also learn something useful. To facilitate their decision, the contractors were told that contributing to the project would surely help their standing with EADS, a promise which Francis would have to make good on, without really knowing how he would do that at this point in time. Once assembled, Francis's team was told a story which would explain the work they were going to help do. There was no way that the real purpose of the effort could possibly come to light.

■ ■ ■ ■ ■

Though it may be hard for a naïve observer to believe it, constructing an aircraft is much more akin to an assembly operation than to pure manufacturing. Very much as one would argue in the automobile industry, the main thrust relates to bringing together parts which are almost always manufactured in several different locations.

In the case of an Airbus A320 or any of its shorter or longer derivatives, there are final assembly lines in Toulouse (France), Hamburg (Germany), Tianjin (China) and Mobile, Alabama (USA). All the final assembly lines are similar and comprise the same number of stations. Each of these stations performs a specific task in the aircraft's assembly and systems testing. A320 fuselages arrive at the line in two segments that are joined to begin the aircraft build-up sequence. The joined fuselage is lifted into a position where the two wings are mated to it, and engine pylons and landing gears fitted. Soon afterwards, cabin fitting, engine installation, fuel and pressurization tests and engine run-up are followed by flight testing, aircraft acceptance and delivery. In between all these activities, the electrical wiring harness is installed. One may not realize it, but a mid-size aircraft like an A320 can have more than 250 miles of wire in it!

Another anecdote illustrates the complex nature of an assembly process where parts must be brought to a central assembly plant from many different initial locations and of the huge logistical issues that can create. EADS, Airbus Industries' parent, originally built five Airbus Beluga aircraft—aptly named as they look like a fat beluga whale—huge, ugly behemoths which they needed for the movement of oversized aircraft components like wings. These are being replaced by a new version, the even larger Airbus Beluga XL which entered service in early January 2020. The new version is no less ugly than the first.

■ ■ ■ ■ ■

Paradoxically, the only difficult question to which Francis Lefors had to find a suitable answer looked absolutely trivial. It concerned the painting of the aircraft. There was simply no way the obvious livery would not raise questions. The solution was a simple "white lie." He told his team that the project was the first in a future series of tests to determine the feasibility of developing a remote-piloted commercial aircraft; Saudi Arabia was leading that charge along with several other countries because of a serious intellectual interest in the issue and as the large amount of desert in the Kingdom made testing easier.

Little if any work was going to be done on the inside of the plane, other than elementary clean-up and the removal of most rows of seats; the narrative for the team was that the plane would be fully appointed when in Saudi Arabia. Most of the work was going to be done inside the cockpit. Again, the fact that the aircraft control systems were based on a fly-by-wire principle meant the work which Francis was going to have to complete was simply to link every control element, switch, joystick, throttles, and others to some external control module. Ostensibly, a number of the controls which may be used by pilots in the case of emergency, or if having to deal with unusual circumstances, would be dispensed with. The idea was that, when completed, the aircraft could be made to take off or land, as well as cruise, with the radio functions being bounced from inside the cockpit to an outside operator.

Once the project was virtually completed, the plane had been transformed into a drone, which was eventually painted in the colors of Saudia, the national airline: a white body intersected by a wide grey line, and a dramatic dark royal blue tail, with a golden palm tree above two golden scimitars. The royal family had indeed understood that there was no point drawing attention to itself with a different livery for its fleet. Practically, and from the outside, it was virtually impossible to distinguish this aircraft from the sole A318 currently in the Royal Fleet.

CHAPTER.02

SINGAPORE, WASHINGTON, DC.

"Roy, can you come here, please . . . Urgent!"

Roy Pierce was the senior man on the trading desk of the Harbor Bank; in fact, he headed up the whole Treasury function, whose role it is to fund the bank. The Harbor Bank, based in Singapore, was probably the largest local bank with the strongest connection to Hong Kong and China. It always had a solid Singaporean, overseas Chinese ownership. It had inherited a lot of the activity that previously took place in Hong Kong while it was still a British Colony, particularly as Hong Kong was perceived as **the** gateway to China. Roy was now nearing retirement and had in fact carried out a large part of his career in Hong Kong before moving to the Island Republic shortly after the then British Prime Minister announced that Hong Kong would eventually be allowed to revert to China.

He had read this announcement and the decision it revealed as a precursor of the ultimate demise of the Colony as a truly global financial center. Without having much to point to in the recent Chinese political moves, he had seen the behavior of many communist regimes: they seem to sign agreements to win some time and yet have no real intention to be bound by their commitments. He fully expected that this would apply to this Sino-British agreement in due course. In his view, Hong Kong would become a province of China, and its free-market system would only be allowed to keep operating for as long as it suited China's needs. In short, profits could become elusive if the activities needed to generate them did not coincide with China's perception of its needs. The opportunity for the business to move to Singapore seemed too good to pass on. He strongly argued in favor of it and was rewarded with a position on the Board of Directors of the bank in Singapore.

The individual calling him was Teh Kok Min, one of his young traders. Like most of its competitors, Harbor Bank's Treasury Department comprised a proprietary trading function where traders managed a "book" funded by the bank's capital. Theory has it that a financial institution must stand ready to meet the needs of its customers, and that this required being permanently present in markets, buying and selling. Thus, even when making large trading profits was not the order of the day, all banks had a battery of such traders, focused on different segments of the global financial market. They were constantly buying and selling the instruments for which they were responsible. The overall market brought together these many traders in a worldwide merry-go-round, as trading did not stop; it simply moved from one location to the other, following the sun. Each trader would put up a price at which he or she was a buyer of the securities in which they were active, and a price at which he or she would be willing to sell. Thus, any outsider seeking to buy or sell would see a large number of bids and offers from a wide variety of broker/dealers on a computer screen and could thus contact the desk which offered the best deal. Kok Min called Roy because he had just noticed a few surprising trades. He felt he could not participate further in the market without his boss's guidance. Roy walked to Kok Min's desk and asked:

"What's up? Anything wrong?"

"Well, maybe nothing; maybe a lot. I don't really know. But we've seen three major trades with what looks like a Chinese entity, or rather someone who usually deals with and for the Chinese. They're selling large amounts of U.S. Treasury bonds."

"How large?"

"Well, we really don't know as it's just a bid and ask quote. But I called one of them to see and was offered 10 yards nominal, or face value. Way larger than usual."

Bond traders have a custom to refer to any dollar amount greater than $1 billion exchanging "yard" for "billion." Here, by saying 10 yards, Kok Min meant $10 billion.

"10 yards, that's huge!"

"I know, I know. I've never seen that before either. Typically, we look at $100 million or thereabouts . . ."

"Right."

Roy paused for a second and added:

"OK. You're right. That's not normal. Be careful. Tell you what, if I were you, I wouldn't participate in any of this stuff. When you don't know, let others make the profits . . . or take the losses."

Kok Min nodded. Roy smiled and asked:

"Keep me posted, please. Market direction, activity, the works!"

■ ■ ■ ■ ■

The next day, Roy was again called upon, this time not by one but by two of the members of his team. First Kok Min reported another series of offers of U.S. Treasuries, presumably from China, as the offer came from the same Hong Kong-based broker, known to have a close relationship with the Chinese government. Yet, the interesting twist was that the offers were not nearly as large as the prior day. Roy was asking himself: *"was yesterday simply a fluke?* At about the same time, Vijay Tong, a senior currency trader, was astonished and needed his boss right away. Roy walked calmly to Vijay's trading position and asked:

"Yes, Vijay, what's up?

"Look at this, it seems that someone is selling a few billion U.S. Dollars, exchanging them for CryptNotes. The bid for CryptNotes is up 15% and there's no seller. Don't know where the market is!"

"How big?"

"As I said, I saw a few billion dollars. But, in truth, I don't know, but way more than usual . . ."

Roy was initially quite perplexed. The proposed trades in the U.S. Dollar did not seem out of the ordinary, but the trading imbalance in CryptNotes was certainly unusual. It had to mean that the amounts on demand were considerably higher than normal. He was still ruminating when Kok Min told him he was again seeing large blocks of U.S. Treasuries on offer; and this time, the size was again abnormally large. Then the proverbial light bulb went off. There had to be a relationship between the Treasury and the dollar trades. He said to Vijay:

"Bet you the currency trade is nothing other than the settlement of yesterday's Treasury sales. T+1, normal next day settlement."

"Settlement" in the financial markets refers to the moment when the securities bought or sold are actually exchanged for cash. T+1 means that settlement in the Treasury market takes place on the day after the trade. Roy turned toward the whole trading desk and barked:

"We're not buying any U.S. Treasury, at any price."

Seeing his traders somewhat confused, he added:

"Don't know who is selling, but the amounts are way out of the ordinary. Don't want to find myself in front of a runaway train."

To a trader, Wee Ka Shin, who was asking why not take advantage of what looked like an unusual volume, he replied:

"Usually, I'd be with you Ka Shin. We can be contrarians in certain circumstances. However, imagine a scenario where the volumes are large because the seller has a lot to sell . . . Imagine that the seller is China."

"China?"

"Could be, why not? But frankly could be anybody else as well. We sure don't know yet, but we see a connection with China; the selling broker is known for its ties with China. If they're the seller, then there's potentially a lot more to go; they own more than a trillion of the stuff. In fact, they're the second largest foreign owner of U.S. Treasury securities right behind Japan. Prices could literally crater, at least until someone, probably the U.S. Federal Reserve Bank, decides bond prices are unacceptably low, meaning interest rates have become unacceptably high. Don't want to guess when that happens . . . Much too dangerous to try to catch a falling knife."

He paused for a few seconds pondering his mixed metaphors and added:

"Also, use your discretion to buy as many CryptNotes as allowed under your trading limits. However, buy them only on downticks."

His reference to downticks reflected the normal behavior of markets. Typically, posting interest in a transaction, one would start with the last traded price. If a seller, one would offer at that price, while if a buyer one would be prepared to buy at that price. In a market where there is a lot of activity in one direction or another, the normal interplay between buyers and sellers would lead to each trade being closed at a "tick" or a set increment, for instance 1/16th of one percent, above or below the prior deal. A price above the prior deal would be called an uptick. The converse is also true in down markets; the move is called a downtick. Buying on an uptick contributes to maintaining upward momentum, while buying on a downtick at least does not "feed the frenzy." At most, it slows down a trend reversal.

Roy went back to his office to make a couple of phone calls. Then he walked straight into the office of Chiang Shao Jin, the managing director, or top executive of the bank:

"I don't know for sure, but something very odd is happening in the markets for U.S. Treasuries and the U.S. Dollar. Can't prove anything yet, but my guess is that the Chinese are up to something."

Shao Jin was an experienced banker who had spent the first part of her career at the Monetary Authority of Singapore (MAS), the Republic's central bank. She had climbed the ladder there quite rapidly, having a combination of exceptional professional skills and personal charm. She was quite tough, but never seemed to lose her calm or to throw her weight around, though it was considerable. She was the incarnation of the Asian principle: ". . . never make your adversary lose face" which simply says that one should be humble in any form of victory to avoid hurting the counterparty and thus potentially triggering in the defeated the desire for revenge. She looked straight at Roy and asked:

"The Chinese? What makes you say that?"

"Well, we've seen huge selling volume in U.S. Treasuries. On top of that, with a day's delay, we're seeing a huge demand for CryptNotes against U.S. Dollars. "

"What's the surprise? Bond trades settle the next day . . ."

She paused, looked at Roy calmly and added:

"Sorry, I guess you mean that the huge volume is a surprise. OK grant you that. But where is China in all of this?"

"The counterparties seem to be in China or Hong Kong. They're the people whom we've always thought were fronts for the Chinese, at least in our part of the world. By the way, we're seeing more selling today. So, my guess is that we'll see more demand for CryptNotes tomorrow."

"Sounds reasonable. Anything else? But why CryptNotes?"

"I checked with a couple of friends abroad and there has not been as much volume there. And as far as CryptNotes, can't fathom it either."

"By "there", you mean Europe and the U.S.?"

"Yep. This reinforces my belief that China is behind this. If not, why would someone else choose to trade only in Asia?"

He paused and offered his personal guess:

"I bet they know we'd have a terrible time trying to embargo any of their money here, in Singapore. We'd need an unimpeachable proof."

Roy here was jumping ahead several steps. He was assuming that China was taking an adversarial approach toward the U.S. He further assumed that the U.S.'s reaction would be to try to retaliate, freeze their assets or otherwise embargo certain transactions. Thus, carrying the trade away from the U.S. might appear to offer a bit more room. He assumed that the Singapore monetary authorities would not freeze China's assets without some solid proof, which, in his mind, would give China the time to take the money out of Singapore and move it home. He looked at Shao Jin. She was smiling, so he continued:

"They might not trust the U.S. or Europe to do the same thing. I've still not been able to reach anyone in the Middle East, but that's next on the list."

"Any change in trading policy because of that?"

"Yes, but I'll want the Executive Committee to confirm it as soon as you want to call a meeting. In the meantime, I've decided we aren't buying any U.S. Treasury bonds, except if a critical client relationship is involved and requires it . . ."

"Good idea. Anything else?"

"We're buying CryptNotes on any downtick."

Roy's jargon simply meant that he would not chase CryptNotes up if its price kept going straight up. He added:

"I am still going to be quite prudent. Assuming this is of Chinese origin, I don't think they're dumb. So, even if they've decided to cut back on their holdings of U.S. Treasuries and selling some of their U.S. Dollars, they've got to know that they can't do it all in one fell swoop. In fact, a smart trader would put in a buy order for a small amount here and there just to confuse the market. So, in other words, I don't want to chase CryptNotes; I'm willing to buy on weakness until I have a higher conviction of what's happening, but I'm not trying to shoot the lights out."

Shao Jin replied with a broad smile:

"Couldn't have said it better myself."

Out of the blue, Roy asked:

"By the way, do you know what happens when you try to shoot the lights out?"

"Not sure, but I bet you're gonna tell me . . ."

Roy deadpanned:

"You've got to be prepared to live in the dark!"

And he let go of a good belly laugh. Shao Jin smiled too and added:

"Let me schedule a meeting of the Executive Committee to advise them of your decision. Also need to schedule a special meeting of the full Board of Directors by phone or Zoom to make sure everyone is fully in the loop. Plus . . ."

She paused and added with a wry smile:

"You never know what you may learn."

She shifted in her chair as she was turning toward the phone and with a wink in her eyes added:

"I'm also gonna talk to my friends at the MAS. It'd be interesting to see if they've picked up any of this. I suspect they have as it'd not be like them to miss it. Even if they didn't see it directly, another bank is bound to have called them. However, who knows, we may be the first this time; your team's pretty sharp."

As Roy was stepping out of her office, Shao Jin let go of a last piece of friendly advice:

"One last thing for you; don't go past your risk limits.

THE CRYPTO TRAP | 17

It did not take terribly long before the news of what appeared like a new Chinese financial strategy reached the U.S. Jack Turnbull was the Director of Operations within the CIA; his group was thus responsible for collecting foreign intelligence and for covert action. Jack decided that his first call should be to Simon Rabinowitz with whom he had worked on several prior occasions. He had, of course, previously had all the internal conversations he thought he should have, but that only involved his own boss and the President's Chief of Staff. He had deliberately avoided any talk with any staff, as he did not want to risk any leak. He told Simon what they knew so far.

Simon initially wondered in his own mind why Jack would call him on such a matter. He knew that they were good friends, but he kept thinking *"how can Mossad help the U.S. on a U.S. financial matter?* He still elected to accept the implicit compliment and went ahead with the conversation asking:

"This is really serious. Could it be a part of a broader pattern?"

"Broader pattern?"

"Yes, skirmishes, or at times a bit more than that, just to test the enemy. You know my old point: many developed countries play checkers, Russia plays chess, and China plays go; many more possible moves . . ."

Though he still did not know—in fact had not even thought of it at that point—he came to see that his last comment, about skirmishes, might be more insightful than he realized at first. He brought Jack into the confidence of the developments on the Saudi front, in as discreet a way as he could; specifically, he told him of the rumor, but held back anything that might touch upon a solution. He could not help adding that the word "skirmish" was a bit weak for such an attempted aggression against a senior royal figure. As he was thinking aloud, suddenly a new thought came into his mind. He verbalized it:

"Wait a second. Just had a thought. There is a new and increasingly visible link between China and Iran. We saw it at work a while back in the underwater missile launcher episode[3]. We've also heard of Houthis shooting at oil installations in the United Arab Emirates with drones. You know and I know that Houthis don't have drones other than supplied by Iran. Could the three events, the financial strategy, the Houthis shooting at the U.A.E and the Iranian attack on Saudi Arabia be linked?"

Jack remained silent for a while and then replied, in a characteristically cautious fashion:

"My dear Simon, everything is possible. Clearly, you're assuming that Iran gets drones from China. May well be correct. After all, we know that's where they got their missile technology. However, I prefer to hold off on that conversation until we know more."

"Couldn't agree more. At the same time, there is no harm in keeping it at the forefront of our thoughts. This is the third time we may be seeing the dark shadow of China in the Middle Eastern region: the virus[4], the underwater missile launcher drones and now a possible direct attack on the U.S. financial system."

Simon paused and then concluded:

"We need to change our original strategy; I need Ariel's agreement on this. So far, we've just been dealing with Iran and the Middle Eastern terrorists. Now, I think we should definitely be ready to expand it to their masters, and that includes not only China but also Russia. The time for proxy wars with no response from the developed world has got to be over . . . And if not now, at least quite soon!"

He paused again and then almost immediately added:

"But we cannot do that in a visible way. Remember, plausible deniability; plausible deniability is the key as President Clinton used to say. We'll also need to involve the real political powers that be.

---

[3] From the same author, see "Below the Surface," Barringer Publishing 2022
[4] From the same author, see "The Shadow Experts," Barringer Publishing, 2021

We can't be rogue. Too dangerous. Don't ever want my name associated with starting WW III . . ."

Jack could only reply:

"Hey, you and me both. But since you mention them, I've got to tell you that the powers that be in Washington, as you call them, are quite upset."

"About what? The financial aggression?"

"Of course."

"Well, imagine how the Saudis feel. But, back to the U.S. and financial markets, frankly, who allowed China to buy so much U.S. government paper? Your government was happy to take advantage of it when it allowed them to run massive budget deficits and to maintain artificially low interest rates. Well, now's the time to pay the piper."

"I can't say I disagree with your analysis, Simon, but you've got to know that I can't talk that way, at least officially."

"I know, I know. Don't think I want to shoot the messenger. Simply, you need to make people there know that we're not really surprised. Yet, that's not the burning issue now; we'll have enough time for this later. Do you mind my setting up a conference call with you and Countess Renate to see what can be done."

"Sounds great. Thanks."

CHAPTER.03

Countess Renate immediately called Colonel Abdul el Wahabi.

"Abdul? I have news for you. And this time, it's hard news, not informed speculation."

"What is it?"

"My plan can work technically. In fact, we have located an aircraft we can use and put a team to work. I did not see any way around purchasing it. So, I bought it. I'm sure that this is well within the means of the Kingdom given the challenge and we will bill you for it."

"Sure. We've already covered that."

"I know, I know. How about an airworthiness certificate? Just for travel within the region . . ."

"You've asked before as well. I'll take care of that, too. Probably don't need it, but, at worst, it'll be an order from the Crown Prince."

Countess Renate had called on a traditional phone line and thus could not see the smile on Abdul's face. Yet, she "heard it" in his voice. They hung up.

❚❚■❚❚

Reporting to Countess Renate, Francis explained the crux of the work that was being carried out, focusing, as he should, on benefits, not engineering details.

"The trick for us was to have external pilots move the replicas of the onboard controls, with the movements of their toggles being transmitted by radio to the computers on the plane. With what we've done, we'll just need some decent internet connectivity. We'll use Wi-Fi to have the external pilots and the aircraft communicate. Not so long ago that would have been simply impossible, but now, that's no different than what we use to fly drones."

Countess simply replied:

"Seems we have most of it under total control, correct?"

■ ■ ■ ■ ■

As expected, Francis had started with a used, older A318 which EADS had accepted as a trade-in on a newer aircraft and parked in Tarbes-Lourdes-Pyrénées Airport. A hangar had been made available to allow the team to work. The only downsides were weather which could be notoriously fickle in that location and a runway which was a bit short in certain wind conditions for some larger aircraft with a full load of fuel, which was not an issue for Francis. Verification that everything was working properly required the external control module to be loaded on a truck which was parked in the vicinity of the aircraft, yet outside of the hangar. The pilots sent out the orders by radio and technicians would be sitting in the cockpit to check that the plane's controls were responding as anticipated.

Francis who was well-known to the local officials because of his new job at BEA had no difficulty securing a clearance to take the plane on a test flight. It did not need to be very long and exhaustive. Yet, it had to involve all the motions that would be expected during takeoff, cruise, and landing. For the test, the work set up was repeated: the two external pilots were in control, but two other pilots sat in the cockpit of the plane, ready to take over if there was any obvious communication problem. The remote pilots went through the complete test routine with no difficulty other than a minor hiccup as they were taxiing the plane to the end of the runway: the interaction of the nose steering wheel on the left side of the cockpit and the rudder pedals did not work as well as expected. The response of the small steering wheel would need to be recalibrated. Other than this minor problem, Francis was satisfied that the aircraft could be made to take off or land, as well as cruise; the radio functions were effectively bounced from the outside operator to the inside of the cockpit.

Francis called Countess Renate and observed:

"The plane is almost ready, Countess, but there is one area of testing that I still do not feel we've done well enough."

"Which one?"

"We conducted the test flight within a less than one-hundred-mile radius from the airport. However, the plane will need to be considerably further from its external control module in real life . . ."

"I understand, but the technology you are using is pretty well-known. Isn't it the same as for drones?"

"Yes. I understand all that. But you know the basic principles of aeronautical engineering: "fail safe." I'd love to test it further."

"Tell you what. Do you have to carry out the tests in France?"

"No, not really."

"Well, then. Why don't we plan on completing the full testing program in Riyadh?"

"Ah. That's a thought. The flight from Tarbes-Lourdes will be piloted from within the cockpit, though the drone pilots will be onboard as well. They'll be able to verify they see the same thing on their instrument panel as the actual pilots see on theirs. So, the only final thing we need to be sure of is the communication between the external pilots and the plane and that we can indeed do from Riyadh.

And, as you said, that should almost be routine as there are plenty of drones being flown in that part of the world."

"Well, then, it's agreed. You'll do a complete test flight when we're there. I don't want you to draw attention to it in France."

"Understood. That should work."

■ ■ ■ ■ ■

"Abdul? Countess Renate here . . ."

"Ah! Countess. Where are we in the project?"

"The plane will be flown to Riyad tomorrow morning . . ."

"Incredible. You did everything in less than two weeks?"

"Frankly, we took a few shortcuts. We can carry out most routine maneuvers. But we elected not to worry about those that a pilot would encounter in an emergency, like a system breakdown, the loss of an engine or something of that nature."

Abdul was clearly delighted. Countess Renate added:

"A funny detail, we only applied one coat of paint and only paid a limited attention to small details. Yet, unless you come very, very close and suspect something already, there is no way anyone would think this is other than the real thing . . ."

"Great. What's next?"

"We're going to need permission from the Kingdom to fly an Israeli drone just above the plane when the Prince's trip starts."

Abdul could not hide his surprise and replied in a slightly higher than usual tone of his voice:

"What?"

"We'd like to see as much of the developments as we can . . ."

The idea which Countess Renate was discussing was to shadow the plane from far enough above that the drone could not be detected by radar, other than by the plane's radar of course, or, worse yet, by naked eyes. At the same time, the drone should be able to see the plane below and effectively take a movie of the whole flight. The focus would not be on the plane, though it would occupy the center of the picture. After all, it had in effect become eventually expendable if the rumor of the impending attack was correct. Rather, the focus would be on everything around it, and more specifically below it. The drone should be able to "see" and thus to film any missile before it hits. It should be able to pinpoint where the missile was launched. Providing as it would real-time coordinates of the aggressors would allow Saudi Arabia, if it so wanted and if the aggressors were then on its territory or within its territorial waters, to launch an air strike against them. Abdul still had to ask:

"What kind of drone?"

"I'm not sure, but I suspect it will be a Kovesh, the Israeli version of the RQ 170 Sentinel. Simon tells me it's the only one in their fleet that can do the trick."

Though the RQ Sentinel, or the Israeli-modified version, called Kovesh, for "conqueror" in Hebrew, is not always used as a surveillance drone in this kind of capacity, it did seem to be the most appropriate solution at present. Indeed, powered as it is by a turbofan engine similar to those that power jet aircraft, it could fly at the same speed as commercial aircraft. Other drones, such as the Eitans, which are propeller-driven, have major advantages over the Kovesh in that they can stay aloft much longer, but their cruising speed is about half that of an A318.

Abdul, always focused on practicalities could not help but note:

"We'll need to work on the logistics with you, but I am sure it will be authorized."

"Thanks. Now, let me run you through the plan in detail . . . We can't afford any mistakes."

CHAPTER.04

"Abdul? One last thing."

"Yes?"

"For the plane's arrival tomorrow morning . . . Any curfew issue that we should worry about?"

"Not at the air base. Just let us know all the information we need, and we'll have air traffic control ready for you. By the way, I'm amazed at how fast you were able to proceed . . ."

"Not unhappy myself. We always try to meet our clients' deadlines. My team tells me the engineering was pretty straightforward. The technology is well-known, It simply hadn't been applied to that situation. That's all. The biggest challenge was to get the various parts . . . Thank God for 3-D printing!"

Abdul knew what 3-D printing was but did not really understand Countess Renate's last comment. He elected to let it slide as he did not feel he needed to understand each and every detail. He just said:

"Impressive anyway. What's next?"

"Well, high priority . . . Make sure the other A318 is hidden in a hangar. You do not want to have two of them next to each other.

People know you've only got one. Plus, I checked, Saudia has no A318 in its fleet, just three A319, forty-seven A320 and 15 A321 . . ."

"Boy, you guys do your homework . . ."

"Sure do. The more prep work we do, the luckier we get!"

"And then?"

Countess Renate then provided more detail on the logistics of the plan going forward. She explained that the two French pilots who had brought the plane from France would remain in Saudi Arabia until the end of the mission. With a wink, she added:

"If they're here, they cannot be a party to any leak . . ."

She continued, arguing that there would be a need for an office from which the drone operators could work. She added that the sole requirement would be that the office had absolutely first-class communication and radio coverage. They would also need overnight accommodations and a discrete return flight to Toulouse adding:

"The same applies to the two French pilots and the few technicians who accompanied the plane to Riyadh, just in case anything went wrong, and it needed to be fixed quickly. We'll need discrete accommodations. Assuming the return flight is private, they can all be on the same plane."

"By the way, Countess, why did you need two sets of pilots, those who flew the plane to Riyadh and the drone operators?"

"Simple, we wanted the crew that would deal with the remote controls, the drone operators, to be in the cabin and make sure they saw exactly what they were supposed to see on their own replica of the cockpit. Think of it as a cheap dry run . . . Plus, frankly, actual pilots must do things drone operators don't know how to do, and vice versa."

"Didn't you worry about the risk of accident? More people on the plane had to mean more potential victims?"

"No reason to worry about that. The plane was in perfect working order when we, or rather you bought it. We just added what was needed for the controls to be activated from outside the plane."

∎ ∎ ∎ ∎ ∎

The next day, Countess Renate was in Riyadh to supervise all the activities. She landed her own jet at the Riyadh Air Base, which was formerly known as Riyadh International Airport before King Khalid International Airport was commissioned in 1982 and all commercial flights moved there. All royal flights typically took off from and landed at the base, as it was obviously both much more discreet and much easier to secure. This was going to be the day of the Crown Prince's flight to Dubai.

Everything needed to be perfect. Simon had agreed to provide a Kovesh for the surveillance of the flight. Its cargo bays had been emptied of anything that was not mission critical thus allowing it to triple its standard 800 nautical mile range. He had obtained permission from the U.S. Fifth Fleet, which is responsible for a territory which includes the Arabian Gulf, Red Sea, Gulf of Oman and the western end of the Indian Ocean, to use one of its two aircraft carriers, the *Ronald Reagan.*

The plan was that the Kovesh would first land on the *Ronald Reagan*, refuel and stay there until the Crown Prince's flight was scheduled to depart. It would then fly over Saudi Arabia and expect to reach the Riyadh airspace at about the time the royal flight was ready to take off. It would have enough fuel for a short holding pattern if there were any delays for the Prince's flight on the ground. From there, it would shadow the Prince's flight, at an altitude about 10,000 feet higher than the A318 aircraft; the Prince's exact flight plan would be communicated to the Kovesh operators as soon as finalized. If the information intercepted by Mossad was correct, the drone would be able to film the whole flight and thus to see when, where, and how the A318 would be brought down. It would then immediately return to its 50,000-feet cruising altitude and fly straight back to Palmachim Airbase, its home base. There, *Mossad* would analyze the data it recorded and share its results with Countess Renate and the Saudi Security Services as soon as available.

About a half hour before the Prince's scheduled departure, the pilots, selected from the usual team used by the Royal Family, arrived at the plane as if it was a normal flight. The aircraft was, as usual, parked away from the terminal. They used rolling stairs set against the L1 door (the left forward door of the aircraft) to board. They were initially surprised that a curtain partition was set up inside the cabin just right of the entrance door. They could not know that it had been designed as a temporary measure to prevent them from seeing the inside of the passenger cabin, which was effectively empty. However, to the pilots, that was not routine. So, mindful of their duties to ensure the Prince's safety, they called Security, which was manned by one of Abdul's men. They immediately received confirmation that the change was OK.

They did not think any more of it and went through their pre-flight routine, including ensuring that they had the proper amount of fuel pumped into the aircraft. They inputted the flight plan into the aircraft computer, which immediately, unbeknownst to them, shared it with the drone pilots, safely and quietly installed in a very nice, air-conditioned office in the terminal. The pilots were chatting with each other when the next step occurred, the arrival of the cabin crew and the caterers' trucks.

Countess Renate had explained to Abdul the importance of everything looking as totally routine as possible, though she and he fully recognized that nothing was truly routine when it involved such a senior member of the royal family. She had argued:

"We've got to assume that someone will be watching the whole process. Most likely, he'll be using binoculars. More importantly, we've got to assume that the terrorists have an inside source."

"Inside source?"

"Yep. Inside. Inside the airport administration or worse inside the Prince's staff."

She paused for a second and with great care she added:

"Or inside yours."

She did not give Abdul the time to interrupt although her last sentence had visibly flustered him. She explained:

"Someone must have told them where the Prince was going, with whom and for how long. Otherwise who could have given the information that was eventually discovered by Simon? In fact, that same someone would have told the terrorists of the change of plans and now of today's date for the new flight."

"Guess so . . . Understood. But how do we find out?"

"Frankly, at this time, we don't. Yet, we can manage around it. The first step has to be to ensure there must be no surprise . . ."

She paused and added with a wink:

". . . other than the operational issues which routinely can crop up."

Abdul laughed a nervous laugh and sighed:

"Always do when you least expect them."

Before the actual Prince's entourage boarding commenced, one aircraft-catering-truck was positioned at R1 (the front door on the right-hand side of the plane). Another truck parked along the fuselage, near the right front cargo bay. Containers assumed to contain luggage were loaded into the bay, with a luggage volume in keeping with the nature and length of the trip.

As the cabin crew was climbing up the steps to board the aircraft, they were informed by a security agent who was standing at the bottom of the rolling stairs that there was a change in plans. They would use a different aircraft. They were still invited to follow the agent and climb up the stairs and enter the A318 normally. Once inside the aircraft, however, he motioned them not to stay in the plane, but rather to keep walking and climb into the catering truck which was parked at the opposite door. They were told that this would expedite their transfer to the aircraft that would be used. They bought that line, as the bus that had brought them to the airplane had by then already departed back to the main terminal. The two pilots were told the same story. They were asked to leave the cockpit and follow the cabin crew. They were asked not to make any change to what they had already set into the A318 computer. Everyone was surprised but only up to a point. It was not the first time that a last-minute change had been orchestrated. They all assumed it was a security issue. And, in fact, they were right!

The first catering truck transferring the crew then departed the front right door. A short while later, a different catering truck returned, in fact, this time, accompanied by another. They were placed at the front and aft doors on the right-hand side of the plane, R1 and R2. Inside the cabin of the A318, security had ensured that all window shades were down. Again, that should not have surprised anyone as it is routine in hot climates for the shades to be lowered to keep the cabin from getting too hot as the aircraft sits on the tarmac. And this is so even though an auxiliary power unit is still in use to provide power both eventually to start the engines and to keep the cabin from getting too hot.

The boarding then continued with the few people who were traveling with the Crown Prince. People walked in through the left front door and then exited through one of the two catering doors on the opposite side of the plane. Most people had to walk through the empty cabin and used the rear door. That left the front catering truck reserved for the Prince and his security detail. They were certainly surprised to note that the interior of the cabin was bare, but they were informed that they were part of a safety drill. Countess Renate added:

"By the way, we've made sure that the catering trucks are of the variety which is totally tight to the plane. We couldn't have the usual platform that protrudes from the front of the truck: nobody outside of the plane must be able to see anything."

Abdul nodded.

After the Prince, who boarded last and was discreetly moved to the catering truck, had arrived, an outside observer could note that the two catering trucks drove away from the plane at about the same time, though neither aircraft door looked like it was being shut fully. However, another truck quickly came along and briefly docked at the R1 door. This reflected a routine provision in the security protocol for this mission. A member of Saudi security services walked into the airplane to verify that all doors were appropriately secured, and the emergency slides set to flight mode. This task is typically done by the cabin crew in commercial flights, but, in the circumstances, the Kingdom preferred for a fully accredited member of the Security Apparatus to have that responsibility. They did not want to have to explain more things to more people than absolutely necessary. Once he had done his inspection, he ensured that the front right door was locked and armed, at which point the catering truck left for the last time. The security agent then exited through the front boarding door, closed it from the outside and walked down the rolling staircase, which was then rolled away from the aircraft. Ostensibly, the front left door would not have its slide activated, but nobody really worried about that; any outside observer would assume that the cabin crew was taking care of it. From the bottom of the stairs, he made a thumbs up sign towards the cockpit, as per routine. He could not see, but also neither could anyone else that the cockpit was, in fact, unoccupied. Francis Lefors and his team had placed a coating on the cockpit windows and windshield to prevent anyone from seeing inside. There was no need for the plane to be pressurized, as there would be no one on board.

Abdul breathed an audible sigh of relief when the process was completed. The remote pilots who had been selected to ensure that they did not have a French accent, took over from there, from their office in the terminal. They communicated with the control tower as expected, sought permission to start the engines, the left one first and the right one afterwards. They received permission to proceed to the runway, after having done all but their last check list. Just before take-off, they completed their final pre-flight check list at the top of the runway. They followed the instructions of the control tower, set the various radio frequencies as instructed and eventually took off. From then on, they scrupulously followed the flight plan, only making the changes communicated to them by air traffic controllers if needed. Two Saudi Air Force jets were escorting it, one on either side.

Countess Renate had warned Abdul:

"I would expect the terrorists to strike before the plane starts its descent phase. We don't know where they are. Let's assume that airport security is such that the takeoff phase is probably safe. But, after that, who knows? In truth, they could attack during climb, cruise, descent or even approach. I doubt they would hit early, as that would mean they're in Saudi Arabia. I also assumed that an attack on approach is unlikely, as that would mean they're attacking from Dubai, which I personally doubt."

"What if our information was incorrect?"

"You mean, what if the plane hasn't been hit and is about to land. Well, it will abort landing just above 3,000 feet and fly back to Riyadh requesting an emergency royal clearance."

"Will they have enough fuel?"

"Sure, no big deal. The maximum range of an A318 is about 3,000 nautical miles. A flight from Riyadh to Dubai is a bit less than 480 nautical miles. We have actually pre-fueled the plane for a potential return flight and did that away from prying eyes. The remote pilots will enter the corrected aircraft total weight into the computer. There will be plenty of fuel to return to Riyadh. "

"Won't it look odd?"

"Depends. I assume you mean odd for a plane to abort landing at that point."

Abdul nodded and Countess Renate continued:

"Sure will, but we sure as heck don't want anyone to know that this was a pilotless converted aircraft, do we? So, we'll duck all questions and bring the plane safely back here."

She added:

"But Simon's intelligence is pretty specific, he tells me. So, I'm going to assume that the terrorists will carry out their plan. Frankly, if they don't, we should be worried that some leak might have developed somewhere along our planning chain."

"Leak?"

"Yes. Could be a direct leak with someone telling the terrorists that their plans were uncovered."

"Hold it. Who could it be?"

"Your guess is as good as mine. But someone must be leaking if somehow Simon found out about the Prince's flight as we've already established. Let me add that it could also be some indirect leak. Like someone observing the activity surrounding the flight here in Riyadh and feeling that something unusual is happening. I can't think of where our plan could be flawed. I checked it in detail with Simon who concurs. But who knows?"

"Makes two of us, Countess. Could the delay in the trip have changed the terrorists' plans?"

"We discussed that early on, remember? It's sure is a possibility. But we agreed that this would not be the first time there was a delay."

She paused and added:

"Admittedly, maybe not as long a delay. But, in the end, my guess is that people who are ready to do this kind of thing would not cancel it because of a delay."

Abdul moved on to his next question:

"Now, how does the Crown Prince travel to Dubai?"

"That's the easy part as you know. One of the Boeing 757 from the Royal Fleet was readied in a hangar. The crew—which is trained and qualified on all the types of aircraft in the fleet—has already transferred to the new aircraft. The pilots were told that the new destination was Abu Dhabi, not Dubai. The two cities being less than one hundred miles from each other, the difference in total fuel consumption is small and well within the normal margin of safety."

"But he thinks he is going to Dubai . . ."

"I know, I know. And, by the way, if nothing happens to the first aircraft, the Prince **will** go to Dubai. They'll change the destination of the 757 at the last minute. However, it does not matter if the 318 is shot down. Again, as you know, we've told, or rather **you've** told the Prince that the best for him would be to fly straight back to Riyadh. And you've told me he's OK with that."

Abdul nodded. He initially wanted to question why the pilots were not surprised by the choice of aircraft. After all, Abu Dhabi is north of Dubai and the flight would therefore be even shorter. Why take an aircraft with a longer range for a shorter trip? The explanation was simple: the fleet was not comprised of any other short-haul aircraft, other than the "other" A318. Yet, that one had to remain hidden, if only because one did not want the terrorists to confuse the two aircraft. And in fact, the pilots thought they were on that plane! However, as a further precaution, the pilots were instructed to use a flight plan that went quite a bit further east, partially over the Persian Gulf, and to approach the Abu Dhabi airport on a more direct vector.

As predicted, the boarding of the 757 was quickly completed. The plane was held in the hangar for about thirty minutes to make sure that there was sufficient time delay between its own takeoff and the A318's departure. In due course, it eventually took off in the direction of Abu Dhabi. Saudi Air Force sent up another two Air Force jets and then two others. A couple returned somewhat quickly to base, while the other two stayed aloft. They were going to escort the 757. Yet, Abdul wanted them to be in the air before the Royal plane. Any observer might have been surprised to see a second plane taking off with two fighter jets trailing it. Having the jets already aloft allowed them to close in on the Saudi Royal aircraft and provide the escort needed without having been identified at takeoff. Though, in practice this was partial overkill: it is not uncommon for fighter jets to take off and land from an air force base.

CHAPTER.05

LONDON, U.K.

Hideo Kamatsuka was quietly sitting in his office in London. In fact, it would be more exact to say that "**they** were seating quietly in **their** office in London." Though they were known to the world under a single name, they were in fact two friends, neither of Japanese descent, who were disappointed by the way global central banks were managing currencies, though their monetary policy activities. They had identified the fact that central banks, which were supposed to be above politics and independent, had in fact become the enablers of economic strategies which, the duo thought, would eventually blow up, with dire consequences: an international currency crisis, global rampant inflation or a major depression, or some combination of those. Their disappointment led them to invent the blockchain algorithm and CryptNotes in the 2000 decade, with the expectation that the new global cyber currency would provide a welcome solution to the problem they could see brewing.

■ ■ ■ ■ ■

The genesis of their thought process, whether they would or would not admit to it, could probably be found in the late 1980s. At that time, Japanese authorities had guided their economy toward solid growth, in part by maintaining lower interest rates and easier access to credit for major corporations. Over time, these policies led to many new players entering financial markets. Many have argued that the late '80s Japanese stock market bubble was fueled by a Japanese corporate invention, known as "*zaitech*," or "Financial Engineering," by which equity market speculation became an integral part of corporate activity and the resulting profits a "normal" part of earnings statements. At the same time, the same low interest rate environment and easy credit led to a real estate price bubble, with the land on which the Imperial Palace stood in Tokyo being then allegedly worth more than the whole of California!

Eventually, what had to happen happened: the speculative bubble burst in December 1989. After peaking at 38,915 intra-day on December 29, 1989, the Nikkei 225 Index closed at 7,055 on March 10, 2009, an 82% decline. It might put things in a better perspective to observe that this was about the same magnitude drop in a stock price index as occurred in the U.S. in the 1929 Great Depression.

Though this was the first time in the modern era when a central bank had deviated from its normal line of helping control inflation all the while maintaining economic growth, it was not the last. The next time central banks panicked in response to a difficult situation was in 2008 when the credit crisis which started in the U.S. mortgage market turned into a global financial crisis. Central banks started pumping money into their respective economies, as a means of avoiding the depth of the recession which would have most likely ensued.

While many observers were surprised that this highly unusual way of dealing with an economic crisis did not immediately result in rampant inflation, a couple of adjunct professors at the London School of Economics, Frank Thistle and Nikolai Bernstein, understood way before others that it simply reflected the influence of China and of its then very cheap labor. Much lower labor costs than in the developed world enabled Chinese exporters to keep prices low, or at least as low as raw material and energy costs allowed. These manufactured goods exports competed head-on with the domestic output of U.S., Japanese, and European industries. These were, in turn, forced to keep prices low as well to avoid losing market share. With manufactured goods prices in check, inflation was never able to develop, though certain observers noted that service prices actually rose more than goods prices, not surprising as goods can be imported much more easily than services. Healthcare and education were the most dramatic examples.

Frank and Nikolai understood that this absence of inflation was a matter of luck, not of skill in the management of monetary policy; in other words, central banks had been lucky. The world was reaping the benefit of the reforms initiated in China when Deng Xiaoping started opening the country to the world in 1978.

Interestingly, Deng Xiaoping operated without any highfaluting title; he was, initially at least, neither president, not prime minister, nor even chairman of the ruling Communist Party. He was simply, at 81, unquestionably, as Chairman of the Military Commission, the most powerful man in China. His move to open the Chinese economy to market principles is in fact credited with lifting 800 million people in China out of poverty.

While it was predictable that China's more free-market oriented economic policy was bound to have an impact for quite some time, Frank and Nikolai were concerned that this "inflation depressor" could not last. Eventually, China's economic growth would absorb more and more of its spare labor. That success would in turn force it to raise wages at home as well; the shield it had provided against inflation due to the excesses of western central banks would become much weaker and eventually vanish.

This made the duo lose their faith in the integrity of central banks. While the two compères had hitherto relied on them as the guardian of economic orthodoxy, they now saw them as corrupted by political influences. Central banks had lost—or given up—the independence without which they could not play their assigned role: central bankers must be prepared to confront politicians when they make mistakes in the management of their economy. In summary, Frank and Nikolai started to look for an alternative to a centrally controlled global currency system.

Though nobody knows for sure who wrote it, a quote appeared in February 2009, which, if Frank and Nikolai were not actually the authors, could still absolutely have been from them:

"The root problem with a conventional currency is all the trust that's required to make it work. The central bank must be trusted not to debase the currency, but the history of fiat currencies is full of breaches of that trust. Banks must be trusted to hold our money and transfer it electronically, but they lend it out in waves of credit bubbles with barely a fraction in reserve."

Interestingly, and possibly because they had traced the start of the problem to Japan, they decided to refer to themselves as one person, with a Japanese name: Hideo Kamatsuka. Though there were a few skeptics who believed that Kamatsuka-San was one single person, it was in fact pretty much broadly accepted that the pseudonym hid the identity of more than one person. Moreover, if the pseudonym did refer to a group rather than a single person, many assumed one out of the two, three, or more individuals had to have played a leading role. They were wrong. The two compères had been friends since the early teen years, despite substantially different backgrounds: one was a member of British bourgeoisie, while the other the scion of a Jewish family which had emigrated from the Soviet Union to avoid capture, going initially to Syria, then to Uruguay and eventually settling in London.

Their research led them to an invention which would eventually revolutionize the world of finance; something which would eventually foster a development which would become known as the world of cryptocurrencies, and which would be, quite profitably one should note, embraced by many. A few of these early adopters appreciated the real benefit of the algorithm the duo had created; many others were simply taken out of curiosity or a sense that one must own it " . . . because it is the future." On the surface, it appeared a brilliant theoretical solution to a vexing problem.

The centerpiece of their solution was the concept of blockchain. It is a growing list of records, called blocks, which are linked together in an encrypted manner. Each block contains a variable number of transactions which anyone within the network can create and build. The key element of the concept is the notion of total decentralization: nobody is in control, but everyone **collectively** is in control because of the protocols built into the system. More importantly, the software behind the discovery was provided to users free of charge; it was an open-source system that allowed anyone to make modifications within broad rules.

Blockchain enabled the creation of CryptNotes, still the leading cryptocurrency. In practice, new CryptNotes are created by miners who verify the integrity of the transactions within a block; they are the auditors of the system, though they are all independent from one another. They are rewarded by the system in that they receive newly created CryptNotes for their efforts. This reward is conditional and thus involves an important element of luck. Indeed, to be accepted by the rest of the network, a new block must contain something called a proof of work, which is based on an anti-spam scheme proposed by Adam Back in 1999. In their version, the creator of the block must find a number—a 64-digit vigesimal number—such that the block content and that number are numerically inferior to the network "difficulty target." A vigesimal system is comprised of twenty individual characters, just as the decimal system to which we are all used comprises ten of them. A simple way to visualize what this might look like is to think of the twenty characters as follows: 0,1,2,3,4,5,6,7,8,9,a,b,c,d,e,f,g,h,i,j. A "number" in that system is any combination of any of these characters, whether it comprises one digit or twenty or anything in between.

In plain English, this requires finding a number through guesses that are generated by super powerful computers, at a rate approaching if not equaling billions per second. It is indeed easy to imagine the myriad of possibilities to assemble twenty individual characters in a combination comprising sixty-four of them. If repetitions are allowed and the order in which the characters are put together matters, the number of possible permutations is about 2 followed by 83 zeros! Dizzy already?

■ ■ ■ ■ ■

Though the success of their algorithm and of the cryptocurrency market it spawned was not in doubt, the two compères started to ask themselves questions as the new world evolved somewhat away from their control. In truth, Frank and Nikolai had initially installed themselves as benevolent dictators—reserving for themselves the role of creating operating rules and in effect of controlling that they were followed. Yet, it was clear in their brilliant minds that such a role could not be maintained; it was in direct conflict with the principle of decentralization. It is also fair to say that many of the people informally on their team had also started to resent their special roles and attendant privileges.

Additionally, without going into too many details, suffice it to say that Nikolai had identified and worked to correct a few intrusions into the network, each of which had the potential to expose the weaknesses of the project and lead to questions about its viability. These intrusions, which penetrated through weaknesses in the system's security, allowed intruders to create large numbers of CryptNotes—violating a policy of controlled growth through mining. That ran directly counter to Nikolai's goals when Frank and he created the system. What's the point of creating a decentralized system that everyone should trust, precisely because no one is in control, if anyone can invent a scheme to penetrate the system and potentially defraud everyone else?

Nikolai's worries were in fact further confirmed when it became quite clear that CryptNotes had become a "discreet" manner to conduct criminal trading. The fact that all activity occurs online and thus away from any official record had motivated many criminals to use cryptocurrencies, to the point that, a short few years ago, certain estimates suggested that at least half of all transactions were indeed for illegal activity. Even further, there had been accusations of manipulations by insiders within the crypto industry, though no one had yet pointed a finger to any single one of these cryptocurrencies.

For the sake of their long friendship, they initially agreed to talk the issue through. Yet that very friendship led them to recognize that they had simply grown apart with respect to their invention. Frank remained somewhat of a revolutionary at heart and continued to believe in the need for their creation: CryptNotes. He probably would have gone after some other aspect of "the System" had he and Nikolai not developed CryptNotes. Nikolai, on the other hand, was more of an idealist. Yet, confronted with a few new realities, he was just beginning to have second thoughts. He was unsure that CryptNotes were being used appropriately and went even as far as asking himself: *Did we create a monster?* So, while they both eventually had intended to "move on" from CryptNotes, Nikolai was prompted to make the decision earlier.

Eventually, they sent a final email to fellow developers in the CryptNotes universe. The email was signed by Hideo Kamatsuka informing these developers that he was moving on to other projects. Kamatsuka-San said that he handed over the cryptographic key he had used to send network-wide alerts. However, that was a bit of a white lie. Indeed, both Frank and Nikolai kept their own access to the system, *only to be used in an emergency,* they thought, after having committed to each other that neither would ever use that key without full concurrence by the other.

■ ■ ■ ■ ■

In many ways, this was the end of an era, and the beginning of a new one. The network kept growing after Kamatsuka-San left the project. In fact, the value of CryptNotes went up manifold, and, in a few instances, crashed equally impressively. While many people today swear by the system and argue that the concept of blockchain opens numerous interesting avenues, a number of more cautious people point to potentially serious problems. In particular, they argue that there is the potential for price manipulation, for the whole affair being nothing but a pyramid scheme, or worse. Others, even more cynical, also point to the fact that the blockchain software has been made available free-of-charge for a dozen years, suggesting that breakthrough solutions, if there were several to come, should already be visible.

One thing is for sure: many people still work in the field and make or lose money through CryptNotes and the related cryptocurrencies that have been born after CryptNotes' success. A byproduct of this success is that crypto mining has grown, with as many of two thirds of them being based in China, particularly in Sichuan. China's recent crackdown on crypto mining on the grounds that mining uses too much electricity raises an interesting question: Is the country really against cryptocurrencies? Could it be that the country is simply trying to rein-in the electricity consumed by too many miners, all the while, behind the scenes supporting the development of the market, but to its own advantage and under its own control? Could it be that China would in fact welcome cryptocurrencies which might be the final nail in the coffin of the U.S. dollar as the world's reserve currency? What would a crypto market look like if it was controlled behind the scenes by a single political power?

CHAPTER.06

The stunning press headline reverberated around the world:

"Saudi Arabia's Crown Prince dies in plane crash in Persian Gulf . . ."

No public announcement had been made by Saudi Arabia, though some so-far unknown Islamic terrorist organization claimed credit for the accident. Journalists could not refrain from seeking the dramatic headline, although they were warned by the Saudi Palace that firm information was not yet available. What was factually known was that a plane supposed to be carrying the Crown Prince and a small entourage had gone down about an hour into its flight, while it was over the Southern end of the Persian Gulf. There was an unsubstantiated belief that it must have been shot down by missiles, though a few cooler heads argued that some massive mechanical failure could have produced the same outcome.

Rampant speculation continued, with more conviction vis-à-vis the missile theory when debris from the plane were located quite quickly in relatively shallow waters just a bit more than fifty miles off the coast of Dubai. The debris left no one in doubt as to the fate of its passengers and crew: nobody could have survived such a crash; it had to be preceded by one or several explosions since the pieces that were retrieved were all so small. No human remains were located. It would take longer to analyze the black box and to determine exactly what happened. With any luck, there would be useful signs pointing the investigation in the right direction.

■ ■ ■ ■ ■

The most senior of the two pilots currently flying the Royal 757 walked into the cabin with what seemed like a totally puzzled look on his face. Puzzlement may in fact be too weak a word; in truth, he looked mentally completely lost. He was no longer sure of what he knew and what he did not know. Yet, something told him that he had to do something. He approached the Crown Prince with what appeared to be quite a bit of hesitancy. Without daring to look him straight in the eyes, he weakly mumbled:

"Your Highness, I have just heard that your plane has been shot down and that you and your entourage are dead . . ."

He still exhibited total disbelief as he finished his sentence and awaited his instructions: a bit like someone going through motions automatically rather than in a way which he or she would have thought through. The whole thing made absolutely no sense to him: *how could the Prince, his entourage and crew all be dead? I should be too? And I'm not and I'm speaking to the Crown Prince?* The Crown Prince's reaction left him even more puzzled. A wide smile crossed his face. As a sheer reflex, the pilot even allowed himself a short chuckle as well. The Prince motioned to the pilot to wait an instant. He grabbed his cell phone and called Abdul back in Riyadh to ask for more information. He kept smiling as they were talking. Though no one other than he heard the conversation, the reaction of the Crown Prince was immediate. He politely and quite calmly asked the pilot:

"Please turn the plane around and proceed back to Riyadh."

He paused and added:

"We have enough fuel, don't we?"

"Yes, your Highness. Plenty with at least an extra hour of circling for safety. Plus, we always have King Khalid International Airport if something was wrong with the Riyadh Air Base."

The Crown Prince nodded his satisfaction, and, before the pilot could return to the cockpit, the Prince asked to be given access to the plane's public address system and said:

"Friends, something terrible just happened. Terrorists blew up a plane which they thought was ours. We are all assumed to be dead, which, of course, we are **not**; Allah be thanked. We are flying back to Riyadh, but I am going to invite every one of you to stay away from anyone outside of this plane. We will all be given some private quarters where we shall remain until the Government and our Security Services agree on what should be done. I am deeply aware that some of your loved ones may be left with the wrong idea of our demise for some time. The Palace will not confirm or even comment on the news. It will simply say that it is aware of the news but does not know whether the plane was really ours or another."

He paused and added:

"I dislike it as much as you do. I hope that we can find a way where the most important relatives may be spirited out of your homes and brought back to join you. Yet, total secrecy around our fate must remain out top priority."

One could hear some confused rumbling among the few passengers, but one does not confront, let alone contradict, the Crown Prince . . .

■ ■ ■ ■ ■

Countess Renate and Abdul el Wahabi had not left their positions at Riyadh Air Base since the A318 took off. That was part of the plan, and it was surely not the time to make any change. They were waiting for news. In truth, they were waiting for the announcement that terrorists had shot down the Prince's plane. They were unsure as to when it would happen, but there was nothing more for them to do than to wait for the news. The longer the news was taking to come, the more impatient they were becoming. Countess Renate was starting to worry that something had gone awry, as she had not heard anything, and the plane must have started its descent from 36,000 feet only a few minutes earlier. She had confirmed it with the remote pilots. Internally, she was starting to wonder: *What if the rumor was wrong? What if it was a set up to create more antipathy between Saudi Arabia and Israel?* Abdul, on his end, was even more worried as his potentially misplaced belief in some wild Israeli rumor had definitely inconvenienced the Crown Prince: *What's going to happen to me if this was a false alarm?*

All that internal turmoil ended in an instant. The news, which came straight from the remote pilots was laconic: "Lost control. Plane . . . down!"

Abdul's phone suddenly rang. Countess Renate noted that Abdul was speaking in Arabic and at the outset was wondering who might be at the other end. The demeanor of Abdul, who was bowing to the unseen interlocutor should have given her a clue, but it did not; after all, it could be someone from the palace as well. After his short phone conversation with the Crown Prince, Abdul was visibly relieved, but, at the same time, quite concerned. *What's going to happen next? What would the Crown Prince do?*

Abdul had been partially relieved when the Crown Prince agreed to have his flight return immediately to Riyadh. At least, he would not have to worry about the safety of His Royal Highness. Yet, with that relief came a ton of new work; he had to busy himself arranging discreet accommodations for the travelers. As per routine, the aircraft crew had been instructed to surrender any form of phone or internet communication device they possessed to the Prince's security detail. While these would normally be returned to them as soon as the plane landed, everyone instinctively understood that all forms of personal communications would be prohibited. The decision by the security detail to keep the cell phones, tablets or personal computers of the Prince's entourage made it crystal clear if it was ever needed. A couple of people were discreetly weeping, thinking of the agony imposed on their loved ones. Yet, again, there was no way anyone was going to go counter to explicit instructions from the Crown Prince!

■ ■ ■ ■ ■

A day later, as Abdul and Countess Renate were back together to plan their next steps, Renate asked:

"What do we know at this point?"

"Well, in truth, we do not know all that much, but we have excellent leads."

"What kind of leads?"

Abdul calmly enumerated the facts he felt he knew:

"We know the missile or missiles had to have been fired from within the oilfields, somewhere in a straight line between Doha and Sir Abu Nu'Ayr Island, so about 60 miles from Dubai. We have recovered pieces of missiles that bear Iranian markings."

"Already? Great. Iranian markings you say?"

"Yes, but that's hardly a surprise. We know the Iranians supply most of the regional terrorists with all sorts of weapons, including missiles. They hardly ever bother to hide their provenance."

"That's true. So, what do we think?"

Abdul went on to explain that there was no way of knowing who fired the missiles. The pilots of the two fighter jets did not see anything, though they reported they needed to take evasive maneuvers, as it appeared that missiles were also aimed at them. In his mind, he could rattle off as many as a half a dozen names of potential Iranian clients, each of whom might have been willing to try to shoot down the plane in exchange for some favor or arms delivery from Iran. One thing he added, though, was that there were strong indications that there was more than one missile used, explaining:

"The pieces don't fit together. There are at least a couple of different numbers on them. To me, it's got to mean that there were at least two different missiles, given what we have so far recovered . . ."

Countess interjected:

"They did **NOT** want to miss . . ."

"You can say that again."

Indeed, given the spot from where the terrorists were assumed to have shot at the plane and the fact that it was crossing 15,000 feet, it would already have been a large enough target. A single missile aimed at the center of the fuselage between the two jet engines would have caused an explosion, as this is where the fuel is typically stored in aircraft. The fact that the terrorists shot two missiles must mean that they wanted to be certain. Even if one of the missiles was a dud, the odds of both being "bad" were just not realistic. Abdul, however, added an intriguing comment:

"But nobody really saw anything and that's quite troubling."

"What do you mean?"

"Well, any regional terrorist organization can find a way of firing one or two missiles from any boat. I'm not saying that missile launchers are legion, but they're not rare. And also, they're even hard to fit on a boat; there's a minimum vessel size required to accommodate the launchers. But here, we are told nobody saw a boat launching any missile, and there were plenty of small craft in the area. It's a major oil field, so there are many supply boats going back and forth to shore from the platforms and vice versa. Yet, no one saw anything. That brings into play the possibility that the missiles were launched from a submarine, or at least some mini submarine."

"Wait a minute, Abdul. Wait a minute . . . Unless the missiles were fired from a lot further away than we think, how could a submarine navigate such shallow waters, particularly with such randomly varying depths? I'm told you go from 300 feet to 50 and back in less than a mile in that area, maybe even shallower."

"It's true that the waters are shallow and with varying depth, but our experts believe a small submarine could easily transit through them and fire if needed . . ."

Countess Renate looked pensive, but all of a sudden her face lit up. She said with excitement in her voice:

"Hey! Another thought . . . A while back, *Mossad* intercepted underwater drones that were able to launch missiles[5] . . . I remember Simon Rabinowitz telling us that the missiles they had recovered were Iranian, but that the launchers and the drones were probably of Chinese origin."

"Are you sure?"

"Absolutely. I can't remember all the details, but I know the general outline. Our group worked with *Mossad* to identify the source of the leak that allowed a then secret technology to be used to communicate with the underwater launchers."

She paused and then suggested with great conviction:

"We must bring Simon in on this as soon as we can."

Abdul looked surprised initially, but did not have the time to react, as Countess Renate had jumped to another facet of the issue:

"In any case, we **have** to talk to Simon, Abdul . . ."

Abdul did not seem to connect. She added:

"Remember, we should have a movie of the whole flight. They must have something on the videotapes taken from the Kovesh . . . So, by the way, make your "mini submarine" an underwater, remote-controlled missile launcher of the kind I'm talking about and the whole thing begins to make a huge amount of sense. The real or host submarine might have stayed further out in the Persian Gulf and

---

[5]   From the same author, see "Below the Surface," Barringer Publishing 2022

the drone missile launcher might have been positioned closer in, at a shallower depth . . ."

"I see what you mean."

Suddenly, his face betrayed a high degree of anxiety. He explained:

"But if that's true, it would have to mean some Chinese involvement, wouldn't it?"

"Yes and no. We don't know for sure. We know from my recollections, still to be verified by the way, that they provided these assemblies to Hezbollah, in part via Iran."

"So?"

"Well, Iran may have provided it to other groups, say the Houthis of Yemen, or anybody else. I doubt that Iran would be stupid enough to do it directly on their own. They operate through intermediaries. So, China may simply be an Iranian supplier . . ."

"And if it is not?"

Countess deadpanned:

"Then, it's a totally different kettle of fish. China attacking Saudi Arabia, one of its major oil suppliers would be ominous. Just add some Russian involvement to the mix and WW III becomes unavoidable . . ."

CHAPTER.07

RIYADH, SAUDI ARABIA AND TEL AVIV, ISRAEL

Still the day after the attack, but in the early afternoon, Abdul had been able to have a more thorough conversation with the Prince. The point of the formal meeting was not only for him to report on what was known, but also to get as specific instructions as possible as to what the Prince was prepared to authorize. Interestingly, the Prince asked Abdul to rehash the entirety of the plan that had been put into execution. Abdul was beaming as the Prince said in reply:

"Colonel Abdul el Wahabi, you saved my life, Thank you. Some reward will come when some calm has returned. The king will know of your exploit."

It may not be well-known that the Crown Prince of Saudi Arabia is the second most important position in the Kingdom, after the King himself. In the absence of the King, an order is issued to have the Crown Prince manage the affairs of the state until the King's return. Therefore, technically, the Prince could order virtually anything, including going to war, assuming that he had received the King's permission beforehand, though even that would not be an absolute necessity in theory at least. In the present case, needless to say, the King and the Prince were both furious. An attempt on the life of the successor to the King is extremely serious; the future of the monarchy is threatened.

At the same time, Saudi Arabia had no desire to start a regional war, particularly as they assumed that no one could ever fully and definitively prove the identity of the country which was behind the attack. The constellation of terrorist organizations spawned by Islamism and rivalries between Islamic groups was such that it was almost always possible to hide behind some, thus far, unknown or barely known group, as was the case here with the group that claimed credit for the attack. Some might even go as far as to argue that Kuwait's leadership is closer to Iran than to Saudi Arabia, and that a terror group loosely linked to Kuwait might have sailed south toward Dubai and been responsible.

The directions given to Abdul by the Crown Prince were quite straightforward, though details would still have to be worked out. The terrorist attempt on the life of the Crown Prince had definitely changed the landscape. Therefore, first, Abdul had to figure out as quickly as possible who was behind the assassination attempt, and, in the event it was a minor league terrorist organization, who commandeered it. Second, Abdul had to develop a plan to strike at the terrorists and their backers, even if the main backer was a powerful regional state. The Prince however added an important caveat:

"Under no condition should a potential retaliatory act by us which could be read as an act of war ever be traced to the Kingdom, even if the backer is Iran."

The latter comment reflected the political reality of the region. Iran was well known to be involved with, and supplying, several regional terrorist organizations from Yemen to Lebanon to Syria. Thus, implicitly, but without saying it aloud, the Crown Prince was arguing that the odds favored the theory that Iran was involved in the assassination attempt. After all, Iran saw itself as the "home" of Shiite Muslims, while Saudi Arabia, with Mecca and Medina the two holiest sites for Islam located within the kingdom, was the unquestioned home of Sunni Muslims, the less "pure" version of Islam in the interpretation of the Shiites. Yet, it was equally clear that nobody would really win a regional war between Iran and Saudi Arabia. History had shown how useless the war between Iran and Iraq had been: no winner and massive casualties on both sides; there was no point adding an unnecessary chapter to that book. On the other hand, covert actions that would weaken Iran would certainly be welcome, as would steps which would convince Iran's geopolitical backers that the cost of supporting Iran might be higher than expected.

In passing, the Prince thanked Abdul for finding a way to isolate the fighter pilots escorting the 757, adding:

"I'm glad that they won't talk to anyone, though I am sure that no one explained to them why we were returning to Riyadh. Yet, better safe than sorry."

He paused for a second and sighed:

"But it doesn't take a rocket scientist to figure out what might have happened . . ."

■ ■ ■ ■ ■

Abdul knew that the Kingdom had numerous external consultants. Each of them should be able to provide useful help to achieve the Prince's first objective, though it might take some time. He already knew for a fact that whatever weapon had brought the jet down had left a trace: they had already had access to debris from the missiles, although at this point one was talking of photographs, not the actual piece of metal. Further, all the states that were in any way potentially implicated from a geographical standpoint were more friendly than not; the access to physical evidence should not be too difficult; and, in this case, physical evidence included the aircraft's black boxes. The debris field was slightly south of Sir Abu Nu'Ayr, a small island about fifty miles offshore Abu Dhabi; it is a part of the Emirate of Sharjah, one of the seven emirates in the United Arab Emirates. It sits in the middle of the region's prolific offshore oil territory. The sea in that area is quite shallow, ranging to a maximum of two hundred feet, and most of the time averaging around a hundred feet. The debris of the jet were easy to see, and currents, in the area, were not particularly strong. In fact, a hangar had already been set up on the south coast of Sir Abu Nu'Ayr Island, near the new airport, to collect all the pieces and perform the initial investigation.

Given the fact that the plane was supposed to have the Saudi Crown Prince as a passenger, the local authorities on the island gracefully accepted the Kingdom's request that a couple of Saudi observers be posted on the island to supervise the recovery of the plane's debris. They were all members of the Prince's personal security team. At the same time, many commentators were surprised not to have heard a word from the Saudi Royal Family confirming or denying that the Prince had been on the flight.

Two schools of thoughts emerged. The first postulated that the Prince was onboard that flight and that the Kingdom was waiting to retrieve at least some humans remains, preferably assumed to belong to the Prince, before confirming anything. Inevitably, speculation was rampant as to the likelihood of finding anything in waters which are known to be home to a number of varieties of sharks. Yet, interestingly, statistics suggest that shark attacks are much more common on the Iranian side of the Gulf than along the coast near Abu Dhabi or Dubai, which would at least weaken that narrative. The second school of thought argued that the Prince was not on the flight. He must have had to change his plans. The lack of official reaction probably reflected caution until they knew better what might have happened. There was no point being aggressive if there was a simple explanation; on the other hand, any reaction to a terrorist attack on the life of the heir to the throne would have to be much more strongly worded. The more time passed, the more journalists always in search of a story were leaning towards the second interpretation.

The two flight and cockpit recorder boxes were immediately located and brought to the hangar. The United Arab Emirates authorities readily agreed that these be transferred to Riyadh for analysis. Again, there were few surprises. The cockpit voice recorder did not generate much of anything, as the voices on the tape were those of the remote pilots. Everyone with a need to know within the Saudi security apparatus already had that recording, from the source, the remote pilots themselves. Yet, at the same time, the recorder also reflected the conversations between the pilots and air traffic control. These were sparse as the plane was struck during its descent, a bit more than halfway between its cruising altitude and the ground. One thing was for sure: there had been no emergency that could be identified. In short, the missile theory was becoming virtually incontrovertible.

Countess Renate did not say anything, but she knew that the remote pilots would have told Saudi Security immediately if there had been some sort of warning or failure before the crash. So, from her point of view, the only potentially interesting element would be from the black box which would be recording the settings of the various controls. Yet, the flight recorder did not produce anything of interest. It confirmed that the aircraft was smack on its flight plan and crossing 15,000 feet with its nose up about 2 degrees when it was hit. It did confirm the initial observations on the time and location of the attack. Through there may have been one or two hits, the flight recorder went down almost immediately. This is not a surprise. Flight recorders are powered from the aircraft's electricity supply. After an accident like this, the electrical supply is lost, effectively freezing the data. In addition, it is just the data storage section of the flight recorder that is protected during and after a crash.

■ ■ ■ ■ ■

Countess Renate had set up a Zoom call with David Heller, who was captaining the effort for Simon, and Abdul. She asked:

"David, what is your reading of the Kovesh' s images?"

"Quite interesting in fact. As you know Countess, we have a number of elements pretty much down. First, there were four missiles, launched virtually at the same time from the same place."

"Abdul was talking of two missiles."

"I know, but in fact there were four. That's clear. They were shot from drone submarines, probably remotely controlled sea-to-air missile launchers. The water where they were was shallow enough that we could see that there were two launchers. We can see enough to believe that they were of the same type as planned by Hezbollah when they dropped them off our coastline. Interestingly, it would seem that two of the missiles totally missed their target. Guidance problem or something else."

Countess Renate asked:

"You sure?"

Abdul interrupted:

"Could they have been aimed at the jets escorting the plane?"

David remained prudent in his assessment:

"Quite possible. In fact, more probable than a guidance malfunction. Yet, you're never sure without the physical evidence. We need some more analysis, but I'd be surprised if the story changes materially. Remember, I had more than a few opportunities to see these babies up close and personal. I know what they look like. If they were not the same, then my guess is that they are an upgraded version of the original ones. So, no change in the conclusion."

He paused and added:

"The Kovesh images showed that there was a helicopter hovering in that area as well, and guess what? There was a radio cone suspended from it. Remember what we saw in our own waters a while back, off the coast of Haifa? So, it's fair to assume that this is the same combination that we saw there. Whoever supplies them must have retained blueprints or some inventory."

"Need to find out more about that."

"Totally agree, Simon is actually on the case. This is clearly a security risk. He has not forgotten the Chinese—Iranian link."

"Anything else?"

"Well, there seemed to be a submarine where the water is deeper. We could almost guess a long, dark shadow probably a thousand feet below the surface at most. Note that we're not in the realm of facts here; that's speculation, as the shadow could have been due to a myriad of other causes. We assume that she is kind of the mother ship, which was around to grab the missile launchers once the mission was accomplished. By the way, that would rule out any Kuwaiti connection; its Navy does not own any submarines, just offshore patrol boats."

"Did the submarine grab the missile launchers?"

"We don't know for sure. As you surely remember, the Kovesh had to turn back to Palmachim as soon as possible to avoid having to make a pit stop to refuel probably at Eilat. However, we have clear images of the helicopter flying off as soon as the missiles were shot. The one thing that's surprising is that we couldn't see any markings whatsoever on the bird."

Abdul offered his educated guess:

"Has to be Iranian, but they did not want to risk being blamed in any way . . . Who else would have them and use them in that part of the Gulf?"

Countess Renate shifted gears:

"Can't disagree, but let's not confuse facts and assumptions, however well-founded they may be. Now, given where we are, can we discuss the outline of the rest our project?"

Countess Renate was specifically referring to the retaliatory actions which were supposed to be carried out. Abdul agreed and proceeded to give a general idea of the project which had been approved in concept only so far by the Crown Prince and the Royal Council. He stated the obvious:

"The Kingdom is by now tired of being hit, the latest attempt being in their view a significant escalation."

He continued, indicating that it had thus been decided to sponsor some form of non-attributable anti-terrorist activity which would do to the terrorists and their backers the same as they were doing to Saudi Arabia. He added the major caveat on which the Crown Prince had insisted:

"It must remain totally untraceable to Saudi Arabia . . ."

Countess Renate seemed a bit surprised by the boldness of the idea. She thought for a couple of minutes which seemed like an eternity to Abdul. She then surprised him as she replied:

"The Shadow Experts aren't terrorists. We have historically facilitated fighting terrorist organizations. To some extent, we could see this project as a reply to a terrorist attack. Yet, I know that we do not have the tools to conduct these attacks. We would need to work with some other counter-terrorist organization. *Mossad* immediately comes to mind, though I am really unsure as to how Simon would react. No offense, David."

"None taken, Countess. In fact, I suspect that Simon would want Ariel and probably the War Cabinet involved. As Abdul indicated: Saudi Arabia doesn't want to be identified. I won't surprise you when I say that neither does Israel."

As Abdul was nodding his approval, Countess Renate replied:

"Great. We agree. In fact, I know that Simon wants to talk to me and have his friend the CIA Director of Operations along. Can't think of what they want to discuss, but with Simon and Jack Turnbull, things are always interesting."

She paused for a short minute and, turning to Abdul, queried:

"But I assume this means you must get permission to get Israel in the loop as well . . ."

Abdul simply kept nodding. He knew he needed permission and that permission would be granted given the current mindset in the Crown Prince's entourage. Yet, he did not relish the idea of discussing the idea. However smart the Prince was, and he was quite smart, he was also known to be somewhat impulsive. How would he react to the notion that Saudi Arabia might partner, again as it turned out, with Israel against a common enemy?

CHAPTER.08

"Countess, I'm glad we could find some time to talk . . ."

"Simon, you know that my telephone line is always open for you."
She paused and quickly added:

". . . and for you too, Frank. So, what's up?"

Simon let Jack tell Countess Renate what had just happened in the
world financial markets. He started with the pure facts, discussing the
large trades which had been noted. He then added, though admitting
that there was no direct confirmation yet, that it seemed more than
marginally probable that China was selling some of its very large U.S.
government bond holdings and exchanging the U.S. dollar proceeds
for CryptNotes. He concluded:

"Let's be honest and clear. At this point, we have no proof of
anything. The Chinese are known to hold about $4 or $5 trillion
worth of U.S. Treasury bonds, about 12% to 16% of all outstanding
stock. We suspect that they must have sold at most a few hundred
billion or so."

"How do we know that?"

"Well, Countess, the truth is that we don't. So, let me rephrase this: we have seen a few trades totaling probably more than $100 billion, but less than $300. At the same time, we don't know if we saw all the activity. We only picked up trading that occurred in Asia, in Singapore to be precise. There could be more, but if there was, we haven't seen it. To make things even worse, they could have simply been selling to raise the funds needed to subscribe to new issuance by the U.S. government, although we think they did not . . ."

Countess Renate followed up:

"Same question, but on the CryptNotes, . . ."

"Oh, with those, things are not any simpler; the amount of CryptNotes purchased so far looks close to what they should have gotten from the sales of bonds. Although, again, note that these are traders' approximations."

Jack paused for a second. Then he admitted that, so far at least, there was no way to be sure of anything. However, there were at least two or three elements which did not make sense:

"First, the way they seem to be carrying this out makes no sense. Traders do not normally show their books. They try to get the best prices . . . To minimize their impact on markets. So, if you're doing such large trades, you would normally look for a way to mislead markets . . . Or at least not to be so obvious."

He could see that Countess Renate was not following. He explained:

"Remember that I am not a financial market expert, so, at best, I am repeating what I've been told. You might have a small buy order in the middle of a selling program. Just to see what happens if your order misleads the market into thinking you are through with your sales. Second, why focus solely on one trading location, Singapore? Singapore is an important marketplace, but it pales in comparison to London and New York. That also makes no sense."

Countess Renate replied:

"Unless they're trying to start a panic which would result in many others selling as well. Wouldn't that make sense?"

The question unsettled Jack. In fairness, that was a scenario which hadn't so far at least been raised. Playing it in his mind, he reasoned that the hypothetical Chinese goal would be to scare the U.S.; to show them that they can start a run on the Treasury market or the U.S. Dollar without making much more than a small dent in their own holdings. He paused and asked:

"Wait a minute, if that's what they're doing, aren't they cutting off their nose to spite their face?"

Renate asked,

"Why do you say that?"

"Simple: they would suffer the loss on their whole portfolio, whatever was left after the sales, if both bond prices and the dollar went down. We think these holdings represent a solid thirty to fifty percent of their foreign exchange reserves."

Jack paused again to see Countess Renate's reaction and then continued:

"So, sure. The U.S. would possibly have to deal with higher interest rates. But remember, the Fed has bought trillions of U.S. Treasuries in the last several years. So, a few hundred billion would not matter much."

Jack concluded his reasoning:

"The point is that this does not make sense. Again, at some level, the sale or purchase of a few billions of U.S. Treasury bonds are kind of all in a day's work. However, the fact that they are exchanging the U.S. Dollars for some other currency, in this case a cryptocurrency, suggests that there is more to the plot. And that's what we need to find out."

Though he had some idea already, Simon could not resist asking Jack to expand on the rationale. Jack went back to a theme he had already broached with Simon:

"Well, the big weakness of the U.S. economy is that it has gotten used to living in an absurdly low interest rate environment. Even more, the U.S. Government is running budget deficits which add to that debt, each and every year. They would find it a lot harder to service the debt if interest rates were higher. Think of this, total public debt in the U.S. is just short of $30 trillion dollars. Raise interest rates on average by one full percent and you get an increase in interest payable of $300 billion, not immediately, but quickly enough as bonds mature and need to be replaced by new ones paying market rates. That's about 7.5% of total federal budget revenue . . . Assume that interest rates rise by more than 1%, say 3%, for the sake of argument, and the whole thing collapses. You'd have to double taxes or reduce all the various social benefits in the U.S. budget by some 25%."

Jack paused for a second and then ominously added:

"Or substantially cut their defense spending . . ."

Countess Renate simply said:

"I see. Could be a way to force the U.S. to slip into second place as a hyperpower."

"Damn right. Second behind China! But that is not all. The increase in government interest rates would immediately reverberate throughout the economy, mortgages, corporate credit, consumer credit, you name it. The pain would be horrendous."

Simon interrupted:

"But is there not something the government could do to deal with that?"

Jack could only reply:

"Well, there is. But, in truth, it's only a short-term solution. The Federal Reserve Bank could buy some of the bonds sold by the Chinese. In economic jargon, it's called "printing money.""

"So?"

"There's the rub, my friend. The Fed has already been buying bonds, to the tune of $5 or $7 trillion in the last several years as I just said. That's causing inflation to pick up already. Have them do more, which would I'm sure be the short-term solution, and the risk of hyperinflation is real."

He paused for a minute and concluded:

"When you think of it, it is a diabolically smart tactic on the part of the Chinese if that's what they're trying to do. Sure, too obvious a selling strategy might depress the value of their U.S. Treasury holdings. In fact, the last few days have already put a dent in it. But whatever capital value they lose has got to be a lot less than what they'd need to spend to develop a military capability that is sure to beat the U.S. They found the weakness and they are using it."

Countess Renate noted:

"Wow, that's terrifying. We could go on and discuss how and why the U.S. got themselves into that mess, but that's probably not the right topic at this point."

Jack came straight back:

"Totally agreed. The key now is whether we can find a way of either getting greater conviction on what the Chinese are doing and if our hypothesis is correct, how we can get them to re-evaluate the cost of the exercise or simply to realize that they cannot win."

"Well, gentlemen, there may be something I know which could make this a lot less worrisome prospect."

Jack's eyes widened and he asked:

"You've got my ear, Countess."

Countess Renate retorted that she could not provide much detail without creating a real danger for the Shadow Experts. Yet, she cryptically added:

"Assume for a minute that we may have some inside knowledge of the cryptocurrency market. Then things might change. We might be able to devise a strategy which would considerably raise the costs of the operation to the Chinese side. Now, let me note that there is little I can do or think of doing with respect to the ownership of

U.S. government debt. That, Jack, is for your government to resolve. However, there may be a way to make the proceeds from the sales less valuable. And, if the Chinese cannot any longer eliminate the U.S. Dollar risk, their strategy might have to be revised . . ."

Simon beat Jack to the reply:

"Quite intriguing, Countess. When can we move to the next step in this discussion? Am I correct assuming that you may need to have certain "internal" conversations?"

"Simon, you're always on the ball, aren't you? You're correct. I must first find out what I can and cannot do. Let's just say that my feminine intuition tells me that we may have at least some partial solution."

Simon thanked her and added:

"I won't push you any more at this point. But, if I am somehow on the same wavelength as you, I think we could actually use the current quandary to address at least one if not two other problems."

He paused and added:

"Didn't we need to talk about a new client of yours as we speak?"

"You're right, Simon, but I have not yet received the all-clear signal."

"I see."

"Let me add that the client might actually help you, Jack. He could be a buyer of U.S. Treasuries if asked nicely . . ."

Jack was about to say something, but Countess Renate gestured with her hand that she would not say more."

CHAPTER.09

A while earlier, Hans Koerig, the Head of the Globale PrivatBank in Vienna, was attending a conference at the Hilton Imperial, one of the best, if not the best hotel in Dubrovnik, Croatia. Located on Marijana Blazica, the palace had many rooms offering a gorgeous view of the harbor. Additionally, it offered all the amenities which one would expect from a hotel in which to hold a conference. Finally, its proximity to the walled old town provided great opportunities to take in the local color and view the rightly well-known local attractions, like the guards parading in vintage uniforms, the multitude of ordained ministers of various monotheist religions crossing paths in their respective religious dress or the contrast between the old and the new in terms of architecture.

The Globale PrivatBank was founded several generations earlier by an ancestor of Hans and had remained in the hands of the Koerig family ever since. It had been careful never to offend any power that be, yet to maintain the highest possible standards; "discretion, accommodation and professionalism" might have been the bank's motto. Austria indeed had to experience somewhat of a bumpy economic ride in the second half of the 19th century and the first half of the 20th. The Vienna stock market crash of 1873, which triggered a great depression in Austria, the dissolution of the Habsburg empire that encompassed Austria and Hungary in the aftermath of the first world war and the collapse of the Austrian financial system in 1931, all illustrated the serious challenges which the country experienced. Austria's banks, though helped by the government in that they were not forced to write off non-performing loans, survived but many subsequently became considerably more conservative in the management of their balance sheets. Globale PrivatBank, with its origins at the heights of the Habsburg Empire, maintained an undeniably understated, aristocratic quality to its overall presentation that extended to its "reception rooms" which exuded an air of discreet elegance. The famous slogan created by Citibank Switzerland's advertising agency in the early to mid-1990s would seem to have been crafted for Globale PrivatBank: "money talks, but wealth whispers."

The principal focus of the Dubrovnik conference was cyber security in the banking system. It secondarily included some discussion about bank secrecy and how it was evolving. One session was devoted to the interplay between traditional banking operations and the advent of cryptocurrencies. The fellow seated next to Hans during the first morning session seemed very interested and was frequently alternatively nodding or smiling.

When the session was over and the coffee break started, Hans made a determined effort to meet that individual. In truth, Hans Koerig was quite a traditional banker in an environment where money was generally "clean" and yet somewhat recent. As a traditional banker, Hans was not as fully versed in the new technology or instruments as he could or wanted to be. The gentleman seated to his right in that session at the conference seemed to him to be a godsend. He assumed that he might be willing to help him educate himself in those newer areas which he knew he had to learn. Hans found him easily, sitting quietly in a plush, orange velvet armchair and observing what was happening around him. Hans was surprised that other people had not tried to get close to him and thought: *Is this someone who wants to remain by himself? Can I still try to speak with him?* Eventually, overcoming his hesitation, Hans approached him and asked if he could join him. The gentleman smiled broadly and invited him to sit in the chair right next to his. Hans simply said:

"You seem to understand so much of what was said in the last session. I, for one, probably did not understand more than a small fraction. Yet, this seems to be an important topic."

"I agree with you, by the way you said your name was . . ."

"Koerig, Hans Koerig, from Globale PrivatBank, in Austria."

"Nice to meet you, Nikolai Bernstein here. I'm a financial consultant and I live in London. Back to your point: cryptocurrencies and the algorithm on which they are based are probably here to stay. They are very important, particularly when governments behave badly. Yet, they could also be a source of mischief."

Hans wanted to ask what the gentleman meant by "governments behaving badly," but did not have the time. A hotel employee was walking among the guests with chimes; the discreet sound was meant to tell everyone that the coffee break was over and the next session about to start. Hans and Nikolai's conversation had to stop, but not before they agreed to meet for lunch, which was scheduled for the next break after the session that was scheduled to begin in a minute or two.

At lunch, though they were not alone at their table, they engaged in an ever-deeper discussion of the crypto world, but, somehow and maybe surprisingly, no one seemed to try and meddle in their conversation. Hans was impressed that there was no detail which Nikolai did not seem to know, while Nikolai was fascinated by the eagerness to learn of that nice traditional banker who seemed to be totally unfit for the topic. They sat together again for the next two dining functions, with Hans feeling he was gaining some knowledge, but not nearly enough to become proficient. Before departing Dubrovnik, Hans asked a question which Nikolai found surprising:

"You must have guessed by now that I am way beyond my depth."

He paused as Nikolai was politely making hand gestures to indicate that the assertion was not true, and yet continued:

"Would you mind meeting a friend of mine who could really use your help?"

"I would be delighted, but where does that friend live? Personally, as I told you earlier, I live in London."

"Oh, location should not be an issue. My friend travels all the time. In fact, there are times when I ask myself if she really has a permanent residence."

He paused, smiled and continued:

"So, I'm sure she would have no problem meeting you there in London, or wherever you prefer . . ."

■ ■ ■ ■ ■

Hans's next call, while at Filipe, Dubrovnik's airport, waiting for his Austrian Airlines flight back to Vienna, was to Countess Renate. Though he was in effect quite excited, nobody looking at him there or at the other end of the phone line could guess it. He had "put back" his self-controlled Austrian banker's face and appeared totally calm. He announced:

"Hans Koerig here."

"What an unexpected pleasure, Hans, what can I do for you?"

"Well, I just met someone whom I think you might well want to meet . . ."

Countess Renate was at the same time surprised and not surprised. It was not unusual for members of the Shadow Experts to call her with ideas—and Hans Koerig was a member of the Shadow Experts.

On the other hand, they were not always the best sources of referrals for new experts. She asked:

"Really, who?"

"The name may not be familiar, but his area of knowledge is crucial."

"What is it?"

"Cryptocurrencies and the crypto world in general . . ."

"Really? Really?"

She paused for a few seconds. For her, the potential contact was all the more relevant as she had indeed started to think of the so-called crypto phenomenon and felt very weak on the topic. She had had a few conversations with a few people recommended or not by her experts but had not so far found someone who combined the three attributes she sought: the knowledge she would require, the motivation that is essential to be a Shadow Expert, and the "bedside manners" that make the expert quite effective. She added:

"Indeed, this could be quite interesting. Am I correct assuming that you are thinking of the person for the Shadow Experts and are assuming that we do not have that knowledge in house yet?"

"Absolutely. Sorry, it did not even occur to me to assume the group had that knowledge."

"Not to worry. You're actually quite correct; we don't have the depth we need. Our cyber expert in Singapore has some understanding, but he was telling me quite recently that we would do well to add that arrow to our quiver. What's the person's name?"

"Nikolai Bernstein."

"Never heard of him. Are you sure he knows what he's talking about?"

"Well, you know that it would not be hard to fool me. I know next to nothing. I met him at a conference in Dubrovnik and he seemed very knowledgeable during a session on cyber security and the crypto world. I connected with him afterwards and found him eager to share his knowledge . . ."

"Why would he do that?"

"My impression is that he sees a lot of the good that comes with the development of the crypto world, but also appreciates that a lot of mischief could also result from it. Found it interesting that despite what seemed like a lot of knowledge, he did not ask questions or try to draw attention to himself."

Countess Renate was surprised by Hans's comment. Yet, at the same time, it encouraged her. She had through her usual contacts heard rumors of illegal or at least quite questionable activity in the crypto space. For instance, she had read stories on the use of cryptocurrencies on the black web, with the implication that they probably financed a whole slew of undesirable activities: crime, illegal arm sales, and even a good part of the drug trade. Similarly, another article argued that cryptocurrencies were used by money launderers and others trying to evade capital controls. She had also even read about possible manipulations in cryptocurrencies. In particular, she had been impressed by this piece in the financial press at some point a few years back. It reported on research claiming that a company may have manipulated a cryptocurrency by issuing tokens which they offered without having the backing of real dollars. In short, the message of the piece was that the one cryptocurrency involved in that story might simply have been a sort of Ponzi scheme. Her impression had been that a lot of the buying might have been suspicious, and, even worse if true, narratives had been constructed and spread which had enticed unsuspecting people to enter a market which, in the end, they probably did not really understand.

Countess Renate knew that none of these charges were ever proven, but she kept asking herself what she and many others might be missing. How could she evaluate or help clients evaluate situations in which cryptocurrencies were involved if she did not have the facts and the means to interpret what she was seeing? From that vantage point, the idea of learning more and possibly having a specialist on the team was very appealing to her, provided she could develop the confidence needed to believe and trust that individual. She told Hans that she would contact Mr. Bernstein if Hans could forward his contact information.

■ ■ ■ ■ ■

Countess Renate first met with Nikolai Bernstein in London. Though she introduced herself as Hilde Schneider, an Austrian socialite who was fascinated by technology, she readily admitted that she did not know much about it herself. They met at the Dorchester Hotel, off Hyde Park, in a nod to the status she was impersonating, though, in truth, Countess Renate herself would have had no trouble affording a stay in the establishment. She faked a rather strong Germanic accent and wore sufficient disguise to ensure that she did not look like either Countess Renate or Princess Alexandra. That would ensure that, even if the contact went nowhere, there would not be someone able to associate her face and the names of either of her alter egos. At that stage of the proceedings, it was common for her to remain extremely cautious.

She found Nikolai quite nice and was happy with the way he answered the few technical questions she raised. Nikolai was definitely quite careful to project a solid knowledge of the matter, while his experience as a professor at the London School of Economics allowed him to tailor the specificity of his words to the level of understanding he judged characterized his audience. Thus, he was conveying enough hard information for Countess Renate to feel that she was leaning something, all the while avoiding taking her down rabbit holes where he would unquestionably have lost her. At the same time, he displayed what Countess Renate judged was enough self-confidence not to seek to impress, for the sake of impressing. She interpreted that as a good sign. She kept thinking: *"I like him. He can talk to our clients and will neither seek to impress them nor seem unable to explain things they do not understand."*

Her principal focus was to try and get a read on the character and, without being too direct, on why he was willing to share the secrets he was sharing. His original answer to the first technical question was in fact quite disarming:

"As you know, Hilde, the CryptNotes world is an open-source project; as such, it isn't owned or operated by anyone. Thus, I don't have much of a reason to keep much of anything secret. You can find out most of what you would want to know on Wikipedia or similar sites."

"I see. Wish I had thought of that. Yet, your knowledge has to be worth money."

"I certainly hope it does. However, I do not want to seem to brag, but I have more than enough to live on. I am not a part of the jet set. My needs and those of my family are modest. I come from modest roots, and I am already impressed with what I can do with what we have as it is."

"You're not currently working?"

"Yes and no. I do not have a formal, full-time job if that is what you mean by "working." I still take a few teaching assignments when I am asked and feel qualified. I'll take on this or that consulting project also. But in the end, most of my time is dedicated to keeping current on the crypto world and to understand it as much as I can. I do a bit of research on the side too, just to keep my mind active. You know? There's nothing worse than an idle mind. Moreover, my wife and I have two children and they need a role model; someone who works, just as they will need to work when they are older."

Countess Renate, aka Hilde Schneider, had already decided that, if the first meeting went well, she would have Nikolai meet with Wong Hai Chock, her cyber specialist in Singapore. If needed, Raj Agarwal, her hardware expert in Bangalore could offer his own opinion. Ostensibly, these would be introduced as friends or acquaintances, with pseudonyms which would allow both to keep their identity secret. For her, at this point, Nikolai had passed the first part of the test. Quickly, she shifted her focus to Nikolai's background and the reasons why he was so ready to help her friend Hans Koerig.

Nikolai had originally decided that he would not reveal anything of his real background. Both he and Frank Thistle had managed to remain under the radar since they left CryptNotes. Some truly critical new insight would be needed to revisit the decision to remain anonymous.

Nikolai's reluctance to go into a few of the details about which she asked questions surprised Countess Renate. She suspected that there was something which prevented Nikolai from opening up, but she was unsure what it might be. She hoped she had not misjudged him, effectively having unwittingly exhausted his actual knowledge.

She pivoted and started to tell a story about another friend of hers, who remained nameless. She had started a group of experts to help people resolve situations they could not otherwise address. She provided a few examples, suitably doctored, of the successes the friend had had. She was delighted to see that Nikolai was opening up as she went on. She still decided then that she could not come clean and admit that the friend in question was nobody else but her. She still asked how Nikolai would react if she offered to put him in contact either with her friend or someone she suspected knew more about her. Nikolai replied that he would welcome that as a next step, adding:

"This could in fact be exactly what the doctor ordered for me. Keeping my mind active and contributing to some greater cause."

■ ■ ■ ■ ■

Back from London and now in her castle in Austria, Countess Renate called Wong Hai Chock.

"Hai Chock? Countess Renate here."

"How are you? More importantly, knowing you Countess, what can I do for you?"

"Touché. Well, I have always felt that we lacked sufficient depth in the cryptocurrency field, and I believe you agree with that assessment. Now, guess what? I may have met someone who might be ready to help. I did not tell him who I was. I just said that I had a friend who had created a group which looked a lot like the Shadow Experts we all know and love."

"Cautious and very much in character. No surprise. Where do I come in? Let me guess? You would like me to talk to him or her, right?"

"Indeed. By the way, it's a "he." But let me add one important caveat. You know of a group of experts, but you do not know much more than the fact the group exists. More importantly, you are not a part of it, nor do you suspect I am. I guess this might be a good time to call your old friend, Jim Ng, back to the fore."

Hai Chock smiled. He knew that Jim Ng was an alter ego he had used in other occasions to help Countess Renate without being thus required to reveal his real identity. He replied:

"I see. What do you want me to test?"

"Depth of cyber knowledge, and you should have no problem pointing to your "day job" as a professor/researcher at the National University of Singapore. Jim Ng also works there, correct?"

"No, Countess. He used to work there and is now a consultant. No matter, I, or rather Jim can refer to that earlier experience . . ."

"Good. You see, I understand that Nikolai—that's the fellow's name—was once a professor at the London School of Economics. Academia could be some sort of an initial common ground."

"Sure. Makes sense. Leave it with me, I'll find out what I can and revert. Can you send me his phone number, email address or whatever I need to get in touch with him, please?"

"Sure will . . . He will be expecting your call. Will you use the phone or Zoom?"

"Depends on what he prefers. Doesn't matter much to me, though I kind of like to see facial expressions."

CHAPTER.10

TEL AVIV, ISRAEL, RIYADH, SAUDI ARABIA, AND SOMEWHERE IN THE AUSTRIAN ALPS

Simon had invited David Heller and Marvin Goldstein to meet him in his office at *Mossad* headquarters in Tel Aviv. A veteran of the service, Marvin was responsible for all technological development for *Mossad*. He had an encyclopedic knowledge of the capabilities of each of the branches of the Israeli Defense Forces. He also knew exactly what was being planned for the future and even what research directions were emphasized and those which were not. At fifty, Marvin had worked with nearly all the key players in the service and his reputed friendship with both Ariel Landau, *Mossad*'s Director, and Simon, Ariel's deputy, opened many doors.

He knew his stuff better than anyone and had a mind that thrived on challenges. He loved innovation, even if this was going to stretch his capabilities nearly to the breaking point. He was a man of vision; his vision was focused on technology. His only well-known shortcoming was that he loved technology so much that often he would extend his explanations into levels of detail that many considered unnecessary and often veered away from common Hebrew, or English, to speak in technobabble. Yet, most people still gave him a pass on those, as he was so good at everything else.

The point of the meeting involved discussing a couple of "disruption" capabilities which might be needed, if the decision was finally made for *Mossad* to help strike at one or several of Saudi Arabia's enemies in a way such that no one could point the finger toward either Israel or Saudi Arabia. At that moment, the idea which floated in Simon's and David's heads relied almost entirely on a narrative which still comprised numerous unknowns, as Simon had added:

"Way too many unknowns!"

Neither Simon nor David were ready to commit to anything. They suspected they had most of the required capabilities. Yet, the step involved in moving from actions that directly concerned Israel, to something designed to help Saudi Arabia was a big one: from direct to at best indirect benefits.

As a start, the duo was indeed assuming first that the missiles that had brought down the airliner in which the Crown Prince was supposed to be traveling were shot by clients of Iran, if not directly by Iran. Further, they believed that these missiles were shot from a remote-controlled submarine launcher, which they had earlier determined was manufactured by Iran, using controls which came in part if not totally from China. Finally, they could see and thus knew for a fact that the missiles bore Iranian markings. In short, they were working on the assumption that China and Iran were in the loop at least because they had proximately provided the weaponry if not the execution. Those were the links that could lead them to accept the assignment, subject to political agreement from the government; the old: *"the enemy of my enemy can be my friend even if he does not seem to like me much."*

The one area where speculation was still ripe related to the fact that the helicopter that they believed communicated the instructions to fire to the underwater launchers had no identification whatsoever on it. Marvin offered a hypothesis:

"What if the helicopter was also from Iran? After all, the geography of the place from which the attack was carried out would not be readily accessible to clients of Iran. On the west side of the Persian Gulf, you have Kuwait, Saudi Arabia, Bahrain, Qatar and the United Arab Emirates. I can't believe that any of these countries would carry out anything like an attempt on the life of the heir to the throne, except, but even there I feel I must tread very softly, Kuwait."

He paused to drink from the glass that sat on the table to his right and added:

"You know that the situation in Kuwait is complex. Officially, it is definitely on the side of the U.S. Unofficially, . . ."

Simon interrupted:

"We know, Marvin. We know. If I may add my own two cents worth, I think it is on the side of Saudi Arabia but needs to keep its distances."

Marvin nodded and continued on his previous train of thought:

"If you think of Yemen, it's probably too far, about 800 miles one way. But it would have to fly over Saudi territory and the United Arab Emirates most of the way if it kept to a straight line. Have them fly south first then over Oman and then Iranian territory on the other side of the Strait of Hormuz to avoid Saudi Arabia and the U.A.E. and you can nearly double the distance. So, if it's Yemen, you'd have to assume that it was allowed a refueling and staging stop in Iran. Ditto for the return trip."

David asked:

"So, they're out?"

"Yes, unless Iran is a part of the logistics. That leaves two other options, one of which makes virtually no sense. That's Oman, though the sultanate is an Islamic country, a good part of it is more or less aligned with the west and has diplomatic relations with the United

Arab Emirates. The other brings us back to the Palestinians. Even there, I'm of two minds."

He paused again to check that Simon and David were still with him and continued:

"On the one hand, my guess is that they **could** execute the mission for Iran. On the other, I can't imagine them flying a helicopter all the way from Gaza or Lebanon . . . And back."

Simon interrupted:

"I know what you are going to add . . . The attack was carried out from waters that were within the exclusion zone, but probably from outside the territorial waters, but still pretty close."

Marvin replied:

"Correct. I was going there, but there is a twist. As I just said, anyone else other than Iran would have had to travel a fair distance . . ."

David interjected:

"And we do not know that any of these have submarine capabilities, let alone the sophisticated materiel which we believe was used."

"Precisely. So, for me, it has to be either Iran or China, or, as I said, Yemen strongly supported by Iran. So, it's indeed at least indirectly Iran or China. Now, if it is either of them, we should not be surprised that they would not want to take the risk that anyone takes a picture of a helicopter with national markings."

Marvin paused again to state the obvious:

"By the way, any helicopter from China would have to have come from one of their boats in the Gulf of Oman. Any trade of any such flight?"

Simon replied:

"Good point. We haven't checked but should do that right away."

David immediately said:

"I'm on it."

Marvin continued:

"They, the Chinese, have got to know that the Americans have geostationary satellites focused on this area, and they've got to suspect that we too have similar though more modest capabilities."

Simon concurred, adding:

"They probably didn't know about the Kovesh filming the doomed plane. But I agree with you; they have to be aware that the Americans and others, including us, have satellites that continuously monitor the general area."

He paused and turning to Marvin asked:

"Do we have anything which would allow us to attack and destroy ships without it being traceable to us or Saudi Arabia?"

Marvin beamed. There were two projects on which he had been working, which could come to play an important role. He had been waiting for an opportunity to discuss these new capabilities, and, now, these were offered to him on a platter.

The first involved a drone-dropped torpedo. While most torpedoes are launched by submarines or torpedo boats, *Mossad* had developed the ability to drop up to two torpedoes from the Kovesh drone. And the drone could do that while flying at or close to half its maximum altitude of 50,000 feet. Additionally, *Mossad* capitalized on the invention of Heidi Lamarr which is still in use today in the U.S. navy. With George Antheil, a music composer, the actress-inventor obtained the first patent in 1942 for "frequency hopping" or "spread spectrum" guidance. This allows torpedoes to be guided by wireless signals, which switch quickly among many different frequency channels so that enemies could not jam the signal. Marvin explained further:

"Typically, torpedoes are fired within less than a mile of the target, often just a bit more than half a mile. Now, if you just dropped a regular torpedo from too high, it would get damaged as it hit the water and would not work."

Simon had to ask, with a wry smile and his eyebrows raised:

"So, what have you guys concocted?"

"Well, we made a torpedo which is half torpedo, half cruise missile. We use the same fuel source for the two propulsion systems to save on space, although we do lose quite a bit of range when the torpedo hits the water. We're down to 5 miles at most, whereas regular torpedoes can have a range of 20 or more miles."

"Doesn't this reduce their usefulness?"

"It does up to a point, but remember, their full range is rarely used. Anyway, this is where the combination torpedo-drone is crucial. Because our drones have such a small radar image—remember the Kovesh is designed to have strong stealth features—we can have them fly close enough to the target, from a high enough altitude."

David was still not satisfied. At the same time, Simon was beaming that his "understudy" was doing the job so well. David asked:

"What does that mean?"

"Well, we can drop the torpedo from about 20,000 feet. Initially, the torpedo flies virtually straight down, allowing for the curve associated with its initial horizontal velocity when it is dropped from the moving aircraft . . ."

"Marvin, you're losing me . . ."

"Sorry, David, just making the point that bombs of any sort do not fly straight down from where they are dropped; they initially pick up the original horizontal speed of the aircraft from which they are launched."

David waved the explanation away, though, in fairness, he still wasn't sure it had all sunk in. Marvin continued:

"Anyway, back to our torpedo. When it gets to about 1,000 feet above the water, its engine takes over and, like a cruise missile, it slowly glides down, over as much as 10,000 feet forward until it softly hits the water. In fact, it be better to say that it lands on the water and then dives below the surface as a boat-launched-torpedo would. It can then travel about 5 miles at most under water, although we aim to have it drop silently into the water no more than a half a mile from the target."

"So, the chances of being seen are limited, correct?"

"Absolutely. And it's true for both the drone which climbs straight back to 50,000 feet and for the torpedo which has very small radar image. Now, things would be a bit less ideal if someone were looking precisely in that direction, with the right binoculars. I should add for the sake of completeness . . ."

Simon looked like he was going to interrupt to warn Marvin not to go too far. Marvin noted the virtual comment and simply added:

"I know, Simon, I know. But it is important to note that our remote-drone-pilots can also control the torpedo until impact. So, we can change the target, make the torpedo a dud or even explode it before it hits anything."

David could not contain himself and had to ask with a wry smile:

"I know I'm going to regret asking, but why?"

Marvin smiled as he replied:

"Everything is based on the assumption that we have the right target. What if we discover at the last minute, one way or another, that we don't?"

"I see. Good point. So, we could use that to bomb any ship and thus score against the enemies of Saudi Arabia, right?"

"Yes. However, you know that torpedoes have limitations. They can be detected close to the target, as they do not "fly" very deep underwater. So, they're great against big ships that cannot turn on a dime, but we would have a very hard time using them against the kind of speed patrol boats the Iranians use."

Simon brought that discussion to a conclusion:

"That's great Marvin. Thanks. Now, you said you had a couple of things for us . . . What's the other one?"

Abdul and Countess Renate were discussing the more specific steps which Saudi Arabia wanted to implement to teach a lasting lesson to the Iranians and the Chinese, as it had by then become quite clear that they were the most likely perpetrators or co-perpetrators of the attack on the Prince's aircraft. While it was still possible that some support had been provided by locals who knew the area and the normal flight path of aircraft into the Dubai airport, it seemed unlikely that the sophistication of the weaponry would have been shared with locally based terrorists. Similarly, though Iran and China had shared the technology with Hezbollah, it had been concluded that the chances that there was any direct Palestinian participation were also quite remote[6].

Abdul first provided what feedback was needed from the Prince. He argued that the Prince was quite serious about the unacceptability of the attack. Yet, he also felt that this could not be allowed to turn into a trigger for World War III. Specifically, Abdul said:

"The Prince would like both Iran and China to feel some pain, with a principal focus on Iran, because he had not seen anything which could directly point the finger to the Chinese. He knows about the Chinese connection due to the air/water communication system which you mentioned. Yet, he argues that China could have transferred it to Iran in exchange for something. In short, I think that the Prince would accept an "accident" here or there that saw a Chinese ship hitting a mine or otherwise sinking somewhere in the Arabian Sea, but nothing more. Nothing direct."

He paused and just to make sure he added:

"I guess he means to draw a difference between a missile or a torpedo on the one hand and a mine on the other."

Countess Renate smiled briefly and saw an opening there:

---

6   From the same author, See "Below the Surface," Barringer Publishing 2022

"Abdul, I cannot tell you a lot more, but I can say this. Another assignment for my group could well lead to some attack against China."

Seeing Abdul's eyes widen with what looked like fear, she added:

"I am not talking of anything military. Don't worry. At this point, I am not at liberty to discuss it further, but my sense tells me that these two assignments could well end up overlapping somewhat. Would you mind it very much if we tried to get Simon and his deputy David on Zoom. We need to bring them up to speed and find out what is possible . . ."

Though his body language and, in particular, his facial expression, did not seem totally comfortable, he still, apparently confidently, replied:

"Not at all."

■ ■ ■ ■ ■

Simon was not immediately available when Countess Renate contacted him, but David Heller was. They decided to start the conversation anyway and let Simon join when he could. Countess Renate began:

"David, I believe you know Abdul el Wahabi, Saudi Arabia's Head of Security. Abdul, David Heller is, as you know, the closest associate of Simon Rabinowitz, his deputy in fact . . . David, as you know, we are looking at ways in which you all could help Saudi Arabia inflict some pain on those who ordered and probably also executed the attack on the Crown Prince's aircraft. Without Simon's warning, Saudi Arabia would be preparing the Prince's funeral and mourning his death."

"I know, Countess. I've discussed the topic with Simon. It would be of great help if Abdul told us a bit more of what he has in mind."

Abdul replied:

"Happy to. In short, we have determined with your help, thank you by the way, that there is a high probability, nearly a certainty in fact that Iran is behind the attack, with most likely a strong technological assist by China."

"Sorry to interrupt, but do you have anything pointing to China on your side? On ours, frankly, it's only a conjecture due to the origins of their air/water communication system."

"Unfortunately, nothing more here."

"Then, I am afraid that we are on very rocky ground, both politically and ethically."

"We have to agree . . ."

David continued:

"What do you have in mind . . . ? Ah, Simon. I see that you're joining us."

"Hello, everyone. Sorry to have been late."

Countess Renate brought Simon up to speed, concluding:

"We seem to have come to the conclusion that we should only concentrate on Iran. I mentioned to Abdul that another of my assignments may deal with China but could not go any further."

Simon replied that he understood. He startled Countess Renate and Abdul by talking of something which seemed totally unrelated to the topic at hand. He told them that the Jewish Chronicle recently reported on something that dated to the 2019–2020-time frame. In short, *Mossad* had conducted a sabotage operation which had been aimed at Iranian uranium enrichment effort. He added:

"Interestingly, the story, which was based on official Iranian comments, even named a culprit, who is still at large. I don't need to tell you that no one exists by that name now and that the person they are looking for is out of their reach. Now, the very interesting bit is that they correctly report that about 90% of the centrifuges at Natanz were destroyed. We kind of knew that already. What they are not reporting on, is that our operation actually was aimed at both

Natanz and the other enrichment center, in Fordow. I suspect that they reported on Natanz because the damage was visible from the sky and was known, whereas the damage at Fordow was in caves deep inside a mountain. We know that there was serious damage there as well but have still not been able to find out more details."

"Fascinating, Simon. Where does that lead you?"

"Well, let me finish first; you'll see the connection. The paper further reported that, more recently, an armed quadcopter drone, weighing the same as a motorcycle, had been smuggled into the country piece by piece by agents. Its target was the TESA complex in Karaj, the most important factory building the centrifuges—including advanced centrifuges—for the enrichment plants. Finally, the paper reported that *Mossad* has made it a renewed priority to prevent Iran from reaching the full nuclear state that it seeks."

He paused for a second, ostensibly to drink from a glass of water he had to his right hand. He continued:

"It gave me a couple of ideas after we last talked, Countess. The first is our goals and those of Saudi Arabia are certainly aligned on this point. There might be a way to cooperate. We are not a rich country, and financial assistance might simultaneously help us and provide to Saudi Arabia the anonymity it seeks. The second is that, just as we did in Operation Kovesh—the earlier effort I mentioned— our ability to conduct the attack is made considerably easier if we can use, discreetly, of course, some part of the Saudi Territory for logistical purposes. We used the Khafji base the last time around and would be delighted to be able to use it again."

Abdul interrupted:

"Simon, I assume that the Crown Prince is fully aware of that prior operation of yours, correct?"

"Oh, absolutely. I know the agreement was negotiated with the Kingdom's foreign minister then, but I cannot imagine that the Crown Prince was not somehow in the loop."

Abdul concluded:

"Well, my next step probably is to discuss the outline of this with him, unless Countess Renate or you seek direct contact with him."

Simon thought for a second and replied:

"At this point, for as long as we are dealing with hypothetical issues, we can certainly remain at our level. Yet, I certainly do not have the authority to negotiate at the state level and am sure that our foreign minister, or even our Prime Minister would want to be in the loop sooner or later. In the meantime, whatever we discuss should be absolutely secret among ourselves, in your case, Abdul, the secrecy loop, if I can call it this, should probably include His Royal Highness."

CHAPTER.11

LONDON, ENGLAND, SINGAPORE, AND SOMEWHERE IN THE AUSTRIAN ALPS

Wong Hai Chock had organized a conference call with Nikolai Bernstein, as Countess Renate had suggested. Nikolai had, somewhat to Hai Chock's surprise, preferred a Zoom conference call without his video being switched on. Hai Chock thought *careful fellow. That is good if we can work together.* As agreed with Countess Renate, he used Jim Ng as his name and referred to Countess Renate as Ms. Schneider or Hilde.

"Jim Ng, here. Hey Nikolai, it is good to meet you."

"Same here, Jim. Before we start, can you tell me a bit about yourself and of how you know Ms. Schneider?"

"Sure."

Hai Chock, aka Jim, proceeded to relate the main steps of a career which had started in research and teaching and now saw him spending an increasing amount of time in the consulting world. He explained that academia definitely was great, pointing to the crucial government policy in the Republic that everyone must be properly compensated, whether in the private or the public sector. He said he had very much enjoyed the interaction with students and the opportunities to do research. Yet, as he told Nikolai, he had at one point in the relatively recent past, realized that problem solving was possibly even more important than teaching or research:

"With the growing number of issues related to cyber security and fraud, there is a lot of demand for consulting time. I had to choose one or the other. Consulting won."

He was careful to add that he had ensured that he had not burned any bridges, as things could change, adding:

"Who knows, in a few years, I might return to research or teaching. How about you?"

Nikolai replied with an honest summary of his life, going all the way back to his Russian origins and the need for his family to escape the Jewish persecutions in Europe. He disguised his role in the crypto world, though admitted that he had started participating in it quite early:

"It appeared to offer great opportunities to make significant money, but my main motivation had to be what I saw as insane monetary policy moves on the part of the leading developed country central banks. Add to that the crazy fiscal policies of most the same countries and you'll understand why crypto might look like a solution. I had to be in it one way or another."

He confessed that he had been quite lucky as he had invested most of his savings in crypto and had thus enjoyed a wild but highly rewarding ride. He added in passing that he had not invested more in CryptNotes in the recent past, as he thought prices had become increasingly crazy. He concluded:

"In the end, what has turned me off somewhat has been the fact that there have been reported security breaches in the network and that CryptNotes had been used as payment in numerous criminal activities."

Hai Chock paused for a second to absorb what he had just heard. To that point, there was no reason to disbelieve Nikolai, but neither was there any reason to give him too much information. He decided to turn the situation around:

"Nikolai, there is something which Hilde does not know and which I can broadly discuss, although I will not go into any detail. One of my consulting clients has a specific issue with one of the cryptocurrencies."

"Which one?"

"I can't reveal that but suffice to say it is one of the largest three.

"I see. What's the issue?"

"Well, again, I am kind of stuck. But the question that I am having to address is this: is there a way to penetrate a crypto network without being noticed?"

Nikolai remained silent for a few seconds. He certainly did not doubt that Jim's question was genuine. However, at the same time, he had to question the motives. Could it be that Jim, aka Hai Chock, was just a hacker who was in this case just trying *to make a buck* He decided to offer a broad reply, making sure that nothing that he said was factually incorrect, but still avoiding revealing anything which Jim could not find out on his own with a minimum of research on the Internet:

"As you know, Jim, blockchain, which underpins crypto is an open-source network. Anybody can get in. Once you're in, you verify a block and with that proof of work you get a shot at earning a payment in the form of cryptocurrency. The various cryptocurrency networks do not all do the same thing, but the principle of blockchain is the same across that small universe."

Hai Chock did not waste a second and fired straight back:

"Do you know all of them well?"

"I know the concept behind them all quite well. I even have potential access to people who know even more. But I must confess that the one with in which I have dabbled the most is CryptNotes. So, it's probably the one I know best or the least badly depending upon whether you're an optimist or a pessimist."

"Any reason for that?"

"I assume you're referring to the choice of CryptNotes, correct?"

"Absolutely,"

"Well, the answer is deceptively simple: it was the first that I learned about . . . It worked for me and allowed me to build the capital reserve which makes it possible for me to pick what I choose to do and not to do. You see, I'm a bit like you, a consultant."

Hai Chock jumped on the opportunity. He was totally unsure whether he and Nikolai were playing the same cat and mouse game, but there was at least some evidence that they might. Nikolai suggesting that he was in the same generic business as Hai Chock was an opening that Jim could not miss. He replied:

"Now that's quite interesting Nikolai. Would you be prepared to discuss a joint assignment? My current project is well paid, though we are not talking of a fortune. I would surely be prepared to share the revenue with you if we could do the job better together rather than by myself."

Nikolai did not reply immediately. He did not know it, but the thought that was going through his mind was exactly the same that was going through Hai Chock's. Ostensibly, a prudent individual does not accept this kind of invitation on the basis of a visit with a charming though a bit naïve lady and a phone call with someone posing as a cyber consultant. Yet, the offer was quite tempting. He mumbled a few generalities and, in the end, in somewhat of a non-committal manner, he said that this was something which they should discuss further, preferably face to face. He added:

"Is there anything you can send me on you, Jim? I'd like to do some research to allow me to get to know you better. I am not doubting anything you say, but I'm sure you'll understand that I must remain quite careful."

THE CRYPTO TRAP | 95

Hai Chock was not surprised. In fact, he respected Nikolai both for what he said and the way he said it. He decided that there was only one way to play the situation: straightforward. He replied that he could easily send some material, but nothing he could send would be stuff that Nikolai could not find on the Internet if he simply googled Jim Ng's name. Indeed, when Hai Chock had created the "Jim Ng" cover, he had been careful to set up a website in Jim's name. That website had the appropriate biography as well as links to papers to which he had contributed. Clearly, this was the difficult part, as he could not simply list Jim as a contributor in all publications in the name of Wong Hai Chock. That would have defeated the purpose and people who knew Hai Chock well would have become suspicious. He thus created a few "fake" papers that he posted to the website without mentioning where they were published. Yet, addressing directly the question raised by Nikolai, he had added:

"But my one overwhelming concern will be this: we both have to be careful. We can each open the kimono a bit, but there is a point where we will need to move to some form of trust."

"You know, Jim, I'm glad you just said this. I like your honesty and realism. Let's stay in touch. Any chance you can find yourself in London any time soon?"

"Well, not at this point, but my client is in Europe. So I could probably work a visit around one of my trips to see the client."

"Let me know when, and I'll make myself available. It's not as if my daily schedule is chock full."

■ ■ ■ ■ ■

After hearing from Hai Chock, Countess Renate decided she should call Simon:

"Simon, I may need your help, and, if all goes well, you may need mine."

"Still speaking in riddles, Countess. What can I do for you?"

Countess Renate went on to open up about the lead she had gotten from one of the members of her network. She said that both she and her "man in Singapore" had met someone who seemed quite knowledgeable on cryptocurrencies.

"Gee, that would be quite a coup if you could get him or her into your network."

"Well, let's not go too fast. As someone once said, you never want to have to unscramble the eggs. The problem is that we have reached a point where someone will have to reveal something that could be crucial."

"Crucial to your secrecy?"

"Indeed."

"Ah! I see. How can I help?"

Countess Renate replied that she had had a thought. She was wondering whether it would be possible to isolate one of the trades which Jack Turnbull had discussed. What she meant was setting aside the documentation created around one of the trades, such as number of sub-trades, prices, volumes, and counterparties if possible. Simon could not immediately see why and had to ask. Countess Renate replied that, assuming one could, her man in Singapore would attempt to hire the fellow to whom he is talking as an external consultant. That would allow him to see for himself what that person truly knew and how he could help. Simon interrupted:

"I can't speak for Jack, but this might be a great idea. We get him to take a look at the transaction in all its components and details, and that helps us understand what is actually happening."

"Exactly what I had in mind, Simon."

"Why don't you contact Jack directly and suggest we go down that path. Personally, I would not reveal anything about the other side of the transaction."

"Totally agree. In fact, I would be very tempted to leave that one entirely in Hai Chock's hands. His report on how the project goes and what the fellow contributes would be enough for us to decide where we go."

"Your group of Experts would become increasingly powerful . . ."

■ ■ ■ ■ ■

Jim, aka Hai Chock, renewed contact with Nikolai within a couple of days:

"Nikolai . . . Jim Ng here."

"Great to hear from you so soon, Jim. Anything new?"

Jim reiterated quite a bit of their earlier conversation: the thorny issue he had to resolve, the potential help that Nikolai could provide if he was willing to do so and the need to get it done relatively quickly. He veered into new territory, adding:

"It dawned on me that this could easily justify a trip to London."

He said that he could be in London, the following Tuesday, in other words, four days later. He proposed to bring with him a very specific case, saying:

"I really want to go over my client's question with you and see if you are willing and able to help me. I am prepared to give you a lot of information, though I hope you'll understand that the identity of the client must remain confidential."

Nikolai was in fact impressed by the proposal and welcomed it. He said that, to him, it sounded like quite an interesting idea. Then he added:

"I don't want to seem like I'm always asking for more, but still, is there a way you can open up a bit more already?"

Hai Chock understood what Nikolai was trying to do; he wanted a bit more context. Yet, he did not want to disclose much more to Nikolai because this was going to be a "working interview" and he had to be extra careful not to say too much. Still, he felt he could say just a bit more, adding:

"Not much, but let's just say that my client has picked up an unusual level of activity in CryptNotes in the very recent past . . ."

"I've noted the sharp jump in price myself."

Nikolai went on and surprised Hai Chock with his next question: "Where do you want to meet?"

"Could we meet at Heathrow? I'll be flying Singapore Airlines. They have three daily flights to London. If possible, I'd like to return to Singapore on one of the three return flights, the same day. I fly a lot on Singapore Airlines and can get a seat whenever I need it. I could book a conference room at the SilverKris Singapore Airline lounge. I think it's in Terminal 2B."

"Why not! I'm sure I can find a way to get there, even if it means buying an airplane ticket. Send me a text message with time and place when you have it. See you then."

■ ■ ■ ■ ■

Hai Chock called Countess Renate from Heathrow Airport:

"Countess, I have just spent a couple of hours with Nikolai. Let me tell you. He is brilliant. He had his laptop with him. He was able in a matter of minutes to find the transactions we discussed and tell me quite a bit about them. In this case, there was little attempt to hide anything in that the transactions went through a single "wallet." Now, the wallet does not provide all the detail of the real identity of the person behind the transaction. Yet Nikolai smiled and told me there was a way in. He told me about an algorithm, he called it NoteWay, which could dig that identity out. I let him work quietly for probably not more than fifteen to twenty minutes, and he came out with the goods."

"Really. And?"

"It confirmed what we knew, and that I had not told him. Behind the wallet is an entity related to the People's Bank of China, the Chinese central bank."

"Really? Quite impressive."

"You can say that again."

"OK, Hai Chock. How did you leave it with him?"

Hai Chock replied that he said he was going to go back to the client with the information. He said he promised to share the fee 50/50 with him, and to let him know as soon as he could what the amount was. He said that Nikolai did not initially volunteer any form of banking coordinates but got the impression that they would be provided if asked.

Countess Renate replied:

"Many thanks. Let me reconnect with Nikolai and discuss my project with him. I hope you two will get to work together again soon. If I can, I plan to tell him that your visit was a job interview and that he had passed."

Hai Chock chuckled.

CHAPTER.12

A first explosion shook the Shahid Bahonar Port of Bandar Abbas
in Iran; a missile launcher ship inexplicably exploded. Within less
than a minute, a second explosion confirmed what the first seemed
to have announced. There was an attack on the Iranian Navy or on
the navy of the Islamic Revolutionary Guard Corps, both of which
are headquartered in Bandar Abbas, a port near the entrance to the
Persian Gulf, the Strait of Hormuz. A whole flotilla of small Iranian
crafts immediately raced out of the mouth of the harbor delineated
by two curved sea walls, one to the east and the other to the west.
Whether they were dispersing to present a less concentrated target
or simply leaving port in search of the boat which had to have fired
the missiles, nobody knew. The two ships that had been hit were
still burning and the local fire fighting forces were busy putting out
the fires.

■ ■ ■ ■ ■

A few weeks earlier, Simon Rabinowitz, David Heller, Countess
Renate and Abdul el Wahabi had met in secret, with Ariel Landau,

still the official Head of *Mossad* sitting in as the representative of the Israeli government. The meeting had taken place, exceptionally, on Saudi territory at the Khafji base, on the Persian Gulf. Without formal diplomatic relations between Israel and Saudi Arabia, any such meeting would be expected to take place on neutral territory. Simon had already been allowed to break that rule, and he and Ariel simply kept on going with the precedent.

The week prior to that meeting, Ariel was joined by Simon to present a plan of action to the Israeli Government War Cabinet. Simon had first been thoroughly grilled by Ariel. Though the two were friends, they were both aware of the fact that the plan was not something that should be taken lightly. Ariel, in particular, knew very well that there would be some serious opposition to Israel taking any action to benefit Saudi Arabia. Yet, Simon had convinced Ariel that the end was well worth the means. To prepare for the War Cabinet meeting, Ariel did try to poke as many holes in the plan as he could. Simon reminded Ariel with a smile that Ariel's nickname within *Mossad* was "steel trap" in reference to the fact that he was known to be so sharp that nothing ever escaped him. Ariel laughed out loud, though, as the humble, unpretentious man that he was, he always thought that he did not deserve the moniker.

The plan which was being presented to the War Cabinet was not yet totally specific, as work was still being carried out within *Mossad* to upgrade existing weapon systems specifically adapted to carry out one of the actions Simon was recommending. Simon started his presentation with an honest description of the key targets that had been identified in the campaign he had designed; all of them were in Iran. He also made it clear that, in contrast with their prior effort, Operation Kovesh, which had required *Mossad* agents to be present on Iranian soil and to interact with Israeli resources on the ground, the vast majority of the activity would be technology-driven and thus offshore based and directed. He mentioned the fact that, as was the case in the prior operation, Saudi Arabia would offer the use of the Khafji military base, just south of the Kuwaiti border, on the west coast of the Persian Gulf.

The War Council had been tough on Simon. He kept a solid composure throughout, his confidence boosted by the fact that he had passed the "Ariel test" with flying colors. At that point, the plan was simply to execute a number of isolated actions, each of which would require highly sophisticated equipment provided by Marvin Goldstein's team. The idea was to strike opportunistically at Iran in ways which made any detection as virtually impossible as practical and caused as much serious physical damage on the targets as possible. They were going to avoid human casualties as much as possible as well. There was considerable back and forth during the meeting, though, the fascinating element was they only cursorily discussed both the cost, which would be borne by Saudi Arabia, and the risk of detection, which everybody believed would be minimal provided the same kind of weaponry was not used more than once or twice.

The questions that fused from right and left focused on diplomacy issues, together with the risk of revealing hitherto secret weapon systems. The session gave Simon an opportunity to understudy Ariel Landau, the current Head of *Mossad*, whose deputy he had just become. Ariel deferred right away to Moshe Shamir, the Foreign Minister, and Aaron Spielberg, the Defense Minister. They had been in the loop throughout the planning, although the identity of the "client" had made negotiations a bit harder—not that there were great disagreements, but everything had to take place through intermediaries rather than between the principals themselves.

Directly addressing the question from the Defense Minister on the risk of disclosure of weapon systems of which nobody was aware so far, Simon argued:

"For as long as we are not detected, the risk that we reveal some new weaponry is quite low in my view."

The Defense Minister initially begged to differ simply based on the observation that the attacks would do certain things which many would not have believed possible. He concluded:

"They may not know what the system is, but they will know of a capability which they did not know existed."

Simon replied that he could not argue against the point, but that two conditions should minimize the risk. The first condition was more implicit and dealt with the desire to hide Israel's involvement in the strikes. Simon calmly said that he felt that the plan provided ample protection, although a slip up is always possible. The second condition had to be that the weapons work exactly as planned every time, adding:

"The risk of detection goes up dramatically if we have any form of misfire."

Aaron Spielberg asked the obvious question:

"How do you plan to mitigate that risk, Simon?"

Simon replied that there were two distinct elements in that part of his strategy:

"First, we will not use anything on which Marvin is not 100% sure that those risks are minimal if at all. Second, the way we plan on using the weapons means that any misfire, if it should happen, would happen far from the target."

Seeing that Aaron Spielberg did not fully comprehend what he meant, Simon explained further:

"The key novelty in the weapons we plan on using is that they combine the features of different, distinct weapons. For instance, one combines the features of a torpedo with those of a cruise missile."

Aaron interrupted:

"I know that one. Really excellent."

"Thank you, Defense Minister. The other combines the features of high-altitude bombs with those of a laser guided cruise missile."

"Heard of that one too but had not realized it was ready."

"It is the newest of the lot. But, in our case, it would not be an issue. The bomb is actually dropped at quite a horizontal distance from the target . . ."

Aaron interrupted:

"Don't worry, Simon. If Ariel and you are fine with it, and if you're dealing with the weapons you describe, it's fine with me."

Eventually, the limited nature of the engagement had carried the day, though a couple of final hurdles had to be addressed. Given the history of escalation and de-escalation in the relationship between Israel and Iran, the group was adamant that one would have to expect some Iranian response. Simon had agreed that this was indeed likely, although he had cautioned:

"Remember, Gentlemen, Iran could think we are fully behind it, but they will not have any proof. More to the point, nothing that we will do is out of the realm of what Saudi Arabia could do. Attacking Israel directly would expose Iran to serious risks."

He paused and was happy to see people nodding around the table. He continued:

"From my point of view, and I believe Ariel shares it, any form of retaliation is most likely to come either from Hamas or from Hezbollah, Iran's proxies. They can always serve as fig leaves for Iran. I bet the world would interpret any move on their part as a reflex reaction from Iran and nothing more. Now, I don't want to seem to ignore these risks, but let's be honest: it's not as if we don't know them or don't know what they can or cannot do. At this point, without being cocky, I do not believe that Hamas or Hezbollah can realistically penetrate the Iron Dome."

Simon's reference to the Iron Dome related to Israel's all-weather, air defense system, which was designed, with the help of the U.S., to protect the country against incoming rockets or artillery shells. It had proven its worth on several occasions over time, when it managed to intercept a large number of rockets fired from Gaza or even from Lebanon.

Ariel added:

"To me, gentlemen, this is the key point. Both Hamas and Hezbollah have large quantities of missiles. They will most likely fire a few or maybe a number of them at us. Yet, Iran has always been careful to make sure that their support though visible never extends beyond plausible deniability. Nobody has fallen for that trap, but it remains an important element of Iran's strategy. It would be a giant new development for Iran to launch a direct attack on us. And, by the way, on that, I am still confident that the Iron Dome would do its job. My worry would be if they topped their missiles with dirty nuclear material, not enough to initiate a nuclear conflict, but enough that any piece falling on our territory would present potential danger to our people."

The room was silent. The Prime Minister had no additional question to ask, and his body language was saying that he trusted Ariel's judgment. Simon concluded:

"Thus, I believe that between the Iron Dome and our deadly retaliatory capabilities, this is probably not much more than business as usual."

The meeting adjourned, giving Simon the green light to proceed.

■ ■ ■ ■

Simon, Countess Renate, and Abdul el Wahabi had finalized the specific goals they agreed to achieve. The specific purpose of each of the actions that would follow was to convince Iran that wanton attacks on the Kingdom, directly or through surrogates was a losing strategy. The Crown Prince wanted to extract a high enough price but still without any possible direct link to him or the Kingdom. On that point, he was clearly totally consistent with the position he expressed at the outset, and this despite what Abdul said had included several conversations with the King.

In normal circumstances, Simon might not have been willing to participate and this for two reasons. First and foremost, Israel is not a surrogate for Saudi Arabia; it is an independent country which has more than enough work making sure it remains alive, surrounded as it is by numerous enemies. The fact that many, if not most, of these enemies are believed to be funded by Iran might have been cited as an extenuating circumstance but would not have been enough to convince Simon that the risks were worth taking. Second, Israel had only recently attacked Iran's nuclear enrichment installations; while, initially at least, the general thrust had been a belief that Iranian exiles were behind the attack, it had recently become obvious that, whether they were part of the plot or not, Israel had a hand in the attack. The Revolutionary Government had gone as far as admitting the fact that significant damage had been inflicted, pointing to at least two different strategies used by Israel to achieve their goal and naming a major suspect, an Iranian scientist who was believed to have emigrated to Israel.

At the same time, these were not "normal" circumstances. Israel had been made aware by the CIA of machinations of Chinese origins aimed at disturbing financial markets in general and at weakening the U.S. Dollar and the whole U.S. economy more specifically. Though the two events could appear totally unconnected, the planning which had been carried out on the financial front had shown that some Saudi Arabian help and financial support would be quite useful and send mixed signals which would or at least should confuse the enemy.

Simon had thus negotiated a plan of assistance between Israel and Saudi Arabia, in exchange for carrying out a handful of aggressive actions toward Iran, currently probably their most dangerous enemy. The existence and nature of the plan were state secrets in both capitals and were thus known only to a very small handful of individuals.

■ ■ ■ ■ ■

Simon had also called his friend, Jack Turnbull, Head of Operations at the CIA. After having sworn him to secrecy, he wanted Jack to know what their plans were with respect to what looked like an unprovoked Iranian attack on the Saudi Royal Family. Additionally, and, in particular, he wanted to ask him an important question:

"What kind of protection does Saudi Arabia have if the Iranians decided to retaliate with a shower of missiles?"

Without giving Jack the time to reply, he added:

"You know that we have the Iron Dome, but do they have anything similar?"

Jack replied that Saudi had substantial protection against incoming missiles, but, as the attack against the state-owned, Saudi Aramco oil processing facilities at Abqaiq and Khurais in Eastern Saudi Arabia demonstrated, the protection is not nearly as good as Israel's. Simon followed up:

"Is there any chance that you could offer emergency anti-missile coverage to them?"

"Everything is possible, my friend. But this is a political hot potato. I'm not sure it could be provided without Congress being made aware of it, and we both know what that means . . ."

"Everyone will know about it."

"Indeed. But there may be a way to use some equipment in Kuwait, for instance, without being required to make it public. And even there we must be very cautious, as some people in certain quarters argue that Kuwait has drifted closer to Iran and further away from Saudi Arabia. At any rate, there will be hell to pay if the effort fails, but nobody plans for it to fail, right?"

"You better believe it. I'm really betting my career on this effort working. I believe that the real regional danger is Iran and therefore that the stronger or more aggressive Iran gets, the more the Arab world will realize that Israel is much more their friend than their enemy."

He paused for a second and, considering the risk of the failure of this coming effort, added:

"If it's too obvious a failure, I bet you that the two promotions I asked be deferred might well be deferred permanently."

■ ■ ■ ■ ■

The two explosions in Bandar Abbas were the result of meticulous surveillance identifying circumstances where two Iranian ships were moored in a position that was virtually in a straight line from the Shahid Bahonar Port. Simplifying the geography, from the sky, the port looks like an inverted "T". A channel goes deep into the port directly opposite the entrance to the port. This is where the container port equipment is located, mostly on the right-hand side of the "T." Two other channels depart on either side of the T just after the entrance to the harbor. These offer obviously more sheltered anchoring opportunities, as, short of an attack from the sky, there is no way to shoot at any ship moored there unless a submarine had managed to penetrate deep beyond the sea wall area and to locate itself opposite the two horizontal bars of the "T". One must assume that sonar and other detection equipment protect the harbor against that risk. Furthermore, even if a submarine managed to sneak in, the risk that it could shoot two boats is slim. Indeed, submarines fire torpedoes in one direction only; thus, the submarine would have to execute a 180-degree maneuver to hit the second ship after having hit the first. The odds were simply not there . . .

Simon and David had agreed to use two different pieces of equipment to focus on this target. The first was a geosynchronous satellite which would provide surveillance from a distance. More granular data would be provided by an Eitan reconnaissance drone which would circle at very high altitude over the port using a classical figure-8 holding pattern. The Eitan would be part of a team of two drones, both temporarily based in Khafji. With a range of nearly 4,600 miles and a distance between Khafji and Bandar Abbas of less than 450 miles, the drone could stay on location for quite some time. This combination allowed them to pick up the fact that port congestion had forced a couple of ships to anchor close to the center part of the "T". This allowed the second part of the operation to kick in.

A Kovesh equipped with two cruise-torpedoes was dispatched from Khafji. It initially flew on a southeasterly vector to avoid violating Iranian airspace. Though this added about fifty miles to the trip, it was well worth it. Abeam the city of Gerouk, on the Iranian side of the Strait of Hormuz, it made a sharp left turn to line itself up with the entrance to the Shahid Harbor. The first torpedo was dropped aiming at the ship on the left side of the harbor channel; it went straight down and entered the water about 5 miles from the harbor. It navigated at maximum depth until it got to within a mile of its target at which point it rose to less than twenty feet from the surface. The hit on the ship was below the water line, not far from the fuel reservoirs which immediately caught fire. The Kovesh flew a bit further to the northwest to drop the second torpedo which repeated just about the same pattern, though it was aimed at the ship to the right side of the "T."

Both strikes were intended to inflict physical damage to the ships, though human losses would be kept to an absolute minimum. The torpedoes were aimed at the ships' engine rooms and fuel reservoirs, which would be lower than and away from most living quarters. Yet, there was a hope that the damage would be serious enough that the ships would be immobilized in the harbor for some time.

■ ■ ■ ■ ■

The Iranian press did not report widely on the accident in Bandar Abbas. Local news talked of a couple of explosions followed by fires on two navy ships at anchor in the harbor. Interestingly, though, there was no direct accusation directed toward the usual enemies of Iran, probably because there were still questions as to what had actually happened. Blaming Saudi Arabia would make little sense as it was obvious that no missile had been fired from that far away. Blaming Israel was even less probable, as one would wonder why the Jewish state would have done it and, even more importantly, how. There was always the conjecture about the Americans, but motives and manner of action were at best unclear. The U.S. fifth fleet was known to be cruising in the Arabian sea, but there were no known surface ship within the area of the Strait of Hormuz at the time. This left open only one possible explanation: it had to have been a submarine. In that case, only the U.S. and Israel were known to have any such craft within their fleet. Iran punted and blamed the U.S., but the words were, for once, somewhat less aggressive than usual. One could feel a high degree of hesitancy.

The U.S. responded with a standard denial, which was all the easier for them to issue as they had absolutely no idea of what had happened, other than the fact that they were categorically sure that they had nothing to do with it.

CHAPTER.13

WASHINGTON, DC, USA, TEL AVIV, ISRAEL, LONDON, ENGLAND, AND SOMEWHERE IN THE AUSTRIAN ALPS

Countess Renate had flown to London again for a second meeting with Nikolai Bernstein. The obvious point of the conversation was to ascertain whether there was a fit between what Nikolai wanted to do and the activities for which she was responsible as the founder and head of the Shadow Experts. Hilde Schneider started the conversation, but quickly morphed into Countess Renate when the final question had to be asked:

"Would you be interested in joining the Shadow Experts?"

After a short while, and making a short joke on the sudden disappearance of her heavy German accent, Nikolai turned to Countess Renate with a smile:

"I would be delighted."

But he immediately added a note of caution:

"But nobody can ever know the full detail of my prior life. It is OK to say that I know and understand the world of cryptocurrencies and blockchain well, but that must be where it stops. Frank and I agreed to keep our link to CryptNotes secret. I must continue to honor that commitment. By the way, I do not believe I violated it by bringing you in the loop for as long as you, yourself keep it secret."

"Nikolai, I have no issue with that. I will be the only one knowing and will take that secret to my grave."

Nikolai smiled his satisfaction. Countess Renate added:

"I will not tell you anything more, other than to say that several of our "experts" have secrets that I know and will never reveal either. By the way, you now have a secret too: you know that the Shadow Experts are a reality, and you can connect them to me. That, you **too** should take to your grave."

■ ■ ■ ■ ■

Countess Renate called Jack Turnbull to let him know that the Shadow Experts have the appropriate resources to help with what she mischievously called his "Chinese problem." Incidentally, she mentioned that she expected that Jack would bring Simon into the loop. To her, that meant that he would let Simon know as well that the Shadow Experts were prepared and ready if asked to help the FBI deal with the issue. Jack was, of course, happy; his chances of addressing and solving his problem had in his mind risen manifold. Yet, within a split-second surprise took over from happiness. He remembered that she had told him and Simon earlier that something was up. He thought, *this has to be it*, but still asked:

"What has changed, Countess?"

She replied that she could not discuss any "change" as he put it but added that she was now satisfied that she could help him. She added:

"Let me talk you though the resources we can bring to bear. Hopefully, you will immediately see that we have all bases covered."

She paused for a second and went on:

"One of our experts knows the crypto world inside out. I am sure that he can help figure out the crypto angle of your problem. But that's not all. Another of our experts knows financial markets inside out. So, the Treasury and U.S. Dollar angles are covered as well. Finally, you already know our friend, the cyber expert in Singapore, he was on the case on which we last worked together, though I do not believe you ever met him. That should make a great team for you. Wouldn't you agree."

Jack was delighted:

"Couldn't wish for more."

In fact, he had to concede to himself that, not without some trepidations, he had placed most of his hopes on the Shadow Experts. He knew that others within the U.S. Administration had contacts with other people who would be literally dying to help. Yet, he had obtained carte blanche and asked that no one else be involved until he asked. More than anything else, the clinching rationale was secrecy. He had indeed argued that the loss of secrecy on this project might totally jeopardize it. On the one hand, for China to find out that they had been identified and put on some kind of watch list could be good; it might get them to stop as it would be a really huge step for them to continue that could be viewed as a deliberate act of war. But what if China was not the actual culprit? On the other, it would prevent the U.S. Government winning this skirmish in a discreet way without anyone, other than the Chinese, knowing they had been found out and that they had thus had to pay some price. In his mind, it was quite clear; in a case like this, one wants a discreet win with no one losing face and yet one party definitively wounded.

Countess Renate wasted no time telling Jack that they needed a strategy. She made the point that her three experts had met with her, on Zoom, to discuss the issue in broad terms. Jack interrupted:

"Just a minute, this is secret stuff, Countess . . ."

"I know, Jack, I know. But we can't help you if we can't share the crux of the problem within our network with those people whom I need to bring in to find a solution.."

"I guess so. Sorry to have overreacted."

"No worries. I understand."

"Thanks. Now you said "three" experts?"

She reminded him of the three people she had mentioned earlier. He apologized arguing, possibly with some degree of disingenuity, that he viewed her as an expert as well. She smiled but did not react to Jack's last statement. She simply continued on her earlier train of thought. She explained that her group had identified at least three different issues. Therefore, there was a need to decide what needed to be done in what order and by whom. In short:

"As I said a minute ago, we need a strategy."

Countess Renate went on to introduce and briefly discuss the issues as the Experts saw them. The first was a function of the fact that there was little if anything that was known for sure at this point on the supposed Chinese financial market transactions. She added:

"You and I have speculated on the motives, but, as we speak, I don't see us having moved beyond speculation. After all, China, as you've told me, owns tons of U.S. government bonds. Could they not simply be lightening up a bit? With respect to cryptocurrencies, could they not simply be diversifying their currency risks?"

"You are right, Countess. We need to move closer to certainty as to what they're doing and why. The key issue, as I see it, is that we cannot ask and, I don't know about you, but the CIA has no reliable source in the People's Bank of China."

She nodded and moved to the second point, which dealt with the question of what the U.S. wanted to do. What was their goal at this moment? She paused for an instant and expanded on the point, arguing that one could imagine a range of goals. The first she noted was the always present option of direct talks with China, i.e. the diplomatic solution:

"Asking them why they are doing what they appear to be doing and the like."

Jack replied that he could easily see that option and imagined that it might in fact even be used. Yet, that option was not satisfactory in his view. He explained:

"First, I am not sure that we would believe or trust whatever they would say. What if they simply denied having anything to do with it?"

He paused and continued, becoming almost philosophical for a second:

"So, if one is not prepared to live comfortably with an answer, why even bother asking the question? But there is more: as I said earlier, the problem is that they hold most of the cards."

Countess completed the list:

"Well, that gets me to my third option. Staying somewhat undercover but making the Chinese strategy, if it is what you think it is, so increasingly expensive that they stop."

Jack agreed that these were the three options and argued that the indications he had received seemed to point to the need for an undercover approach. Stressing, first, the totally top-secret nature of the situation and of his own comments, he added that he thought that certain members of the government, but not all, were finally beginning to understand the problem . . .

"The problem?"

"Yes, Countess, the problem they've created over time: overspending from a fiscal standpoint, requiring the issuance of massive new amounts of government debt to finance what we couldn't pay for with tax revenues. With the U.S. not among the most savings-oriented nations in the world, some of that debt could not be financed domestically. Then, guess what? It had to be bought by foreigners, particularly by countries that ran massive trade surpluses. Bingo, that's the description of China in the last ten to fifteen years . . ."

He paused for a second, and sadly observed:

"They, our government officials, would really like to have that problem go away without their needing to negotiate anything. Why? Simply, again, because they do not see what can realistically be offered."

Countess Renate could see the moral dilemma in which Jack was finding himself. She wanted to help, but at the same time she felt the need to return the conversation's focus back to the problem at hand. She was not losing sight of what she needed: a set of goals and a strategy to reach them. Without that, there would be no mission and the problem would remain. She added:

"If you allow me, Jack, I'll venture the guess that they're beginning to realize that a communist regime is never negotiating from the same point of view as more open societies. Maybe, China can be a partner, but it cannot be a partner on the same conditions as the U.K. or the E.U."

"From your lips to God's ears."

Countess Renate then asked:

"Since Simon was involved at the very beginning, do you mind if I bring him into the loop?"

"Of course not. He's a friend and a person full of common sense."

■ ■ ■ ■ ■

"Simon? Countess Renate here."

"Great to hear your voice, Countess. What may I do for you?"

"Your friend, Jack, is asking us for help with the Chinese matter. You know, the apparent financial market machination."

"Very interesting, but, I should add, not unexpected. How do we, and by "we" I mean *Mossad*, come in?"

Countess Renate did not ignore Simon last question. She argued that the major problem had to be that Jack did not seem at this point to have a strategy or even a clear set of goals. Knowing of Simon's friendship with Jack, she added immediately:

"I am not criticizing Jack here. I suspect that left to his own devices he would surely come up with both. However, I worry that he feels caught between the realities of the situation, which are not good and the fact that politicians don't have the courage either to recognize the problem or to formulate a strategy to deal with it."

Simon blurted out:

"Countess, I understand and, if I was asked my opinion, I would probably say that I agree with you totally. But though I have not thought this through quite yet, let me share an idea with you. You and I, or I should say my team and I as David really leads that effort, are involved in another "situation.""

"You mean Saudi Arabia?"

"Exactly."

Simon proceeded to expand on ways in which the two issues might be related in one way or another. Countess interrupted:

"You mean there is a direct link between them?"

Simon hastily reacted:

"Wait, wait, wait . . . Direct maybe not, but indirect? Who knows? I'm not saying the Chinese are directly involved in the attempt to kill the Saudi Crown Prince. I am simply suggesting that their links, the Chinese's, their link to Iran is very hard to deny."

"I see."

"They must know that the Iranians can be very aggressive and quite dangerous. Yet, they do not appear to be doing much to stop them. I don't want to go there, but I see a parallel between that and what we know of their behavior in North Korea."

He reminded Countess Renate of the fact that the Chinese, though technically working to force North Korea not to develop nuclear weapons and thus entice them to return to the community of nations were, in fact, not doing anything visible to achieve that goal, adding:

"A bit as if they enjoyed the North Koreans being rogue . . ."

Simon paused and continued, arguing that there were signs that China was becoming more aggressive. He suggested that this might reflect the fact that the current leadership could be under some domestic pressure, concluding:

"Be that as it may, there could be a way for us to link the two, at our level and not officially."

"What do you have in mind?"

"Let's just say that Saudi Arabia could help us on the financial front as well."

"Simon, I see where you're going. Great idea. Let's talk about it later in more depth."

CHAPTER.14

Countess Renate called a Zoom meeting of her three experts to assess what should be done if the U.S. strategy really was to make the Chinese financial transactions more and more expensive from their point of view. Richard Freeman, her financial market expert was the first to speak.

■ ■ ■ ■ ■

When not involved with the Shadow Experts, Richard had been and, to some extent, still was a well-known hedge fund manager. In fact, he created a group of funds which covered almost the full gamut of the strategies available. He had chosen to base his effort in Dublin for family reasons and because Ireland made the decision financially attractive from a tax standpoint. Richard had grown up in Ireland and then moved to the U.S. to complete his studies, getting his MBA from the University of Chicago. Prior to going to Chicago, he completed a double BS degree at the Wharton School of Management at the University of Pennsylvania, focused on both economics and mathematics.

While in school, he was exposed to what he thought was a fascinating but probably not terribly useful algorithm, at least not terribly useful to him. Richard was by then pretty much determined to make a career in the financial world, and the algorithm that he was shown dealt with advertising. More specifically, that algorithm was designed to help advertisers optimize the structure of "media plans" to maximize the number of "contacts", i.e. times an ad was seen or heard by the target market, subject to costs remaining below some ceiling. It was a classic case of maximizing something (here contacts) while minimizing something else (here costs). A media plan is a mix of advertising media chosen for a given campaign, such as radio, television, print, internet, social networks, and several others. The program evaluated each pair of possible media allocations, by looking at what they called convergence and divergence. The genius behind it is that most people readily look for options that are superior to or better than others, based on a set of criteria. That's what the algorithm called convergence. What people tend to forget is that, based on certain of these criteria, the one alternative that was superior on the whole might actually be a lot worse than others. The algorithm called it divergence. In the end, the optimization involved seeking alternatives with maximum convergence scores and minimal divergence ratings.

Though impressed by the mathematical elegance of the solution, Richard filed the whole thing in a corner of his mind, fully intending not to return to it any time soon. Yet, a few weeks later, as he was lounging in his bathtub, a thought came to his mind. What if I looked at each available investment relative to all the others using that same methodology? He immediately got out of the tub, dried himself and began listing the criteria which might govern a stock decision. He developed a program modelled after the algorithm he had originally relegated to a far corner of his mind and discovered to his surprise that the program seemed to be doing quite well.

The portfolios he constructed based on the list of stocks which the program had selected were definitively doing better than the index or some random selected combination. In fact, what amazed him was that the computer seemed to "know" the industry in which a company operated, though none of the criteria he had used to select the stocks contained that information.

Thinking that there had to be a fluke, he re-ran the whole program penalizing each transaction with exaggerated transaction costs, both on the buying and the selling sides. Lo and behold, the value added was still there, though obviously lower. Finally, he decided to buy the stocks at the top of the list and sell short those at the bottom, both with full transaction and borrowing costs incorporated. The overall value added was quite a bit larger and more than anything he had heard anyone earn. This became the first ever "computer-aided" stock selection model. Years later, Richard was still kicking himself for not having thought of using the term "artificial intelligence" to label his invention. He had indeed mentioned the idea of computer-aided stock selection to a number of potential employers and was politely told not to call back. He had just been a few decades too early.

Upon graduating, he took an analyst position at a reputed long/short equity manager, who initially poo-pooed his "computer signals" just as other potential employers had. His boss however allowed Richard to run "his program" on the side in a simplified manner, though he had added:

"I don't care if you use your program to identify candidates. However, whenever you come up with a recommendation, it has to be based on the analysis as we carry it out here."

Though he was careful never to refer to his signals, Richard was flabbergasted that these "computer recommendations" seemed so good. Quietly, he began to guide his own work through his computer, getting the "investment ideas" from his ordered list of stocks, carrying out the necessary research to convince his boss and then running the capital he was entrusted with having by then become a trader with the same money manager. He was delighted by his own results, and the financial rewards that came with it; not surprisingly, so was his boss, when Richard told him of the first step in his investment process: his computerized stock selection program.

A few years later, after having made his mark as a promising equity trader and emerging hedge fund manager, Richard decided that he should try his approach on a commercial basis for his own account. His experience over the time he had been managing money told him that the signals which his model gave were very powerful, and certainly right more often than wrong. He decided to leave his employer and to create his own fund. He was gratified when his boss not only wished him well, but offered to seed his fund, provided Richard invested all the money he had saved in his first job. That was his boss's way of saying "I'll help you, but you've got to eat your own cooking!"

Richard thought this was a very fair bargain and started a long/ short equity fund. Ostensibly, as a new manager, he did not play in the same league as his former boss, but the contacts he had created with investors helped him build a decent business. He was happy that investment decisions were, in effect, made for him as he originally had to work quite hard on the creation of his technology platform. Yet, with the help of a few excellent hires, both on the trading and the technology side, and an excellent administrator, he proved quite successful. Eventually, the fund grew in size to the point where Richard felt the need to cap assets under management, if only to make sure that he remained able to earn the returns that his investors loved.

One thing which Richard discovered about himself during that time was that he was at least as interested in the creation of investment solutions as by the performance of his fund. He kept wanting to fiddle with the model; eventually this led to a second version of the algorithm, this time focused on credit instruments, i.e.

bonds. Gradually, Richard gave the actual execution of transactions to subordinates and remained focused on the development of new tools, leading to the potential for new decision rules and thus new funds. Being careful not to rely too much on so-called back tests— or historical simulations of the hypothetical performance of the "decision rule governed by the model"—he would seed his new funds with his own money, sort of "incubating" them himself.

Meanwhile, Richard had married a wonderful woman of more recent Irish origin than he, who gave him three children. One day, she told him that she would really love to move back to Ireland, though she would never do it if this created any hindrance to his business. Richard thought for a short while and then wholeheartedly supported his wife's plan.

Richard had indeed just remembered that Ireland had a very favorable tax environment for hedge fund investors, together with a well-developed body of potential administrative and operations employees. Several funds had already moved there, and there even had been an exodus of European funds which chose Ireland as the place to base their business: they would still be in the European Union, and thus take advantage of that whole market, and could escape the punitive taxation regimes which existed in several other places. *Ireland is it,* Richard thought. He uprooted his family and the business from Greenwich, Connecticut where he had established it, and returned to the home country. He was very careful not to burn any bridges and thus kept some activities in Connecticut, as he thought: *for the time being at least.*

The move proved well-inspired. The firm grew quite rapidly, allowing Richard to groom new portfolio managers who could eventually take over when he felt ready. Though fascinated by finance, Richard was a discreet individual who was not into ostentatious consumption; he loved his family life and was sorry that he had missed the first several years of his three children's lives. Now, with the firm mature, two of the senior portfolio managers having been named partners, he felt he could gradually move away from individual investment decisions. Though he never made the decision to "retire" or "let go" as he was still quite involved in his business, the evolutionary process through which he went, led him, eventually, to accept Countess Renate's invitation to join the Shadow Experts. What better way indeed, in his words, "to return some of his luck and fortune" than by helping others?

■ ■ ■ ■ ■

After Countess Renate had briefed her three experts on the nature of the problem, Richard spoke first and argued:

"The main problem for me is that we really don't know much about what the Chinese are doing, other than a couple series of transactions. I would take this further and say that I am very unsure as to how much we could find out without sounding an alarm."

Countess Renate prodded further:

"What do you have in mind, Richard?"

"Well, I would suggest, strictly from a financial market standpoint, that we should move on two fronts, with the second deferred by at most a week."

Seeing the quizzical look on everyone's face, he expanded on the idea:

"First, I would offer to call a few friends, asking about their views on the developments in U.S. long-term interest rates and CryptNotes. The hedge fund community is always pretty happy to talk, except when they think they have something unique. Now, you mustn't be too naïve: you always need to discount views, as people could be "talking their book", a polite way to say: "spreading rumors once their positions are set." Yet, on balance you tend to learn useful insights, if only by cross-referencing the various comments."

Countess Renate was smiling; she added:

"And the second step?"

"Well, assuming that we get a sense that our understanding of what the Chinese are doing is not completely off base, we set up a trap."

"A trap?"

"Yep, a trap."

His colleagues were frankly somewhat surprised that he would be so matter of fact on something which others might have viewed as an objectionable action, on so many fronts. Yet, they let Richard continue with his explanation:

"Frankly, this is quite common in the financial markets. You simply take a few steps to make the market believe that you are doing something, when, in fact, you want to do exactly the opposite. In the same vein, you take advantage of someone having a position that is difficult to hold by pushing him or her to sell. A short squeeze, for instance, involves forcing someone who is short eventually to cover his position—that is to buy back the position he sold while borrowing the securities he was selling—by making it increasingly expensive to hold the short. There have been a few examples, quite well documented I should add—think Pershing Square and Herbalife, a couple of years ago!"

Hai Chock could not stay silent anymore; he had to ask:

"How do you do that?"

"Simple, my friend; you force the price up. Since one must put up some money to cover the book losses you have—it's called margin—there comes a point when the holder of the short position can no longer put-up margin. Then, he or she is forced to buy back the shares. Since you had been buying the shares to push prices up, you have ample opportunity to profit on your purchases while the trader that is squeezed has to take a loss, at times a really big one."

"That's mean."

"Yes, Countess, But I'm afraid it's not so unusual and it certainly is not illegal unless there is some visible collusion among investors or the use of material non-public information. The most classical case, though it was initially not a short squeeze, but a long squeeze involved silver and the Hunt brothers. They had cornered the silver market in 1980, pushing prices up dramatically. Part of their later purchases were financed by debt. The whole thing unwound when the U.S. government started selling from its reserves."

"And?"

"Let's simply say that the Hunt brothers didn't do too well. Now, what I have in mind is a set of transactions that would make China believe that there is a big buyer of treasuries and seller of CryptNotes."

"Why?

"Simple, Countess. We believe that the Chinese are big sellers of Treasuries and buyers of CryptNotes. Their strategy might take a lot more firing power than what they've got if there was really somebody that would be a natural buyer of Treasuries, for instance. They might be able to sell, but they wouldn't push prices down."

Renate interrupted again:

"And?"

"Well, we would have a chance to find out what their intentions are. We believe that China's goal is in part to hurt the U.S. by pushing interest rates up as they sell bonds and the U.S. Dollar down as they buy CryptNotes, correct?"

Countess Renate agreed on behalf of the group. Richard kept on explaining why the proposed strategy would allow them to determine what China was up to, and thus how best to react. This insight might in fact eventually need to be shared with the U.S. authorities. He added:

"Remember, we are to remain below the radar because nobody really knows for sure why China is doing what it is doing. You know that the U.S. cannot react if the transactions are truly carried out in a rational economic manner. But, if China acts in a way that is economically irrational, then it becomes much more reasonable to assume that they have a nefarious purpose. I don't know what you think but I would tend to believe that discovering a nefarious purpose would require us, first, to pause and, second, to go back to the client and ask for instructions."

Countess smiled and simply replied:

"Could not agree with you more, Richard. But where do we go from there?"

Richard continued with his analysis of the possible scenarios, at least as much to check his own reasoning with his colleagues as to inform them. He started:

"Assume that China is simply selling down some of their Treasury holdings because they feel they have too much of an exposure. They could credibly argue that they seek a better balance between U.S. bonds and those of the rest of the world."

Hai Chock could not check himself and asked:

"If that's the case, what do you think they'll do if a big buyer of Treasuries appeared?"

"Excellent question. My guess is that they would keep on selling. They would likely believe that the market is deeper than what they originally assumed . . ."

"Wouldn't they want to know who that buyer is?"

"Good point, Nikolai. "Not sure" is the best answer I can give you. The Federal Reserve Bank has been buying lots of Treasuries for the last several years. The Chinese might think the Fed wants to maintain U.S. rates lower for longer . . . kind of "damn the inflation consequences." I don't think that this would lead them to change their minds. They might think there is another, new, "big buyer." Who? Who knows? The flashes we've been seeing out of the Middle East might be enough to lead the Chinese to the thought that some Middle Eastern power is trying to buy kudos from the U.S."

Countess Renate interrupted:

"Very interesting, but it does not get me any closer to the solution. So, how do we figure out the motives of the Chinese?"

Richard replied:

"Well, this is it. If the Chinese keep on selling, possibly even faster, we won't have a final conclusion."

Seeing Nikolai about to ask a question, Richard paused and added:

"I'll explain in a minute."

He went on:

"On the other hand, if they stop selling, then we'll know . . ."

He could see that his three colleagues were not following. So, he explained further:

"Stopping their selling would mean that they **want** to depress prices. You don't do that if you are genuinely trying sell a position that you have and think it's too big. A market in which there is a big buyer is a godsend to a big seller. But if you do not take advantage of the big buyer, it has to mean that the goal is not to get rid of a position but to bring prices down. We would know what they're up to."

He paused and could see his colleagues nodding their approval. He went on:

"On the other hand, back to the question I bet Nikolai wanted to ask earlier. If they keep selling, it could mean one of two things: First, they might still be in a mode where they're trying to reduce their inventory of bonds without losing too much on it by pushing interest rates up. At the same time, this could still be a basic global repositioning of their portfolio. So, whichever of the two, it does not tell us anything. In short, we've got to keep guessing."

"Eh. Quite clever."

"Thanks, Countess. Nikolai, is there anything in there that makes no sense to you or that I have forgotten?"

"No. But one thing is coming out loud and clear. Though we suspect that the two strategies, selling Treasuries and buying

CryptNotes are related, it's pretty evident that we're dealing with two very different markets."

Nikolai was, in particular, referring to an operational aspect of the investment world called custody. The assets that one trades are not necessarily in the trader's physical possession. In fact, most often, they are not, as that would make it too administratively complex and slow down one's ability to trade. Usually, they are held by custodians—third party service providers. Now, the market for crypto custody is quite new and until recently there were very few good custody solutions, At best, there are "wallet" solutions which have either security or complexity problems. Vault storage is a combination of both types of cryptocurrency custody solutions in which the majority of funds are stored offline and can be accessed only using a private key.

He went on,

"I think that Hai Chock and I should do a bit of initial cyber snooping to try and get more info on the CryptNotes front. As you know, crypto trades are not booked or reported in the same way as others. There is more transparency in the blockchain, though, at the same time, people can hide quite a bit by using a succession of "Wallets." So, Hai Chock and I should probably do a bit of initial work. Any problem with that, Countess?"

Countess Renate was smiling broadly. She only had one thing to add:

"No team. Let's do it."

CHAPTER.15

TEL AVIV, ISRAEL, KHAFJI, SAUDI ARABIA,
IN THE MIDDLE OF THE STRAIT OF HORMUZ

In the first retribution attack against Iran, Israel had used one of the first two new weapons which Marvin had been describing. These hybrid torpedo/cruise missiles, or more simply air-launched torpedoes, provided a flawless demonstration in the harbor of Bandar Abbas.

■ ■ ■ ■ ■

A while back, Simon had brought Marvin's description of these air-launched torpedoes to a close adding:

"That's great Marvin. Thanks. Now, you said you had a couple of things for us . . . What's the other one?"

Ominously, Marvin started with a huge grin on his face. David and Simon could clearly see that he was very proud of his newest "toy." At the same time, they definitely worried that they were in for details that they probably did not really need to know. Surprisingly, after the initial broad smile, Marvin was now starting his presentation almost calmly:

"This one is really quite novel. In fact, I don't think that even the Americans have anything similar . . ."

He went on to say that the idea had come to his team as they were developing the small propulsion engine which was fitted to their new "air to sea" torpedoes:

"These torpedoes as I just mentioned are not intended to fly for a long time, in the air or in the water. The only reason for the new motor is that we can drop them from the sky, as we just saw, and get them to hit the water gently rather than in a big splash."

He paused for effect and went on:

"In them, we have three components: the explosives, the fuel for the motor and the motor which works both in the air and under water. In the air, it sucks air in and expels it after having compressed it; in the water, it does the same thing, but with water instead of air; it's then propelled by water jets."

Simon interrupted:

"That was clear to me already, Marvin."

"I know, but I really wanted to reiterate it so that you can see that the new weapon does not rely on any fancy revolutionary innovation."

Marvin paused and asked a question:

"Tell me, what is the major problem we know we all have with mines?"

Neither Simon nor David replied, as they assumed, correctly as it turned out, that the question was rhetorical. Marvin answered his own question explaining that the big challenge had always been to lay the mines. In saying this, Marvin was in fact going counter to the general logic that laying mines was simple. Indeed, mines could be dropped from the air or from a ship and they naturally found their spot in a vertical sense. Yet, Marvin was in fact totally right from his point of view. The main challenge is to lay the mines exactly where one wants **and** without being seen. Indeed, mine fields can be put in place even during peace time and allowed to lay there until they are needed. Then, it really does not matter if one sees the process of putting them in the water: there would likely be no one watching. Marvin went on:

"As we know, historically, mines have been laid by ship, submarine, or aircraft, in which case a parachute is used to slow the descent. Imagine how hard it is to parachute mines without being detected."

Simon cleared his throat, a subtle indication that he expected Marvin to get to the point faster. Marvin seemingly understood and quickly explained that virtually every means for placing mines have their limitations, something which he claimed now to have solved:

"Here's the nice bit. Ships and even submarines also have their limitations, visibility for ships and the required depth clearance for submarines. We solved all problems in one fell swoop."

He paused and was happy to note that, for once, his audience seemed interested in what was coming next. He continued:

"Our system involves a small, independent "motor" which we tether to two mines with a non-oxidizing chain."

David asked:

"Why two?"

"Easiest configuration, but there is nothing magical about it. The point is that the motor is remote controlled, as a part of a chain of similar motors . . ."

He paused and turning to Simon added:

"We're using the air/water communication system of the Boston group that you helped a while back to communicate with their remote controls when we need it."

David interrupted:

"So, at one point, you must have some aircraft in the air, correct."

"Yes and no. You see, the signal can come from an underwater source or from an airborne source. What we have found is that the radio signal from an airborne source can actually originate from a much higher altitude than what we originally thought. So, we can have a drone flying quite high and providing the signal. But you could also have the trigger activated by an underwater drone, for instance, programmed to send the signal when it reaches a specific distance from the first mine in the chain."

"And then they explode?"

"Not quite, David. The first signal involves getting the mines to move into location, with a GPS based location system used first to program where they should be and second how to get from where they are to where they should be."

"Now I see why this is so ingenious."

Marvin was beaming as Simon improvised:

"You drop them, in some general vicinity probably via submarine or even ORCA or any similar sort of underwater drone, and eventually signal them to go where they should be. At that point, they can lay idle, hidden and ready to hit, and nobody will see or have seen where there may be mines."

"Almost perfectly correct. In fact, they are dropped, as you assume via some submarine drone or a real submarine if there must be many of them. But the signal to get into position is given almost right away, and is given from the ORCA or the submarine, via sonar, bypassing the need to have an airborne vessel. Then, there is a second signal which is passed along the chain, through transponders, and instructs specific mines to explode. It's almost as in a blockchain: each mine is semi-independent from the others. You can explode one, and not others;"

He paused and added:

"Of course, unless two are so close to each other that one triggers the other. But it shouldn't be the case."

Simon came back:

"You still have to be somewhere around to trigger the explosion . . ."

"Again, yes and no. The mines have both autonomous and communication-based triggering systems. I failed to mention that they also have the ability to float at a given depth relative to the surface, irrespective of the tide. So, in fact, we have three, not two signals. The first to move in position, within a given column of water. The second to remain at the bottom or to rise to some set depth level. The third to explode if they were not triggered earlier by some interference by a ship. Note that this last bit is crucial. We can arm and disarm them individually at will. To complete the whole story, the mines are either "strangers" to one another or "paired" with one another. Thus, when two mines are connected to the same motor, they obviously will move as a pair, but whatever that pair is instructed to do will not affect any of the other pairs around them. Am I making sense?"

Simon nodded and said:

"Sure are. I have to give it to you. I'm always in admiration of the stuff you can come up with. How close do you have to be to your eventual target for the engine to have enough fuel?"

"Well, that's the secret behind using an independent engine. The fuel compartment of the engine can be of different sizes: small when we do not anticipate that the mines will need to "travel" a lot, and quite a bit bigger when they must cover a longer distance to their desired location. So, in theory, we can be a fair distance away, from a few miles up to fifty miles, depending upon the circumstances. It's a lot easier to customize the fuel reservoir of these engines to the situation than to modify the mines."

He paused and, though David wanted to interject something, waved it away for then with his hand and continued:

"That's why we typically pair an engine with only two mines. First, two mines are easier to drag along than several more and second, you minimize the risk that a couple of mines might bang into each other during motion."

David asked the question he had earlier:

"Quite smart. Quite smart. Are we operational?"

"Yes and no. We have not received final official blessing, which I guess would come from Aaron Spielberg, the Minister of Defense. So, from that point of view, we only have working prototypes. On the other hand, we are ready to request permission when they are needed. We're waiting for a clear scenario where they would be needed to ask for clearance and start getting permission."

Simon had to ask:

"How long would it take to develop and manufacture some reasonable supply?"

"We have the mines. The engines can be manufactured in a week if that were necessary. As you know, we have some of our own manufacturing capabilities, but we can enlist local help quite quickly. For us, having the right weaponry is not a luxury, it's a matter of survival.

"I am aware of that. Thanks. By the way, can you produce them without any marking?"

"Child's play, Simon!"

"Great. Start the production. I'll get you the formal authorization as soon as I can. Ariel will surely get Aaron to agree, given the current urgency."

As they had moved from the corner of Simon's office where the sofa and side chair were toward the door, Simon stopped and surprised Marvin:

"Tell me, Marvin, going back to your "gliding torpedo engine"..."

"Gliding torpedo engine, Simon?"

"Yes, sorry, you know the engine that kicks in when the torpedo is close to the water surface, glides it into the water and then propels it toward the target . . ."

"I see, I see. What about it?"

"Do you suppose you could fix it to a bomb so that it would be a bit like a cruise missile?"

"A cruise missile?"

"Yes. What I am imagining is this. You have a Kovesh or some other drone, fly very high, 40 to 50,000 feet, It carries one or two, possibly three or four of these, depending on weight constraints. Just as you explained for the torpedoes, the Kovesh drops them. However, rather than them being torpedoes, the missiles are bombs which initially drop vertically until they are close enough to the ground at which point they start to fly horizontally toward their targets. You see that?"

"You bet. That's genius. You're simplifying the function of a cruise missile. Instead of being fired from quite far away, it is dropped, as you say, and then performs like a cruise missile as soon as it has reached a desired altitude. I'm sure it can be done, and I would even venture the guess that we could make one of the existing torpedoes do that with only minor modifications . . . The only limit I can think of is the distance you want it to fly horizontally."

"Great, Marvin. Can you take that project on with some urgency please?"

■ ■ ■ ■ ■

The second activity after the torpedoing of the two Iranian navy ships in Bandar Abbas involved the creation of an invisible mini blockade of that whole area. Bandar Abbas is indeed very near, if not right at the mouth of the Strait of Hormuz, which is the entry point from the Arabian Sea into the Persian Gulf, with Iran on the right-hand side going North, and Oman, the United Arab Emirates and again Oman with the Musandam Peninsula on the other side. The Strait is considered one of the world's most economically important choke points, as it is estimated that nearly 20% of the world's oil supply transits through it. At its narrowest point, the Strait is theoretically controlled by both Oman and Iran, with the width of the channel being less than the territorial water limits prescribed by the U.N. for either country. Additionally, the Strait contains eight major islands, seven of which are controlled by Iran. Iran and the United Arab Emirates disagree as to the ownership of the strategically located Abu Musa, Greater Tunb, and Lesser Tunb islands. Nonetheless, Iran has maintained a military presence on these islands since the 1970s.

Skirmishes which have been numerous in the Gulf of Oman or within the Strait's area are constant reminders of the precarity of the geography and the desire by Iran to assert control, which, deep down, it probably knows it cannot have. Thus, the "Saudi decision group" comprising Simon, David, Countess Renate and Abdul el Wahabi had decided that one of the ways for making it clear to Iran that unacceptable behaviors will no longer be tolerated had quickly focused on the Strait. Yet, they clearly did not want to fall into the trap in which Iran had deluded itself into: wrestling the actual control of the Strait in a visible way was fodder for the start of World War III. Rather, they thought that the partial or occasional blockade of Iranian boats from the Bandar Abbas area was a "peaceful way" to remind the Iranians of the limits to their power. At the same time, the operation could probably be carried out in a way such that nobody could point a definite finger at anyone.

Qeshm Island is the largest island in the Strait of Hormuz and in the Persian Gulf. Somewhat dolphin-shaped, it stands parallel to the north coasts of the Hormuz Strait, the south coast of Iran. Qeshm Island is part of the huge mountain range of Zagros, which has been deformed and folded in the Plio-Pleistocene. The geopark located on it is particularly well-known for having the world's largest salt cave, more than 4 miles long. At one point, the island is only about one mile from the mainland, while Qeshm City is about fourteen miles from Bandar Abbas. The island is known to have important anti-ship missile installations, being one of the three islands where Iran deployed Chinese HY-2 "Silkworm missiles."

The plan that was agreed involved initially using Marvin's smart mines and mining the southwestern tip of the channel between the island and the Iranian mainland. First, the width of the channel's mouth was considerably narrower than at the northeast end of the Island. Second, one could stay in relatively deep waters without being too far from where the activity would have to take place. The mines would be shipped by air to the Khafji Base, which Saudi Arabia had agreed to make available. An Israeli submarine, the *INS Dragon*, would load enough mines from the Khafji Base and convey them to the southwestern tip of Qeshm Island.

Yet, always careful that arial surveillance via drones or satellites might give the game away, the *INS Dragon* stayed submerged about a mile offshore Khafji. They created two "mine chains" for each of the ORCA submarine drones. While still onshore in Khafji, they started with the "controlled paired mines" which Marvin had discussed. They linked each pair to two others, one ahead, the other one behind, repeating the action as often as needed to create a chain that would be long enough to cover the distance they wanted to mine. They used a degradable link which would last long enough for the mine laying process but would quickly corrode and break down after an hour or so in the salt water of the Gulf.

The *INS Dragon* then sailed south until it reached Bandar Moallem, a small town on the Iranian coast with a small harbor, suspected to be home to a few Iranian speedboats. The submarine stayed submerged in the channel, undetectable by any onshore surveillance, unless being specifically targeted. There, the first ORCA was released dragging its mine chain behind it. It sailed straight toward Bandar Hameyran, the point on the Iranian coast from which the mining was intended to start. Its mine chain was approximately equal to half the width of the channel.

The *INS Dragon* then proceeded to the opposite end of the channel, Baisadu on Qeshm island, about seven miles away from Bandar Hameyran. There, it released the second Orca with its own mine chain. Both Orcas dropped their mines as they were travelling under water, effectively toward each other, while the *INS Dragon* was remaining deep in the channel aiming to retrieve both Orcas at the midpoint where they were supposed to meet. That done, the *INS Dragon* moved further offshore to the middle of the Persian Gulf, where it was safely in international waters. The Orcas were positioned in between the submarine and the mines to be able to relay any signal that might be given. Initially, all the mines were set in an off mode as the plan was certainly not to blockade that area, but rather to have the ability to blockade it at will.

The next step involved carrying out a similar operation at the other end of Qeshm. The degree of difficulty and risk was increasing manifold. That part of the mission indeed required sailing closer to the Iranian coast which magnified the risk of detection for the Orcas or even possibly for *INS Dragon*.

CHAPTER.16

SINGAPORE, WASHINGTON, DC, U.S, LONDON, ENGLAND, DUBLIN, IRELAND, AND SOMEWHERE IN THE AUSTRIAN ALPS

Roy Pierce bounded out of his office and barked:

"Everybody can still trade within their limits, but I want all portfolios square this evening, and every evening for that matter until further notice."

Most traders understood that market developments had led Roy to decide that he did not want to take any "overnight" risk.

■ ■ ■ ■ ■

Any trader on a proprietary desk in a financial institution is provided with a set amount of corporate capital which he or she trades. The size of the capital together with broad control rules effectively determine the amount of risk which he or she can take, and, correspondingly, the amount of profit he or she might generate. Practically, there are two kinds of trade: those which are intended to remain in place for a very short period of time, minutes or hours, but never more than a day and those which are intended to be kept overnight or longer. Traders indeed usually find themselves continuously taking and unwinding positions, based on their personal reading of short-term price moves or trends. The risk in such a transaction is limited, provided the position remains within the trader's trading limits, as it can almost always be instantly unwound if markets "go in the wrong direction." In fact, there are times when having unwound a losing position, a trader takes exactly the opposite stance, hoping to capitalize on what might be viewed as a trend reversal. Nobody ever said that traders do not need to have steel nerves!

Occasionally, traders take positions which they do not close at the end of the day when they leave the office. These are known as "overnight positions" and present a greater risk as things can happen while the traders are away from their desk—for instance when they sleep. These could see a sudden price move, to which the trader may not be able to respond immediately. Indeed, there are many opportunities for unexpected developments, frequently in some other marketplace, as financial and many commodity markets can be said to be continuously open, with trading books passed on from one time zone to the next, among the major global markets such as Singapore, Dubai, London, and New York.

■ ■ ■ ■ ■

Thus, Roy's message was heard to mean that all portfolios should be risk-free at the end of each day. Virtually every trader was surprised as they had seen some significant market gyrations, but not enough, in their views, to be so drastic. Tommy Koh, a recent hire, was the only one who thought he understood why Roy had put in place the new rule. This was not because he was smarter than anyone. He had in fact just made a mistake; a big one that could have been quite costly, both to him and his employer.

The prior instructions, "No long U.S. treasury position," had been clear to most traders. However, Tommy had in fact unwittingly not adhered to it. He had misinterpreted Roy's earlier rule, coming as he did from a financial institution which was known to be more aggressive with its capital. So, he had taken a small upside bet on the 10-year U.S. treasury futures contract as a day trade. As interest rates were moving down following their sharp earlier upward move, his position scored a nice profit. His decision to "go long" on the U.S. Treasury market had been pretty much an automatism, a second nature. Traders look for small bounces or dips within any trend, whether down or up. In this particular case, he had judged that the market had gone down too far and too fast, and that it was therefore the time for a small bounce. Traders usually draw a relatively modest salary but receive bonuses that are in part at least driven by the profits they make on the amount of bank capital with which they are entrusted. Thus, he had originally calculated that his small bet, should it work as he hoped would mean a nice bonus for him. Had the trade not worked, he was ready to liquidate his position and take a small loss. He thought indeed that the loss would be small, as he still believed that, at some point, there should be a bounce—he would just have mistimed it.

Suddenly, Tommy shuddered. He had not asked himself whether Roy's original instruction allowed any intraday trade in the U.S. Dollar. He thought: *What if the trading rules of the day were not to hold **any** long position in U.S. Treasuries?* He started to worry as he realized he might simply have violated the rule out of a habit acquired in a different environment—his previous employer's. He decided that he should immediately report his trade to Roy, apologize and sincerely claim that he had reacted automatically, saying that in his own head he had understood that the instructions meant that no trader should hold positions overnight. He thought—but now realized that he might have been wrong—that he was still allowed to carry out intra-day trades. His reaction was the mark of solid traders: while everyone can and does make mistakes, the typical human reaction to try and hide an error can be catastrophic in fast moving markets. It can be even worse if the effectively unauthorized trade leads to a loss. Then, one can compound the original mistake, a small firecracker, into full-blown massive fireworks, by escalading the position or even at times violating one's trading limits. Coming clean immediately allows the boss to do what has to be done while the situation is still manageable.

Roy listened to Tommy and smiled. He told him that he indeed meant that **no** long position should be held, whether that was overnight or intra-day. Yet, he added with a smile:

"You're new here and I know you're a good trader. I recognize the instinct."

Tommy felt immediately reassured but was still surprised that Roy did not expand on the issue. He simply asked:

"Where's the market now?"

"Still going up."

"Thanks. Don't let this worry you, my friend, but remember to ask next time you are not sure before you take a position . . ."

Roy Pierce had then walked straight into Chiang Shao Jin, the bank's MD, initially sticking his head into the open door and asking:

"Shao Jin, time for a quick word?"

"Sure, Roy, what's up."

"Something's very odd in the U.S. Treasury market. We had seen steady erosion in prices over the last few weeks. As you know, I think it's because of Chinese selling."

"Remember that. So?"

"Well, looks like a big buyer stepped in. I continue to think the Chinese sell order is still out there. But the new buyer seems to have been able to trigger a market reversal. The market went up sharply and, surprise, surprise, the Chinese order disappeared from the screen. In short, the 10-Year went up fifty basis points . . ."

"That's a ton, 3% or so in price terms, correct?"

"Just about."

"Did we lose any money? Shouldn't, right? You had asked everyone not to trade in that market; correct?"

"Well, No. You're right, we weren't supposed to be in the market at all. And yet, in fact, we made money. Tommy Koh, one of my newest traders was long on the contract."

"Wait, as you just confirmed, I thought you asked them not to trade in Treasuries."

"Correct. He misunderstood; he thought no **overnight** position when I meant **no position period**. He's a good guy who made an honest mistake. He realized it as soon as he booked the profit. He came straight into my office to discuss it. Did it on his own. I had a quiet talk to him. Everything is fine. May or may not knock these profits off his bonus, but not sure yet."

He paused and then added:

"In fact, frankly, had it not been for his profit and him coming straight to me, I might have missed the reversal. It was that sudden."

■ ■ ■ ■ ■

From the very beginning, Jack Turnbull was well aware that he did not have the authority to put in motion the plan he was hoping Countess Renate would devise. Yet, he was intimately convinced that the only chance he had for the project to work had to be total secrecy. He thought, *Washington leaks like a sieve, the fewer people in the loop the better.*

He knew that his boss's position was at least partially political and had concluded that certain politicians would therefore need to be brought onboard. After having ruminated on his strategy for some while, seeking informal advice from Simon and Countess Renate whom he knew to be friends, totally trustworthy and politically savvy, he drew up a list of the six people he could not avoid having in the loop. In addition to his own boss, the Director of the C.I.A., they included the President of the U.S., the Treasury Secretary, the

Chairman of the Federal Reserve Bank, the White House Chief of Staff (as his conduit to the President) and the Secretary of State because of the international dimensions of the challenge. He had specifically decided that unless absolutely forced to violate his own preference, he would not include any member of Congress. He had nothing against any one of them, though he certainly had his personal political preferences, but he knew that a crucial source of leaks is found in the various congressional offices. Similarly, he had asked for the people in his six-man "control group" not to involve any member of their staff, offering his help if they needed any form of supplemental briefing.

Luck had it that he was sufficiently convincing and was granted his wish; the circle would definitely be quite small, at least at the outset. As his boss told him:

"The moment some of the results of this hits the top of the media agenda, I can't guarantee that we'll be allowed to keep this to ourselves."

Jack understood and was happy with his boss's decision. Jack's main rationale was simple: China had accumulated these dollar reserves over time. They had done it in the open. Everybody should know that any holder of any security can very well expect that he or she would be allowed to sell it when desired. Furthermore, any possible adverse interpretation of the current Chinese move could be denied with ease and expose the U.S. to global ridicule in the face of an accusation that China was not playing fair. His boss had agreed and noted:

"There's no point giving our adversaries ammunitions to hurt us."

On the other hand, discussing previous successes of the Shadow Experts and the group's totally discreet pattern of behavior and contacts around the world, Jack was able to show that, though they did exist, the downside risks were limited. At that time, he was not aware of the assignment which Countess Renate was receiving from Saudi Arabia. (Interestingly, though Jack clearly did not know it, that link between the two missions could add quite a useful dimension to their arsenal, over time.)

■ ■ ▬ ■ ■

Countess Renate called a meeting of her three experts to focus on their next step, which she knew would involve the crypto market. She fully expected the conversation to involve Hai Chock and Nikolai mostly. Yet, her confidence in the financial instincts of Richard and his knowledge of markets made her feel that his presence was reassuring. Nikolai and Hai Chock, indeed, when they were together were very much wont to shift to jargon which she found totally incomprehensible. Richard could, if needed, offer the role of a translator or even of moderator.

The initial conclusion which they reached was simple. She stated it to make sure everyone agreed:

"Our goal is to figure out the motives of the Chinese."

She paused and with a smile added:

"Or at least try to . . ."

The group unanimously agreed and took it to the next step: they should first work on the U.S. Treasury market to get a sense of whether the Chinese were simply rebalancing their portfolio or doing something else. Nikolai agreed and added:

"We'll always have time to work on CryptNotes, but it is going to take more time and be quite a bit more complex.

CHAPTER.17

The market reversal which Roy had just noticed was the first result of the strategy which Richard Freeman had suggested. The Shadow Experts had secured a line of credit with the welcome help of the U.S. Fed and of Saudi Arabia. They needed the funds to posture as big buyers of Treasuries.

Richard realized that there was one likely risk in the strategy he was going to implement. He was going to be buying Treasury bonds, effectively to counter the influence of the Chinese seller and, if possible, more than offset it. He was expecting thus that whatever he had bought would eventually appreciate. That was the good news. The bad news was that, when he had finished the buying and was seeing a reasonable paper profit, he would still have to sell the portfolio back to the market in order to repay the line of credit he had used for the purchases. Unless he was very careful in the selling, he might very well trigger a reverse market move, transforming his paper profits into real losses, and negating the impact of the initial strategy.

He thus decided that he would first discreetly accumulate a portfolio of U.S. Treasuries "for himself, i.e. the group." That portfolio would hopefully be accumulated as prices were still falling. This might take a week or even more. Though he might have a paper loss on that portfolio when he started the major buy program, he fully expected to reverse the losses if his buying succeeded in moving prices up. He was using the futures market, effectively making the commitment (here to buy, but he could just as well make the commitment to sell) to a given amount of Treasury Bond amount at a set price and at some set date into the future. Since he was using the futures market, he was not required to pay the full price of the position he was acquiring at the present time; he would only need to pay the full price at the set date in the future. Now, he was only required to "post margin" a sort of "good-will payment" which represents the commitment to make good on the order when he had to. In short, he had to put down only between 1% and 5% of the value of the contract he was buying, depending upon the time to maturity of the bonds underpinning the contracts he was purchasing—the longer the maturity, the larger the margin, which makes sense as longer maturity bonds have more price volatility and, thus, risk than shorter term bonds. In practice, he was able to leverage the money he had set up for the portfolio by a factor of nearly forty. The idea was that the profits he would make would add to their firing power later on, while any loss they could incur if markets went against them would still be manageable. Once that portfolio positioned, Richard started the bigger buying program. He did not try to hide his activity, and its visibility led to the reversal which Tommy Koh had noticed.

■ ■ ■ ■ ■

Richard knew very well that cautious traders try very hard to be subtle and discreet, often hiding their intentions to minimize their impact on the market. Typically, whenever an investor needs to execute a transaction that is large relative to daily trading volumes, he or she will contact one trusted broker and give him or her some idea as to what they are trying to achieve. They will instruct the broker not to "show his hand" to the market, asking that the order be "gradually fed" to the market. This helps ensure minimum market disruption. Indeed, failing to exercise such care and showing to the broader market that one has a large order to execute would lead several brokers to know or think they know about the big buyer or seller. These traders would in turn try to "front run" the large order—front running involves buying or selling for one's own account rather than for the client's account. Whether it be their trading or the market impact of the large order, prices would move, allowing the front runners an easy profit as they would eventually take advantage of the price change to take a profit. In short, front sellers hope to be eventually "bailed out" by the large investor.

■ ■ ■ ■ ■

Richard had initially read the Chinese trading as being of the careful type. They seemed to have used only one major broker. Also, they appeared to have concentrated their selling in the Pacific markets, which comprise three time zones, ranging from Sydney in Australia to Tokyo in Japan and Singapore. He could not help but be surprised that the Chinese had, so far at least, avoided London arguably the largest center for offshore dollars. He thought: *Why would a careful trader not spread an order across all market centers?*

When he shifted to the so-called major buying strategy, Richard had elected to be the clumsiest trader possible. He made sure that the size of the order was not only known, but in fact appeared bigger than it was. He contacted the twenty largest brokers, across the four major trading geographies in the world. He made sure they all knew that the order was potentially huge. These brokers then, effectively, started to compete with one another, moving prices much faster than the executed size would warrant. In fact, it took less than one day for prices to jump by around 5%. Yet, to the extent that he did not have unlimited buying resources, he started selling from the portfolio he initially created, but very discreetly, using only one broker. Thus, the market continued to think there was a very large buyer around, not realizing that some of the sales they were seeing came from the same source as the buying.

He was not able to complete the sale of his initial portfolio, because, at some point, someone must have thought they could see that there was both a major buyer and a major seller. Richard smiled at the irony, thinking: *little do they know it's the same investor*. He then used all the funds he had collected, together with the profits he booked to repay as much of the line of credit as he could. For the small bond portfolio that was left, he remained as discreet and careful as possible. He was slowly feeding each trade to the market, making sure he operated across all possible time zones and markets. He occasionally reversed direction to confuse possible counterparties. Thus, he managed to sell down all that he had bought without causing interest rates to fall too materially. On average, the strategy netted a nice profit which was deposited with the Globale PrivatBank in Vienna.

■ ■ ■ ■ ■

The Treasury market reversal led the Chinese to stop their selling. This was the signal the Shadow Experts expected but feared. It was a clear indication that the Chinese were not selling just to reduce their inventory. If they had just wanted to manage down the size of their portfolio, it was totally irrational for them not to take advantage of a big buyer; with that big buyer, they could sell without negatively affecting the market, and thus reducing at the margin the balance of their portfolio. The Shadow Experts were able to confirm the halt in the Chinese selling, when the buying of CryptNotes seemed to go dry at virtually the same time. In short, Richard's ruse worked, and more importantly, it confirmed what they believed: the selling of Treasuries and buying of CryptNotes were linked. **And** there was quite likely some nefarious ulterior motive in the strategy. Countess Renate asked:

"Where does that leave us, Nikolai?"

Nikolai immediately made the case that they had to shift to the cryptocurrency market. He could see all his colleagues nod their approval. The group further agreed that the next step in the strategy would be to try and create some negative publicity for the crypto markets. Nikolai had indeed argued:

"I don't know enough about real volumes to be prepared to mimic the strategy so successfully used by Richard in the U.S. Treasury markets. Deep down, I believe that the crypto market is currently driven by speculators and people who follow the broad narrative without having really thought the whole thing through. So, we need them to start questioning their rationale for buying."

With a whimsical eye, he added:

"They may well eventually do the job for us . . ."

Hai Chock asked:

"You mean liquidate in bulk once they've lost confidence?"

Nikolai could only reply with a big smile and a single word:

"Bingo!"

To create negative publicity, they felt that the simplest approach would involve perpetrating a fraud and eventually publicizing it. The principle behind CryptNotes, for instance, is a blockchain, a shared public ledger where transactions are conducted. These transactions are conducted from individual or group wallets. Essentially, a transaction is a transfer of value from one wallet to another. Each wallet is supposed to have a secret data sign-in, which allows the owner of that wallet to prove that he or she is indeed the owner of the wallet.

Hai Chock and Nikolai had quickly focused on these wallets and their sign-in as a way into the system. Nikolai was ostensibly less gung-ho than Hai Chock, as one of the two creators of CryptNotes. He knew that there were two types of wallets: cold and hot. A hot storage wallet is accessed via the internet services and is thus less secure because there are more avenues to hack into a wallet through the internet. At the same time, it offers more liquidity and convenience. A cold storage wallet is more secure as it is not connected to the internet. It is also more cumbersome for its owner to access. Most cryptocurrency attacks have occurred when a hacker hits an online wallet service and transfers the secret keys to their own wallet—essentially transferring the associated funds.

Hai Chock, on the other hand, as an expert cyber-superstar, had never seen a code that would resist him too long. He had, in a previous assignment, managed to break into a bank account in Aruba using his ability to generate "passwords" at random. He agreed that the most intuitive route, at the outset at least, would be to find a way to hack into one or another of the various internet-based crypto exchanges. After all, that's where major thefts had already taken place in Japan and in the U.S. He added:

"Why make it more difficult than needed . . . until we have to?"

He was broadly smiling as he finished his sentence.

■ ■ ■ ■ ■

Nikolai asked that any execution be delayed for a couple of days and told Countess Renate that he wanted to have a personal conversation with her. Renate was a bit surprised but was surely not ready to reject the request.

"So, what's up?"

"Well, you may or may not know, but there has been rampant speculation that Hideo Kamatsuka . . ."

"Hideo Kamatsuka?"

"Yes, the name which the public gave to the presumed founder of CryptNotes. As you know, the name covers not one, but two individuals. And, as you know from the beginning, one of them is me."

"I see, I see . . ."

"Well, have you heard of the speculation that Kamatsuka-San has a large, personal cache of CryptNotes?"

"In truth, I haven't. Does he? Or rather, do they?"

"Yes and yes."

"So, what do you want to do?"

"Quite simple. I will sell my wallet as quickly as possible; it will not take more than a couple of days, particularly if the big buyer is around."

He paused, and Countess Renate could easily see that he had some difficulty coming to his next point. She encouraged him with a smile. Nikolai then said:

"There's something that's a bit more difficult . . . I need and want to have a conversation with Frank Thistle."

"Frank Thistle?"

"Yes. The other half of Hideo Kamatsuka . . ."

"Can you have it without giving the whole thing away?"

Nikolai clearly looked sad. He first said that giving the whole thing out was not the issue. There were a sufficiently large number of issues circling around the crypto world that concocting a story that would explain his decision to sell would not take a lot of imagination. He added that what made him sad was his belief that his friend, Frank, would probably not listen to him, or at least not listen to him in full. He added:

"I will tell him a story which will convince him to sell enough to never have any money issues . . . The story will have nothing to do with our strategy, but I know he will likely initially not buy it. The clincher will hopefully be when I tell him that I am completely selling out. That should shake him."

He paused, noting in passing for Countess Renate's strictly confidential information, that both he and Frank have more than enough to live very well for quite some time. But he had to add:

"Yet, when I am honest with myself, I try to imagine how I would react if the shoe was on the other foot. I think I would most likely hedge my bets: sell some and keep some. It pains me to think I will be hurting a friend, but what the Shadow Experts are about to do is exactly what I feared might happen when I decided to call it quits . . ."

CHAPTER.18

David Heller was surprised by a call from Barack Decker, the captain of one of the two ships, the *Charm of the Sea*, which Israel had dispatched into the Persian Gulf. They had transited through the Suez Canal and then simply sailed down the Gulf. Captain Decker went as far south as the general vicinity of the site of the attack on the Saudi plane. The other ship, *Sailing Princess*, captained by Moshe Aaron stopped short of the area, chiefly to serve, if needed, as a halfway point between Khafji and Qeshm.

■ ■ ■ ■ ■

These vessels, which appeared to be run-of-the-mill supply ships, could be transformed to look like fishing boats, when the crane that normally rested horizontally on the aft deck was raised. Such a minor change provided an initial opportunity to confuse any enemy who might be keeping tabs on them. Originally, Mossad was pretty sure that no one would suspect anything. However, unfortunately, in their prior joint mission[7], both vessels had had to use some of the more sophisticated features which would inevitably have sent a signal to the enemy that these simple supply ships might be more than what they appeared to be. Would these enemies make the connection?

The additional features that make these ships quite special started with the fact that they were much more than regular supply boats; in reality, they were fast boats which could transform into hydrofoils with a couple of simple maneuvers. The foils, which at rest were folded into the hull at the bow of the boat, could be extended. On these foils, the boat would rise to a higher plane on the water, with less friction and higher speed. To accommodate the fact that the boat could rise higher on the water, the angle and length of the two propeller shafts could also automatically be altered so that they could still operate at full power at top speed. These secret modifications allowed them to outrun virtually any boat, particularly as their twin engines had double the power of most boats of that size. Unfortunately, with the need for more power came the requirement that fuel capacity be substantially raised as well. The classic physics principle: "you burn more fuel to carry more fuel."

Additionally, the vessels were equipped with an air lock which allowed the boat to pick up or deliver loads underwater. Usually, this feature was used to transfer loads from one boat to another, but it also allowed the boats to be resupplied in food or water from a submarine without the operations being visible on the surface. In addition, the lower level of the front deck, under the bridge tower, hid a full gamut of electronic surveillance equipment. This provided space for a couple of operators to work all the while allowing them to move undetected to the modest living quarters on the bridge.

Finally, these vessels had more than one identity. They each had three names on rotating supports on each side of the bow of the ship.

---

[7] From the same author, see "Below the Surface," Barringer Publishing 2022

Simply rotating the support allowed the ship to change its name. At the same time, each of the names corresponded to a country of registration, Malta, Panama, or Gibraltar. Thus, the flagpole at the very aft of the ship displayed the correct flag through a clever mechanism inspired from the multi-color ball point pens of the past: each flag rolled around its own axis until the flag was fully folded; then the whole assembly retracted into a sheave. The least complicated, but probably most visible feature dealt with the color of the middle section of the hull. The top of the hull was always white, while the bottom, the part most often immersed into the water was always black. The middle section, however, comprised vertical rotating triangles displaying one of three colors: red, dark green and white.

■ ■ ■ ■ ■

At that moment, Captain Decker was sailing the *Charm of the Sea*, a white, Malta-flagged ship. The vessel was moored to the west of the main channel in the Persian Gulf, off the coast of Sir Abu Nu'Ayr Island, a small island belonging to the United Arab Emirates and near where the missiles that downed the Royal Saudi flight were fired. The island was almost perfectly round with a long extension at its southeast end, where a small harbor was located. Further, there was an airfield making life simpler to keep the vessels fully supplied. Interestingly, it was a protected environment under the Sharjah Environment and Protected Areas Authority and had been registered as a wetland with international importance, particularly as it was one of the most important hawksbill turtle nesting sites within the entire Arabian Gulf.

The vessel, which was not more than one hundred miles from where the mines had been positioned at the top of Qeshm Island, had picked up some increased activity in that area. Satellite and drone pictures suggested that a small group of Iranian speed boats were sailing toward them.

"David, I don't know what they're up to, but I thought you should know."

"Thanks. Quite useful. Keep monitoring. By the way, have you positioned two Orcas at the bottom of the main channel so that they can relay your signal to the various mines?"

"Yes, sir. In fact, they are on either side of the main channel. They cannot interfere with shipping activity and are too small for anyone to pick them up on radar or sonar. I'm gonna get closer to the one closest to me to ensure the optimal sonar signal transmission, if we need to send one."

Barack knew that David was aware of the range of sonar systems. These sound waves can travel for hundreds of miles under water and can retain an intensity of 140 decibels as far as 300 miles from their source. However, when in use with transponders which can "bounce" the signal onto another target, one usually preferred not to exceed a range of fifty miles for accuracy reasons. David replied:

"Great. You know the plan, so be ready to execute if it seems to be what we expected."

"Yes, sir."

■ ■ ■ ■ ■

David then called Simon to bring him up to date, after which they conferenced in the Countess and Abdul El Wahabi. David discussed the call from Captain Decker. Turning to Abdul, he explained:

"As you know, we have delayed placing the mines at the other end of the Island because we felt it would be too dangerous without a diversion."

"Diversion?"

"Yes, Abdul. We want to attract as many of the speedboats of the Revolutionary Guard away from Bandar Abbas: **that** kind of diversion."

Displaying a mix of satisfaction and pensiveness, Abdul replied:

"I see."

"Well, I would suggest that we get ready to start that operation there now. The Iranians may just be handing us exactly the kind of diversion we were looking for."

"How?"

David simply replied:

"Seems a few their boats are sailing at high speed toward our mine-screen at the southwest end of Qeshm. What if they ran into some trouble?"

The next laying of mines would occur at the northeast end of Qeshm island. It had a geography which was nicely suited to the operation they had in mind. There were indeed two islands in the channel going from the tip of Qeshm to the Iranian mainland: Larak island and Hormuz Island. David explained that they had decided to place mines in the seven-mile-wide channel between the islands of Hormuz and Larak. This left quite a bit of space between the eastern tip of Qeshm and Larak Island on the one hand and the northern tip of Hormuz and the mainland on the other. However, both channels were relatively narrow, and shallow, which could be guarded by torpedo-equipped submarines or, more likely, submarine drones. Additionally, the channel between Hormuz Island and the mainland was **always** too shallow, while the other could be too shallow depending upon the tide; a difference of more than two meters between high and low tide.

Abdul had to ask:

"I don't want to go back on issues which have been settled, but I'm still wondering whether there would not be an option to place less intelligent, maybe more plain vanilla mines in those two channels as well . . ."

"Everything is possible. We made the original decision based on two considerations. First, the two channels can be too shallow as we just discussed; larger ships will usually not take the risk to navigate in them. Also, as you know, our major concern is the risk of the larger

Iranian Navy ships attacking one of our two boats, if they were to sail in that area. We do not have to worry about Iranian speedboats attacking them. Our boats are much faster in hydrofoil mode. I don't see how they could go after submarines, except with their own submarine forces, which would also have to use the center channel. So, mining the two smaller channels does not add material strategic advantage, but increases the risk that they pick us up on radar or sonar while we're laying the mines."

"OK, David. I get it. Was just a thought . . ."

David replied that there still was a danger they had to protect against. He explained:

"We are going to have to monitor the silkworm missile sites they have on Qeshm, Abu Musa and Siri islands. We know the Iranians installed them quite a while back, initially only setting them up as mobile firing sites. Now, we know that those missiles have always been powerful. And they have become a lot more accurate. The Iranians have moved from mobile to permanent firing sites, a few of those carefully camouflaged."

He paused and looking straight at Abdul added:

"Simon and I would like to suggest another potential escalation of our activity."

"Escalation?"

"Yes, Abdul, we're thinking of using one of our new weapons to destroy at least a few of the missile firing batteries. Despite solid satellite intelligence, we are not sure where all the firing sites are. Yet, there are enough tell-tale signs that we can easily identify a sufficient number of them to create the kind of damage we believe the Crown Prince is looking for."

Countess Renate interrupted:

"I assume that you will want to discuss this with the Crown Prince, Abdul."

"Yes, Countess, but, as you know, the orders may be strict, but they are quite simple: inflict as much pain as you can without leaving any fingerprints."

David noted in passing that he could provide more detail offline if the Prince needed it. He readily admitted that the tools they would be using were relatively new weapons, but added:

"We are pretty sure they fit all the requirements, particularly the lack of ability to track them back to us and thus obviously to Saudi Arabia. Obviously, we can't go into details now, as they are still classified."

Abdul was beaming.

■ ■ ■ ■ ■

Satellite images clearly showed now that a small group of six Iranian speedboats were approaching the line southwest of Qeshm, where the first set of mines had been placed. They followed one another not more than thirty yards apart. Their formation did not give away whether they had any hostile or friendly intentions. Yet, they represented the opportunity which Captain Decker had been awaiting. He started implementing the original plan.

■ ■ ■ ■ ■

Marine mines had been around for quite some time, but the newest iterations were considerably more sophisticated than in use as far back as a century ago. For instance, the mines to be used in this operation were electronically controlled, using sonar reception. They also had their own electricity supply which they used to vary the depths at which they laid in wait. Most mines had indeed historically been buoyant, incorporating some air within the structure, which created the buoyancy. They had tended to require some form of tethering to ensure that they could remain at an inoffensive depth until they were ordered to rise. The current versions were a variant on the original oscillating mines, which were hydrostatically controlled to maintain a pre-set depth below the water surface independently of the rise and fall of the tide.

The new feature allows these mines to go through a couple of cycles or rising and moving back down and do that without requiring any tether. The real limit to the number of cycles is the electrical capacity of the battery. Simply expressed, a container of compressed air is placed within the structure, together with a small pump. To command the mine to rise to some desired depth, compressed air is pumped into a cavity, displacing water that filled it heretofore, thus increasing the mine's buoyancy. To command the mine to return to some greater depth, water is pumped back into the mine; the water flow compresses the air which thus returns into the container. That increases the weight of the mine, as water weighs more than air.

▌▌■▌▌

Tracing on the GPS map where the small flotilla was likely to pass through the mine field, given the current course of the speedboats and allowing a modest variation in their heading, Barack sent a signal which brought eight mines, four sets of two, closer to the surface. They rose and hovered about six feet below the surface. His sonar signal was relayed by two submarine drones located between the *Charm of the Sea* and the mine field. He intentionally let the first two speedboats pass through unimpeded and resumed the ascension of the mines so that they would reach detonating depth just after the passage of the third speedboat. He then successively triggered half of the mines when the fourth boat was in range. The next sets were triggered immediately thereafter, to increase the chances of hitting the moving targets.

As expected, there was limited damage to the Iranian flotilla, but Captain Decker's action had two visible effects. First, the three speedboats that had passed through the mine field unscathed did not dare retrace their steps, fearing that other mines would detonate. After having rescued whom they could, they veered to port and started sailing along the coast of Qeshm. They would look for a safe harbor—and there were plenty—and await further instructions. Second, two of the last three boats raised the alarm and retraced their steps back to base. The fourth boat, however, was the one most impacted by the explosions and was simply sunk; it would have to be salvaged at some later date.

The damage which the fourth boat suffered was due to a phenomenon known as bubble jet effect, It occurred when a mine detonated in the water a short distance away from a ship. The explosion created a bubble in the water, and due to the difference in pressure, the bubble collapsed from the bottom. Being buoyant, the bubble would rise towards the surface. As it reached the surface when it was collapsing it created a pillar of water that was at least a hundred feet high. It effectively broke the ship's hull in two when it landed on it. Seeing their partners in trouble, one of the first three boats steered back toward the site of the accident and was able to rescue the crew, but not much else.

This Iranians responded by sending two minesweepers to clear the area. One can only imagine what was going through the various commanders' heads. Frequently, these mine sweepers aim just to trigger unexploded mines. However, in this instance, it appeared likely that they would try to retrieve at least one unexploded mine to be able to trace its origins. They would be disappointed; the mines carried no markings.

CHAPTER.19

SINGAPORE, WASHINGTON, DC, U.S,
LONDON, ENGLAND, DUBLIN, IRELAND, AND
SOMEWHERE IN THE AUSTRIAN ALPS

With the help of Nikolai, Hai Chock set out to take over the accounts of customers of the largest internet-linked exchange they had identified. Though many in the industry know the danger of hot storage and advise against storing any cryptocurrency balance in online wallets, there are enough people who do not heed the warning that one could still create a major disruption using that route. Their first critical decision was to limit their effort to the CryptNotes market. Ostensibly, this would only cover a fraction of the universe. Yet CryptNotes being the largest of the cryptocurrencies, it was probably the best target. Countess Renate had added with a smile when she was brought into the loop:

"And by the way, Gentlemen, this is the one in which the Chinese are trading, at least currently."

They all smiled, as, paradoxically, they had not considered that fact in their decision. Nikolai went as far as saying:

"At times, I wonder how I can once in a while take my eyes off the ball so much."

With the strategy in place and the various steps well understood, Hai Chock started his tedious work. What made the work tedious was the fact that success would come not so much through skill as through luck. Ostensibly, this last statement substantially understates the value of skills. In particular, the work required fewer skills now because enough skills had been deployed **before** to create the right tools. It was a little bit like the classical double question: "What would you rather **use?** A computer or an abacus?" Once the answer to the question has been given, one moves to the second: "However, which would you rather **build?** A computer or an abacus?" The computer is easy to use because all the complexity has been incorporated kind of "under the hood." An abacus is easy to build, but one is left with a tool that requires knowledge and experience to use effectively.

First, Hai Chock needed to find a way to hack into the major platforms that host wallets for investors in CryptNotes. That was not the hard part. Indeed, though these platforms were designed and managed by professionals, few if any could match the skills of Hai Chock. These professionals had used cyber protections that were all well-known. And, as Hai Chock used to say: "show me a system that is commercialized, and I'll show you a way around it." So, as expected, he was able to get into the largest of them in less than an hour. He had decided that he would first work on one platform and then move onto others if he could not reach his target intrusion total with just that first one, though he hoped that would not be the case.

Once access was gained to the platform, the hard and tedious work started. He accessed the list of files on the platform's server; each of these files represented a wallet. Hai Chock was delighted to see that it looked pretty much exactly as he was expecting. It showed an account number with a blank field next to it. He had imagined the first column to be where he would find a list of client usernames or a list of client account numbers; he was not sure which he would find, but he was pretty sure it would be one or the other. The blank space next to the identifiers had to be for passwords or crypto keys. That was the main challenge for him. Indeed, he had to find a way to discover the correct password for each account. His major worry was that certain systems lock you out after you have tried too many times to enter a password unsuccessfully. In this case, that elementary safety was not there. Hai Chock still noted in his own mind that the Shadow Experts have so many servers they can use around the world that for any server to be blocked would have made the task more complicated but not impossible; he would simply have had to bounce the work from one server to another.

He went straight to his random password generator and connected it to the list. A random password generator is a brutal but very simple tool: quite simply, it randomly selects all the various possible combinations of letters, digits and even possibly symbols to generate the correct password to get into that one account. There is very little nuance in the system—just brute force, which here translated into time and electricity usage. In the prior iteration of Hai Chock's generator, he had to work individually with each account. The process involved selecting an account, generating all possible passwords until one found the correct one, making note of it and returning to the top, i.e., restarting the same process with the next account on the list. A crazy and time-consuming routine, but that was all that could be done then! There were instances where it took as long as a couple of hours for the correct combination of characters, the correct password, to be generated for one account.

The new generation tool he had created carried out the same process but did it in parallel and, thus simultaneously, on as many as a thousand accounts. When the computer stumbled on a correct password for one account, it would immediately pair that password with that account, and keep working until there was a password generated for each account on the list. Thus, instead of having as many process iterations as there were accounts, there would be only one search for passwords, with the system noting the reference of each pair of account number and password once found.

While his new system was a huge improvement over the prior one, Hai Chock knew that there were always circumstances that could make the search more challenging. The most frequent source of complexity involved the risk of "funky" characters being used. For instance, French or German keyboards would typically have keys for vowels with some accent or symbol above them, both when capitalized or not. Then there was the issue of all the Asian and Middle Eastern keyboards, each with their own alphabets. Thus, it was totally possible that he would not find a match for certain accounts in his current search, as he had used only the characters found on a typical QWERTY English keyboard to save time. Raising the number of possible characters indeed could add, potentially considerably, to the number of possibilities that would have to be tested. Once he had completed the work on the first one thousand accounts, it was time to turn to the next batch, and so on until he had gone through the whole list.

He would argue that any account for which he had found the "right" password was an account over which he had what he called "joint-control." He called it "joint" because he did not exercise any control yet but could as soon as he wanted. Indeed, he did not want to start manipulating the accounts themselves until he was done with the part of the work that was the longest: finding the passwords. Once he started manipulating inside any account, the risk of being discovered rose. So, he had elected to carry out the project in two steps. First find as many passwords as possible and then retrieve as many CryptNotes as possible.

So, while the one computer was busy working on password discovery, Hai Chock had worked on another to create a program that would allow him to transfer the CryptNotes assets from all accounts at once. He set up a "cold" wallet for the Shadow Experts, which was intended to be the ultimate, if temporary, beneficiary of the cryptocurrency transfers. He started transferring all holdings of CryptNotes to that wallet as soon as he had completed identifying the passwords on the second series of thousand accounts.

Within less than a week, he had been able to take control over CryptNotes balances in excess of $10 billion, and that with just a hack into the largest platform. While an apparently big number, it was only a fraction of the total size of the cryptocurrency market which was estimated to be worth around $3 trillion at the time. He and Nikolai had discussed at length, bringing Countess Renate and Richard in the loop as well, whether it was better to focus on one platform or several of them. In the end, Nikolai argued:

"I think we should only focus on one platform, for at least a couple of reasons. First, there is always the risk of being discovered. We'll move onto another one if we cannot achieve our goal on the first try. Second, we do not want all platform managers to revisit their safety protocol. Better to have only one go through the effort."

Hai Chock interrupted:

"I agree, though I think we must realize a couple of things. First, I still bet that all platform managers will look at their security setup when they hear of the hack. And second, by having one rather than several platforms, we will have a smaller impact. But let's face it. Who cares? We plan on repeating the exercise a few times, so let's keep as much flexibility as we can."

Countess Renate agreed and suggested that the better approach was probably to target a large enough amount of money to transfer, without worrying about hitting too many targets. In the end, she won the argument, as her solution was by far the most practical.

The original press headline was quite powerful as soon as the news spread that $10 billion worth of CryptNotes had disappeared:

"Are cryptocurrencies as safe as believed?"

The genius behind the operation was in part that the team had decided that they would publicize as widely as possible the result of their work. The press had a field day talking of the major theft. It even originally failed to mention the second half of the announcement, which might have eased the panic. Eventually, this second part of the statement was noticed. But surprisingly it seemed not to have as much of an impact as it should have had: the press and the public remained seemingly confused. Event-caused panic seems never to be far away from Narrative-based euphoria!

Indeed, the statement by the perpetrators announced both that they had the money and, ominously, that their "incursion" into these accounts, as they put it, was meant to demonstrate the lack of safety of the crypto infrastructure. Their intent was to warn owners of these wallets that the area was much riskier than commonly thought. The clincher was that the announcement included an invitation to the owners whose wallets had been emptied to contact some encrypted email account which would make sure that the funds would be returned to them.

Initially, certain owners contacted the suggested website and were able to recover their CryptNotes assets, though the actual dollar value of their holdings had fallen substantially in the market turmoil following the theft announcement. Others, however, did not react right away. They feared that the suggested website was the second leg in a scheme which would allow the thieves to steal even more. Eventually, encouraged by stories of people who had seen their money returned, most owners did recover their funds; confidence grew in the validity of the thieves' invitation.

CHAPTER.20

SINGAPORE, LONDON, ENGLAND, DUBLIN, IRELAND AND SOMEWHERE IN THE AUSTRIAN ALPS

Crypto markets had dropped furiously when the announcement was made that an unknown hacker had gained total control of $10 billion in CryptNotes, thus depriving their rightful owners of assets they thought they had. Though the "theft" related solely to CryptNotes, all cryptocurrencies took a major hit, falling by as much as 50% for the least liquid and still a massive 38% for CryptNotes. In fairness, one had seen similar price drops in the past; yet it had never happened over a period of two days as was the case this time. Also, in the past, the market tended always to bounce back higher after a major drop; however, this time, it seemed that market participants were loath to buy on the way down. One could clearly see some loss of confidence.

More critically, several observers or commentators who had been increasingly inclined to view the crypto world as an unshakable part of a prudent portfolio started to eat some of their earlier insights: was crypto really an investible asset? Interestingly, the issue was not so much about the theft; there had been two substantial instances earlier when significant amounts had been stolen. What really surprised, and in fact shook people, was the surprising comment which the thieves appended at the end of their claim of responsibility:

"Be careful in the future, we can hack into your wallets again whenever we want. The next time, we may not return the money. And don't think that cold wallets are totally safe, we have ways . . ."

The plan which Nikolai and Hai Chock created and executed was definitively having its desired impact in more than one way. Ostensibly, the first impact was the price decline; the key issue, looking ahead, would have to be whether prices went down further, stabilized, and stayed down or eventually went back up as if nothing had happened. Nikolai summarized the situation:

"Will the confidence return? Probably, if not most likely. Therefore? We'll have to repeat the exercise."

The second possible impact was that, even with CryptNotes prices much lower than earlier, the very big buyer did not seem to be in the market any longer. A good indicator of his "taking a holiday" away from the market was that there had not been any material sale of U.S. Treasury bonds. Finally, the consensus, which prior to the hack had initially emerged and recommended that all cryptocurrencies and crypto assets should constitute as much as 25% of all balanced portfolios, was suddenly pointing to much more modest targets if any. Experts seemed scared; would they be permanently scarred?

Hai Chock and Nikolai reported this as a great success via Zoom to Countess Renate and Richard, who surely did not disagree. They all noted in passing that the market had seemingly focused primarily on the temporary demise of the cryptocurrency market. The corollary of that was that the sell-off in the U.S. bond market went almost unnoticed. This led Richard to comment snidely:

"We'd already concluded that the Chinese have a nefarious goal. I'm starting to believe that they really want U.S. interest rates to go up. For me it's almost a given. Now, I'm frankly wondering if they're not even more interested in weakening the U.S. Dollar . . ."

Countess Renate simply replied:

"People have said that having your currency as the world's reserve currency has been a huge advantage for the U.S. I suspect the Chinese understood that. If true, they would have decided to engineer that move away from the dollar. That would make it harder and more expensive for the U.S. to run budget deficits and could thus lead them to moderate their defense spending. They probably knew that the market for their own currency, the Renminbi, was way too shallow for it to be the next reserve currency."

Richard agreed:

"Couldn't have said it better. So, they had to reverse their position which was, I believe, originally pretty negative vis-à-vis the cryptocurrency market because crypto miners used too much electricity!"

He paused and added:

"And, by the way, if bringing the U.S. Dollar down is really their goal, they don't want to push U.S. interest rates too high."

"Why?"

"Well, Countess, remember that higher interest rates in the U.S. would have to mean one of two things, both of which would be bad for them . . ."

"I'm sure you're going to explain this."

"Of course."

Richard went on to explain that higher interest rates in the U.S. would either push all interest rates up across the globe or push the dollar higher. If all countries were forced to raise rates to avoid rising inflation, that would kill or at least substantially weaken the global economy. With a fake triumphal air, he exclaimed:

"And that, my friends, would hurt the Chinese ability to grow exports. Which in turn would weaken the whole Chinese economy and potentially stir enough popular discontent to threaten the rule of the current leadership . . ."

The other three participants smiled at Richard's comical theatrical conclusion and spontaneously marked the point with a round of applause. Going back to his earlier discussion of two possible outcomes linked to higher interest rates, Richard pointed to the fact that higher interest rates in the U.S., if that was the only country that had them, would attract foreign capital which in turn would either bring the rates down or strengthen the dollar. In Richard's word: "That would be a lot of work for next nothing; the square root of bugger-all in fact, as we say in the high-tech world!"

And he exploded in laughter as he cracked the last joke.

■ ■ ■ ■ ■

Less than a few weeks later, CryptNotes prices started climbing back up again; modestly and gradually, but steadily, nevertheless. Richard understood what was happening from his long investment and trading experience and he promptly decided to begin to accumulate CryptNotes, mostly using the group's earlier profits and the same credit line as earlier. CryptNotes prices came very close to reaching the previous high. Countess Renate had called a conference call of the four of them and asked:

"Time to repeat the exercise?"

Nikolai was the first to reply:

"Which one?"

"Exposing the weakness in the system to theft or fraud."

"I don't see why not, though I have been reading several blogs that talk of enhanced safety."

Hai Chock volunteered:

"Let me first do a bit of snooping. We don't want to attempt anything and fail. That would be worse than nothing. I can imagine the headline: "Thieves try again to steal CryptNotes but fail. CryptNotes are safe after all."

"How would they find out?"

"Simple, Richard. Failure in this case would simply be caused by our being detected. Imagine this: someone in one of these online sites finds out that there has been a failed attempt at penetration."

Countess asked:

"I see that. Is there any way to go after what you call cold sites?"

Hai Chock was ready with a reply:

"Not really. What makes them "cold" is that they're not connected to the internet. I need the internet to have a point of entry unless someone can tell me where the wallets are and how they are protected."

Nikolai smiled and mused:

"I wonder whether this is something we could find out. Hai Chock, we should get together offline and discuss this. I'm thinking of the very big buyer. Hmmm. Couldn't we find out more about him and where the crypto assets are stored . . ."

Hai Chock asked:

"A bit like what you showed me once at Heathrow?"

"Maybe that, maybe something else . . ."

■ ■ ■ ■ ■

Tommy Koh called out to Roy Pierce:

"The big seller of U.S. Treasuries is back."

"Size?"

"Nothing specific, but I'm told it is big."

"Who did you call?"

"Talked to a couple of the big U.S. banks, usual suspects. They confirmed that the seller is big and has placed the order with everyone. I'm told he said that bids under $100 million will not be entertained."

"Holy cow! That IS big. By the way, still points to China?"

"Yes, at least so far. There is still only one broker representing the seller. The one known to have strong ties to China, and he has offers out to everyone . . ."

■ ■ ■ ■ ■

Aside from trading, and from his family, Roy had one passion in life—golf. As was frequent for senior management, his employer had agreed to buy him a membership at the exclusive Singapore Island Country Club. In 1932, it was the first multi-racial club in Singapore and offered other facilities beyond the sole focus on golf, somewhat of a novelty at the time as British golf clubs traditionally were only focused on the game; there was no room for any other activity which one would find in American country clubs, such as a pool, tennis courts or squash facilities. Eventually, it grew to be the premier club in the Republic, with two club houses in two different locations, and a total of four eighteen-hole championship golf courses. Until more recently, it was the location of choice for most international tournaments in the Republic, though a few of the newer venues had become strong competitors, being better able to respond to the need to lengthen courses to deal with the greater distance achieved by leading professionals on most of their shots, and to offer sufficient parking spaces for patrons and easier access.

Maybe because of the weather, maybe because of historical traditions, playing eighteen holes of golf at the Island Club takes place according to a ritual that might surprise many golfers in other countries, though similar routines can be found in many clubs in tropical or even equatorial Southeast Asia. A halfway house is reached, after the first five holes, offering drinks and shade. Hydration is crucial year-round. After the front nine, players stop back at the main clubhouse to have a drink and, frequently, to change shirts. Certain individuals have been known to take advantage of that stop to skip the drink and take a quick shower. The year-round heat and humidity of the Republic indeed leads to heavy perspiration. And this is true for everyone, including the caddies, though their roles have diminished with the advent of motorized golf carts. The back nine holes are played following the same principle, with the same halfway house after the fourteenth hole. Then, one regroups at the main clubhouse to collect on bets, and to enter one's score for handicap purposes.

As many of his friends and acquaintances did, Roy had a group who liked to play together. There were usually eight of them, with one volunteer agreeing to register the group for their preferred Saturday tee times early in the week. That Saturday, one of the eight was traveling, but a guest filled in the full complement of players. Roy found himself playing with the guest, Peter Lane, the head of Southeast Asian Treasury operations for a U.S. bank. His two other usual playing partners made up the foursome: Ong Chew Wee, a senior officer at the Monetary Authority of Singapore and Ho Siew Wah a deputy in the Internal Security Department whose duties were to look after domestic and counter-intelligence issues.

Though the game was always played quite seriously, Roy's foursome found themselves talking about a variety of local issues. The fact that Peter Lane and Roy were effectively holding the same jobs at different banks, led them to focus on the recent financial market activities which had not yet been reported in the local press, though it was well-known to many: the large selling of U.S. Treasury bonds and the purchase of CryptNotes with the U.S. Dollars assumed to be generated by the bond sales. They were talking about it when they finished playing the fifth hole of the Bukit course, a mid-length par 3, with a severe out-of-bounds into the jungle with its full complement of snakes and occasional monkeys to the right, and a well-bunkered green. They departed from the green walking to the left in the direction of the halfway house to order drinks, next to the sixth tee. They could see that the group ahead of them was leisurely walking toward the tee getting ready to tee-off, while the group behind them was calmly walking toward the fifth green. They knew that they could enjoy their drink with no hurry but were also fully aware of the fact that courtesy required no languishing; slow play was frowned upon at the Singapore Island Club.

While Peter and Roy were still on the same topic, their two playing partners joined them in the shade to the side of the thatched hut. Suddenly, Siew Wah, who was the only one of the group that had not been really involved with the trades exclaimed:

"Gentlemen, this is big stuff."

Turning to Chew Wee, who coincidentally was as good a tennis player as a golfer and had played on the national tennis team in Davis Cup competition in his younger days, Siew Wah asked:

"What do you people at the MAS think of that?"

Chew Wee lackadaisically replied:

"Well, my friend, to a large extent, we have left it alone. We have become one of the busiest financial trading centers in the world, and these kinds of trades are not unusual."

Peter interrupted:

"With all due respect Chew Wee, the size and clumsiness of these trades are a bit out of the ordinary . . ."

■ ■ ■ ■ ■

The fact that Peter had to phrase his observation so cautiously reflected two important realities, one universal, the other quite Singaporean. It is universal for a guest who plays with people with whom he has never played before to avoid any form of bluntness, particularly in the genteel world of golf. More typically Singaporean is the fact that foreigners temporarily working in Singapore are especially respectful of government officials. Singapore is a democracy which has prospered despite the country's small size and a lack of real resources other than its people and a unique location: at the southeast tip of the Straits of Malacca, between Malaysia and Indonesia. Its prosperity is directly a result of the vision of its founder, Lee Kuan Yew. While always fair and incorruptible, he was capable of forcing certain decisions, in order to move the Republic in the right direction. Thus, certain observers, frequently from outside the Republic, would remark that decisions might occasionally seem capricious, with little or no way to contest them. Therefore, people always felt it better to speak with caution, if only to open more fully later after having a better sense of the 'lay of the land.'

■ ■ ■ ■ ■

Ong Chew Wee replied:

"You're absolutely correct, Peter. We've been noticing the size of the trades. Why do you call the execution clumsy?"

"Well, at least in my personal experience, typically, when you're working a big order, you do not broadcast your intentions to the whole market. You choose one, maybe two intermediaries and farm your order gradually."

He paused and encouraged by the look on the face of his Singaporean playing partners, he added:

"Here, every time they have come to the market, prices have gapped down for Treasuries and up for CryptNotes."

■ ■ ■ ■ ■

The concept of gapping up or down for the price of a security simply refers to a move materially below or above the prior level. Technicians define a gap as an area discontinuity in a security's price chart. It occurs because the size of an order or the appearance of some piece of news make the prior price no longer a good basis for starting negotiations.

■ ■ ■ ■ ■

The group began walking to the sixth tee to ensure that they would not slow the pace of play. The conversation pretty much died, as the focus had returned to the game, and on the various bets that were on.

As it was not unusual to bet on the front nine, the back nine and the whole eighteen holes, the attention of all players was sharpened. On the front nine of the Bukit course, this was particularly true as the sixth and seventh were two of the most challenging holes; a win on the front nine might be entirely decided on this short stretch.

The conversation, however, resumed in earnest after they sat down at the terrace of the main clubhouse, awaiting their drinks and the time for their back nine tee-off. Roy had added that he totally supported Peter's analysis and was himself bluffed by the seller's strategy and execution. He added:

"Plus, we're told that the trade has only been placed in Asia so far. Why are they not trading in the Middle East, Europe, or the U.S.? These markets are global after all, aren't they?"

Peter countered:

"That's in fact the one thing that argues against their being clumsy; they broadcast their size to all the market, but they only do it in this region. I wonder whether they are worried that they could be caught in another jurisdiction."

Chew Wee, with his MAS hat on, could not resist asking:

"Why? Do you think what they're doing is illegal?"

"Not necessarily. Not necessarily. Frankly, we still don't know enough. But let's play a game. Imagine with me that the big seller is China . . ."

Chew Wee interrupted:

"Wait, before we go there, I know it's been rumored, but do we know this as a fact?"

"No, but we know that the broker they are using is very close to the Chinese Government. But I am picking China because, in this part of the world, it would make sense and we are all probably quite familiar with their financial status and position."

The group nodded. So, Peter went on. He argued that a large investor, such as China, trades virtually every day. There is a lot of maintenance which has to be done in such a large and diverse portfolio, because bonds mature or interest payments are received; that cash needs to be reinvested. Some trading would therefore, in Peter's view, make a lot of sense. Peter surprised the group next:

"Now, assume with me that they are not doing this for portfolio reasons."

Chew Wee was increasingly interested:

"Why then?"

"Well, there can be many reasons, but let me offer an iconoclastic thought. What if they were doing this as a way either to test how the U.S. Fed or the U.S. government would react directly or indirectly to some activity designed to try and jack up interest rates in the U.S., depress the value of the U.S. dollar or both?"

The group was initially flabbergasted at the suggestion, but quite quickly it became very clear that Peter was only saying out loud something that others might have been quietly thinking. Ho Siew Wah was growing more interested by the minute. While Chew Wee was immediately thinking of Singapore's reputation as a global financial center, Siew Wah was worried that there could be trouble with respect to the security of the Republic. Singapore had always been very jealous of its reputation as a place where everyone lived by the rules. They did not want to take an obvious side in any geopolitical dispute if they didn't have to, but surely would not want to be seen as facilitating an aggression against the U.S. Siew Wah surprisingly volunteered:

"Just had a thought, gentlemen. My deputy, Yeo Yap Min, dealt not too long ago with a group that knows how to get results on the global security front. Let me bring him into the loop. Let's see, tomorrow is Sunday, so how are you all fixed on Monday? Everybody around?"

All three other players nodded their support. Siew Wah added:

"I'll call him today and set something up for 9:00 a.m. on Monday. Shouldn't last any longer than thirty minutes. All onboard?"

Peter asked:

"Can you push this by an hour or so? I really need to be on the desk at the opening but can easily make time afterwards."

Everybody seemed amenable. Siew Wah concluded:

"OK, then. We're set for 10:00am on Monday. I'll sent a Zoom invite to everyone . . ."

CHAPTER.21

Though they ostensibly did not know it at the time, the minesweeping strategy of the Iranians was unfortunately doomed to be a complete failure. This demands some explanation. Typically, minesweepers (either purpose-built military ships or converted trawlers) would drag a sweep through the mine field. The sweep would either be a contact sweep, a wire dragged through the water by one or two ships to cut the mooring wire of floating mines, or a distance sweep that mimics the sound of a ship to detonate the mines. Each run would cover between one- and two-hundred-yard width of water. The ships had to move slowly in a straight line, making them vulnerable to enemy fire. Again, typically, minesweepers, though not terribly efficient, do the job well with most categories of mines, especially those that are deposited on the bottom of a body of water, those that float on the surface, and those which maintain some desired depth tethered by a cable to the bottom.

In this instance, the mines which Israel had laid did not fall into any of these three categories. They were neither on the surface, nor were they tethered to the ground or on the ground. Their depth was controlled hydrostatically, while any drift would be corrected by the underwater torpedo-like engine that connected any pair of mines. Thus, any surface or shallow depth netting would fail, as would any cable-based sweep.

To add insult to injury, David had instructed Captain Decker to torpedo the two minesweepers as and when there was an opportunity to do so without risk of being detected. The main reason for his decision, which had been approved by Simon, was to maintain uncertainty in the minds of Iranian Navy commanders. Ostensibly, the accident to the minesweepers would prevent them from returning with any "sample mine." But the blame would be placed not on the mines being impossible to catch, but rather on the belief that the torpedoes hit before any mine could be captured. Would the Iranians send another couple of sweepers? Would they stay put and accept that there were mines in that area? Only time would tell, but Captain Decker was ready, all the more so, as the white-hulled, Malta-registered *Charm of the Seas* had just been transformed into the dark-green-hulled and Panama-registered *Sea Dragon*. In fact, if the situation lasted much longer, the plan had been to replace Captain Decker's boat by Captain Aaron's, which should provide for enough confusion in the Iranian ranks.

In the end, the boat switch was not necessary. Captain Barack Decker had called on *INS Dragon*, a Dolphin class Israeli submarine, to help with the covert torpedoing activity. The *INS Dragon* was already close enough that it only had to sail a few miles and rise a bit closer to the surface. The two torpedoes were launched virtually at the same time, and each hit its target with almost perfect precision. Several fast patrol boats were immediately dispatched to rescue the crew of the minesweepers, though the vessels themselves were left in the canal, half sunk.

■ ■ ■ ■ ■

The next conference call bringing together Countess Renate, Simon, David and Abdul el Wahabi quickly dispensed with any form of self-congratulations. It was well-recognized that the campaign was going as well as could be so far, but the key was to try and figure out what was happening in the minds of the Iranians. *Mossad* had a deeply imbedded agent in the Bandar Abbas area, Solomon Bandari. Simon and David had hitherto preferred to keep Solomon totally out of the loop. He was extremely helpful in terms of information on new weapon developments. For instance, he was very early in letting *Mossad* know that Iran had developed the capability to manufacture its own version of the Chinese Silkworm anti-ship missile. He was also the source of the information according to which China had stopped supplying Iran with the HY-2 missile, though it was then that he figured out and told *Mossad* that the Iranians could manufacture the missiles. At the same time, working as he did directly for the Iranian Navy as a civilian, Solomon could only be used sparingly, to avoid any risk of his being discovered.

Simon articulated the obvious concern of the group:

"We must find a way of knowing what the Iranians are thinking."

He paused, smiled briefly and offered the solution:

"Without going into unnecessary details, let me suggest that David or I will contact a friend in Bandar Abbas and get back to the group as soon as we can."

Though the Countess and Abdul attempted to ask questions, Simon was crystal clear. This was a crucial Israeli asset, and nothing could be done that might in any way jeopardize him. He continued:

"This is why I cannot even make a firm time commitment. He is equipped with our standard communication systems, but I suspect elements of it are hidden and used only when needed. Mostly when he needs to contact us."

With a wry smile, Simon added:

"I know that he has a periodical routine, as he eventually responds when we send him a signal. Hopefully, his periodical check will be soon. But no promise."

The group had to agree to give Simon carte blanche. He thanked them. Yet, afterwards, he realized that he was being quite curt and possibly a bit confusing. So, he felt he needed to add:

"The program stays on track. We know what our next few steps are. No action is envisaged for another week. Let's regroup then. I hope that I will have established contact with our friend by then."

■ ■ ■ ■ ■

Simon was correct when describing the routine of Solomon. Though of Jewish origins, Solomon Bandari, whose name really was Solomon Meyers, had ended up in Iran after having emigrated from Lithuania to Scotland. His family had fled Vilnius, the capital of Lithuania, in 1939, when it became clear that the future for Jews there was extremely unsure.

■ ■ ■ ■ ■

The Soviet Union and Nazi Germany signed the Molotov-Ribbentrop Pact in August 1939. This was a non-aggression agreement. It divided a large part of Eastern Europe into two occupation zones. In June 1940, the Soviet Red Army marched into Lithuania and fully annexed it to the Soviet Union. In the days before the diplomats had to leave Vilnius, the Japanese and the Dutch consuls cooperated with local Jews and issued visas that allowed for the escape of the Mir Yeshiva rabbis and students to Shanghai.

Soviet communism brought painful changes to the region. They began a campaign of terror, targeting people declared to be enemies of communism. Politicians, intellectuals, and community leaders were purged and executed in an atmosphere of lawlessness and extreme violence. They sent tens of thousands of Lithuanians to Siberia, with nearly 7,000 Jews among them. However, it is important to remember that these Jews did not face systematic extermination. They were taken away not because they were Jews but because they were capitalists. Little could they imagine that they were the fortunate ones. More than 90% of those who were not deported by the Soviets were murdered by the Germans and their collaborators. Of the 104 synagogues that once were in Vilnius, only one remained after the war.

■ ■ ■ ■ ■

The Meyers family therefore fled, aiming first to settle in Edinburgh which they assumed would be safer, being a small "country" on an island which it was, in a way. However, the family worried it had chosen the wrong safe haven when the Nazis attacked England. Somehow, Scotland was no longer viewed as so safe. But there was no way to escape; so, the family stayed put and kept hiding as well as they could. Edinburg was where Solomon completed his education. His focus was on marine engineering. His sister, in fact, still lived there remaining even after his parents died. Somehow, the contact with his sister was partially lost as he drifted away from Judaism.

He eventually elected to go to Iran when the rule of the Shah, who had taken over from his father in 1941, seemed well-established. Iran under the Shah post World War II seemed to him to offer great opportunities. In keeping with the Iranian naming custom, he chose the name of Bandari, as he was settling in Bandar Abbas. He was concerned that his real name would give him away, though, interestingly, he did not seem to think that a given name such as Solomon would be suspicious. His engineering knowledge and drive helped him gain a strong position in the naval work carried out in this major Iranian port city. It gained him a senior civilian position in the Iranian Navy. He married an Iranian woman. Though abandoning Judaism, he never fully adopted the Muslim faith, though he and his family would attend the Mosque with some regularity, particularly after the fall of the Shah and the onset of the current theocratic regime.

The return of the strict Muslim Shiites to power and the radical version of Islam they imposed, however, made him seriously uncomfortable. He considered leaving but would surely not abandon his wife and two sons, all of whom were much less critical of the behavior of the Mullahs, though not necessarily supportive of the regime's most extreme actions. A coincidental meeting with an Israeli agent on a trip to Tehran marked the first in a series of increasingly detailed exchanges with an individual whom Solomon did not know was from *Mossad*, though the agent, Farzad Ghasemi, had confessed at one time that he had a Jewish background. Solomon and he developed what could almost be described as a casual friendship. Eventually, Solomon became himself an agent, though neither his wife nor his family were ever aware.

He ensured that the secret equipment he needed was carefully "managed." The two most important elements of the kit were the secret light flash communication tool with its external miniature receiver and a computer tablet, with the appropriate application for sending and decoding messages. This tablet also had a voice activation feature that allowed the owner to dictate messages rather than having to type them. Solomon had two different tablets, although apparently quite similar from the outside, save for the color of the case, were dedicated to two completely different purposes. One was used for his real life, in conjunction with his cell phone and computer desktop at the office. The other, which he kept away from the house in a locker in the gym where he went to exercise, was related to his unofficial activities. He did keep the secret light flash communication tool in his briefcase, as he would normally with a standard flashlight—as the tool really looked like a flashlight and could in fact be used as such.

His wife had surely used it once or twice as a flashlight, leading her to comment with some poorly hidden cynicism:

"Why would an engineer like you keep a flashlight that's heavier than most others you can easily find at the hardware store?"

"I'm used to it," was all he could meekly reply.

Returning home, one late afternoon, Solomon noticed a series of small vibrations in his flashlight. He concluded that messages had been received in the external receiver which was hidden next to the base of the sole chimney on his roof. As soon as the flashlight was in range, the receiver forwarded the messages to the flashlight. He still could not read them as he needed his "unofficial" tablet, which was at the gym. He told his wife that he had not had the time to go to the gym that day. She was not surprised as something similar happened at least once a week, though she never suspected it was part of a routine, as it did not occur on the same day each week. He went straight to the locker room when he got to the gym. He took the tablet and went into one of the toilet stalls. He expected the message to be from headquarters, but was surprised that it came directly from Simon:

"We need to talk. How can we arrange that ASAP?"

He thought for a short while and typed his reply which would not be sent until he was back home where the external transmitter was. The message would transit now to the flashlight and wait until the flashlight was in range of the receiver to transmit it further. He wasted no words:

"Have no reason to travel. Can we talk with this equipment?"

It was obvious to him that he would need his tablet when he returned home. He fully expected Simon to reply one way or another to his own answer. He then decided that the risk was manageable and took the tablet home rather than replacing it in the locker. Once home, and the message to Simon sent, the reply was almost instantaneous:

"A bit dicey. In short, what are people thinking? Torpedoes, mines and the like . . ."

Solomon was a bit surprised, but oddly, Simon's reply was giving him a context he did not have. As someone who worked quite closely with the upper echelons of the Iranian Navy, he had been aware that there had been a couple of "issues." He had heard of the hits on two boats in the Shahid Bahonar Port; he had been asked to assess the damage on the two boats. He was the one who suggested that the most likely cause of each explosion was a torpedo, though he could not explain how they could have been launched. There was no straight line he could find between the boats and the entrance to the port. At the same time, however, he did not have any knowledge of whatever had happened at the Southeastern tip of Qeshm. He had noticed some activity among the higher ups, but nothing more. He replied to Simon:

"Confusion with respect to torpedoes. Know nothing about anything else, though rumors are circulating that there has been a problem in the Revolutionary Guard navy unit."

The next question came straight back:

"Erase immediately after reading. Mines blew up a speedboat and two minesweepers torpedoed at the southeast tip of Qeshm. Need to get a read of reactions and hypotheses."

Solomon thought for a brief minute, and then erased the whole chain of messages, before sending his next question:

"Who is behind this?"

Simon's reply puzzled him:

"We may or may not be involved, but, if we were, it would never be not for our own account."

He could not understand how *Mossad* would partner with anybody else. It was not the normal *modus operandi*. Yet, as a good soldier, he did not question. Rather, he immediately understood that the mission which Simon was handing him, this time, was truly critical. He could not make total sense of why *Mossad* would engineer two different strikes on Iran. After all, he had read on the internet that a plane carrying the Saudi Crown Prince had been shot down, but he did not know who was responsible. With details sketchy at best, he had assumed that some Iranian "client"—the Houthis from Yemen, maybe—was behind it, but could not imagine such an act of war, against Saudi Arabia. He had seen, as had everyone, the reports of the damage caused by a couple of suspected Israeli strikes against nuclear installations. Yet, similarly, he could not imagine why Israel would set out to hit Iran in a place where there was no major nuclear nexus.

Still, he decided that he had to become doubly careful. He took the "sim" card out of his unofficial tablet. Since his house did not have access to wi-fi, the tablet could not operate without a sim card. He was careful to erase everything that could be accessed if someone found the tablet, which he was going to place in the right drawer of his desk. Additionally, he changed his password to comprise SM, his original initials, followed by the current year and month, using the Hebrew calendar. He correctly assumed that the combination would be hard to guess for anyone in his family, or even anyone who did not know of his Jewish ancestry. Just before completing all these precautionary steps, he sent a last message to Simon:

"Will do my best. Don't call me, I'll call you."

CHAPTER.22

The quick meeting which Siew Wah had organized by virtual conference zoom was even quicker than originally expected. The group agreed to put all the information they had on the table, with a guarantee from the MAS that nothing would ever be disclosed. Peter Lane originally was a bit reluctant and even incredulous, but he was kindly reminded that, in Singapore, things that are expected to remain secret remain as such, and that the alliance between the government and the major economic actors who cooperate with it is always on the level.

Siew Wah had invited Yeo Yap Min to join the meeting. Siew Wah introduced him. Yap Min was obviously not able to delve into any sort of detail, but he still told the group about a prior piece of work which bore some similarity to their current circumstances. He explained that a while back the Military Security Department of Singapore could see that their main server had been hacked. Yet, they were somehow unable to trace or counter the criminal intrusion. He added that their last line of defense had been a secret organization which is known to have an exceptional pool of talent. The group, often called Shadow Experts even though nobody knew whether this was or was not its real name, was comprised of specialists in a wide variety of disciplines. Each of these specialists was reputed to be at or near the top of their profession. Each maintained a normal, official activity which allows them both to support themselves and to stay abreast of all new developments in their field. Yap Min continued:

"Their focus is on what they call "good causes," which I guess means cases where they help catch criminals. Well, again maintaining the secrecy to which I am sworn, let me report that their cyber expert was able to find the agent responsible for the hack."

He paused and then added with a wry smile:

"The one thing that struck me the most was what that individual told me when I asked him for his help. And I am virtually quoting from memory: The value proposition behind our network is that we bring the "best" experts to those who need them. With all due humility, I am supposed to be "it" on the cyber security front . . . But I never take myself seriously. It's just that I haven't seen a hack that I haven't been able to break . . ."

The golfing group had a short laugh and quickly agreed to have Yap Min call on the organization, if not to help immediately at least to tell them whether there was something that could be done.

■ ■ ■ ■ ■

Hai Chock had used his own car to go to Yeo Yap Min's office at the headquarters of the Military Security Department at the MINDEF Building on Gombak Drive. Gombak Drive is the name of the road which veers off Upper Bukit Timah, a large Singaporean thoroughfare, to enter a restricted military zone within the Hillview District of the City-Republic. He called Countess Renate as soon as his meeting was over, and he was in a place where he could talk freely.

Given what he anticipated would be the contents of the call, he waited until he was back at the office:

"You won't believe this, but I just heard from the Singapore Government. The Internal Security Department, in fact . . ."

"Your old friend, Yeo Yap Min?"

"Precisely. We're being asked to help them figure out what is happening with respect to big trades in U.S. Treasuries and . . ."

Countess Renate interrupted:

"Don't say it. And CryptNotes?"

"Bingo! Is there anything that I don't know which I should know?"

Countess Renate gave Hai Chock a quick rundown of what she knew, most of which was not a surprise to him as he and the two other "Experts" had already been working on it, concluding:

"Not really. The two key elements are that the trades go through a broker in Hong Kong. Also it seems a lot of these trades are taking place in Singapore. But, again, none of this is news to you, right?"

Hai Chock nodded and immediately jumped on the last point:

"Totally right, but that's where I may have news. At the very least, I feel that Yap Min confirmed our original assumption. He told me that the key players from his point of view are the MAS, two banks who had agreed to cooperate with them, and his own boss at Internal Security."

The Countess immediately reacted:

"Now, wait a second. You're right. This is big. Let's have a quick call with Richard and Nikolai to bring them up to speed and ask for any insight they want to offer. Afterwards, I think I should fly to Singapore and meet a couple of these characters."

■ ■ ■ ■ ■

Countess Renate flew on her own jet to Singapore and had been granted special permission to land at Paya Lebar Air Base, on Airport Road. Prior to 1981, when Changi International Airport opened, Paya

Lebar had been the Republic's civilian airport. It was converted into an air base then, and is in fact scheduled to remain so, until 2030 when the site will be moved. Her team had quite easily agreed to help, but they wanted to be sure that everyone knew everything there was to know about her various assignments. She concluded that she had to have an open and honest conversation with Ho Siew Wah. He had organized for a conference room to be made available to meet her, with Yeo Yap Min and Wong Hai Chock. After the usual banter, the conversation started in earnest. Countess Renate made it clear that her group had a minor conflict of interest in the matter which she, however, thought was manageable. She explained:

"Without going into details which I'm sure you'll understand are strictly confidential, let me disclose a couple of things. On the one hand, we have been hired to identify who is behind the trading you just discussed, Siew Wah."

He interrupted:

"So, you're saying that someone else has figured that out."

"In so many words, yes. Though I'm saying that they've figured out there is an issue. They're still unsure of who is behind it all. In fact, ideally, we were asked to find a way to frustrate it."

She paused and looking straight at Siew Wah she added:

"That puts us on the same side of the table if your interests and those of our client are the same. That's something we shall have to clarify in due course. I should add that, given what I know of Singapore, I would be stunned if we were not all on the same wavelength."

She paused again to drink some of the piping hot, fragrant, yellow jasmine tea which had been placed next to her before the meeting had started in earnest. She went on to disclose, in very broad outline only, that her group had another current assignment which though on the surface totally unrelated, might have at least one common feature. She smiled and said:

"Somehow, in one way or another, that other assignment may also have tentacles extending to China. So, again, I actually think that we are all really on the same side and can proceed, but I must reserve the privilege to stop our cooperation if I see diverging interests."

Siew Wah reacted:

"That sounds just fine, Countess, but I'm not sure I understand what you mean . . ."

"Well, let me put it this way. We have reason to believe that the Chinese are behind the trading in U.S. Treasuries and CryptNotes. We suspect nefarious motives, or, said differently and more accurately based on what we know rather than what we surmise, that their trading is neither natural nor driven solely by reasons of portfolio composition or investment return motives."

"This is quite serious; do you have any proof as of yet?"

"Unfortunately, not. They have not told us anything if that's what you mean."

She smiled and paused for a second. She then continued:

"We have solid indications, but we do not have absolutely conclusive proof. Let me be clearer: we have indications that suggest that the seller did not do something he should have done in the prevailing market conditions . . ."

"Hard to follow . . ."

"Sorry, Siew Wah. What we know is based on our interpretation. Given recent market conditions, the seller should have sold more if his goal was just of a normal portfolio nature. He didn't. So, we postulate that something is amiss. However, we need more information to get to where we would need to get. I should add that we are meeting with our client very soon to discuss our current conclusions. Anyway, it seems to me—but I'd like to hear you confirm it—that you may be concerned about the role that Singapore is playing. And you wish to be as well-informed as possible."

Siew Wah replied:

"This is right. But there's more to it. I must confess that we had already done some thinking, particularly since this meeting with you was set. We developed a few scenarios that might explain the behavior of the Chinese. The preliminary conclusion you seem to have reached is, unfortunately, fully in line with one of our scenarios, the one we hoped was the furthest from reality."

"You and we both . . ."

Siew Wah went on to explain that, at the outset, the Singapore Government was only concerned with the integrity of its global financial trading platform and its reputation. At the same time, he argued that nobody can ignore the saber rattling and outright aggressiveness which China had displayed in the region. He added:

"Again, so far, that aggressiveness has been centered on Taiwan and the China Sea, you know, the islands, reefs, and banks of the South China Sea, including the Spratly Islands, Paracel Islands, Scarborough Shoal, and various boundaries in the Gulf of Tonkin. China, Vietnam and the Philippines are the countries most involved, though Brunei is in the loop to some extent as well."

He paused to check that Countess Renate was onboard, as he knew very well that none of what he said would be news for Hai Chock. She nodded. He took a deep breath and concluded:

"We certainly support our friends in ASEAN, you know, the ten-country Association of Southeast Asian Nations, Brunei, Cambodia, Indonesia, Laos, Malaysia, Myanmar, Philippines, Thailand, and us. At the same time, we have viewed this as something that required careful diplomatic efforts."

"I can imagine."

"Thank you. Now, unfortunately, though I cannot believe that China would be trying to confront us, we could well find ourselves to be 'collateral damage.'"

Countess Renate could not agree more with Siew Wah's assertions. Yet, she also noted that the moment governments in general and diplomatic relations in particular are involved, the situation has to be viewed differently, saying:

"We are not equipped to address diplomatic problems. We focus on issues that have some criminal nature, whether in international law or simply on basic moral grounds."

Siew Wah was nodding his total concurrence. She continued:

"We would be delighted to help you, if we all agree that the various participants all are aware of who is involved directly and indirectly. And, and, and that no one objects. If you agree, my next step would be to discuss this, again, in total confidence with our other client and revert to you."

"Countess, what's quite hard in this case is that you are telling me, unless I misunderstand something, that your client will know who we are, without our knowing who he is."

"I understand that, and if it were what I did say, I would not accept it if I were you."

She paused and was delighted to see that Ho Siew Wah seemed relieved. She continued:

"No, my strategy must be more subtle. What I would do is discuss the fact that a potential client in the Pacific Basin Asia is concerned by the trades and wants us to help. Obviously, that client could be Singapore, but, frankly, he could also be Australia or Japan. I think we can all agree that Hong Kong would not be credible and that the other regional financial markets are too small to matter."

"I see. Well, if that's all you would say, go right ahead."

■ ■ ■ ■ ■

The Countess organized a video conference with a small group of people: Jack Turnbull, Ho Siew Wah, Ong Chew Wee, Wong Hai Chock, Richard Freeman, and Nikolai Bernstein. She went straight to the point:

"Gentlemen, as you all know, we have discussed this question of alleged Chinese financial market trading among all of us, though never with all of us in the same cyber room."

She went on to argue that her main concern at that point was to ensure that everyone was aware of what the Shadow Experts were doing, who was helping them, and in what way. Turning first to Jack, she said:

"I fully understand that your interests, that is, those of the U.S., are not exactly the same as those of Ho Siew Wah and Ong Chew Wee. At the same time, I think everyone is on the same side, though for different reasons. Am I correct?"

Everyone nodded their agreement. She continued:

"I would like to invite Jack, Siew Wah and Chew Wee to outline for the group their major concerns and goals. Clearly, feel free to hold back anything, though I would ask you to disclose anything which could have a bearing on the others."

Jack spoke first. He articulated the view that the U.S. was both surprised by and disappointed at what the Chinese seemed to be doing. He made sure that this premise was conditioned fully on the current analysis of the Shadow Experts as it stood being correct. He did not develop alternative explanations, but noted that there were other, credible scenarios. However, they all, to him at least and certainly to the Experts, seemed to be less probable or even sensible than the other. He admitted:

"We know that China and we are adversaries on the global scene. Skirmishes are bound to happen, that's how the world works. Yet, we feel that their current action, if confirmed, is beyond the pale."

Countess Renate asked:

"Where does that lead you?"

"Well, we really want to teach them a lesson. We will not tolerate externally imposed monetary policy decisions. Neither will we tolerate a direct assault on the credibility or the value of the U.S. Dollar."

Siew Wah had to raise the obvious point:

"You're not thinking of a military option I hope, are you?"

Jack could be seen on the screen gesticulating with his arms to convey that the message that nothing of that nature was being considered. Though he did note that they might at one point be forced to consider such an avenue. He cautioned however:

"In truth, any and all these decisions would be way above my paygrade."

He allowed himself a smile and, resuming his reply to Siew Wah, argued that his brief has been twofold. First, he wanted to find out who was behind this and, to the extent possible, what their motives were. Second, again if possible, and if the motives identified in the first step were not only unfriendly, but downright aggressive, he wanted to make sure that the perpetrator was punished by loss of capital, without any official action taken by the Fed or whoever else.

Siew Wah asked:

"You said without official action. Does that mean that you would not want anyone to know the U.S. was involved, or simply that . . ."

Jack interrupted:

"Plausible deniability, plausible deniability. That's all. Nothing public. Would not prevent certain frank discussion at the ambassadorial level, but nothing that would ever be visible to the outside. So, no official action by the Fed, or public pronouncement by any government official. Nobody should be made to lose face."

He paused for a second and added:

"Obviously, this assumes that the issue is not brought to the fore by the Chinese in some official fashion. We don't want them to lose face, but we sure as hell don't want to lose face either."

"Well, if that's the case, we are indeed on the same side. Countess, can you share with us at least the outline of your plan?"

"I'd love to, but I cannot, simply because we are working on a trial-and-error basis."

Siew Wah had to ask:

"What do you mean?"

"Fair question. We feel, but are not certain yet, that CryptNotes is the weak link. We doubt very much that there is anything we can do to prevent China selling all its Treasuries if it wants to. At the same time, alliances may be formed to absorb as much of these sales as possible if needed. The one thing that we believe is that there is a way to lower the value of any crypto holding they build."

Ong Chew Wee had to ask:

"The ulterior motive?"

"We are hoping that China will at one point realize that their strategy is failing and that they are weakening themselves rather than their adversary. After all, in a global economy, countries will hold reserve assets, and these usually involve financial obligations of other countries."

Richard interrupted:

"The crypto world was initially created because there was a sense that one could not trust central banks. Some of it is still quite genuine, but I am convinced that there is a lot of froth . . ."

"Froth?"

"Yes, Hock Chai, froth in the sense that many traders and holders of crypto are not fully aware of what they are doing. They're either so convinced by their technological rationales that they fail to appreciate how they could, in fact, bring the whole edifice down. Or, they are so focused on making a buck that it doesn't matter what ultimately could happen. Can you imagine a whole world working on open source blockchains. Who could and would police it? Who is sufficiently naïve to believe that criminals could not highjack some, if not most, of it?"

CHAPTER.23

PERSIAN GULF, TEL AVIV, ISRAEL, RIYAD, SAUDI ARABIA, AND SOMEWHERE IN THE AUSTRIAN ALPS

Solomon had been invited to a meeting discussing the current challenges that faced the Iranians. He was asked to attend owing to his naval engineering experience and his position as a senior civilian engineering adviser in the Iranian Navy. He found himself surrounded by senior navy officers, a couple of whom he did not know and assumed, correctly as it turned out, to be senior commanders in the Revolutionary Guard. The most senior Iranian Navy commander first turned to Solomon and said:

"This is absolutely top secret. We need your help to understand what is happening . . ."

"Understood, but what do you mean by "is happening"?"

The commander, Admiral Reza Pashtani, waved the question away with his hand and simply said with a severe frown just above his nose:

"You're about to find out. Nobody other than this group knows the full story. Any leak, if there is any, will have to have come from this room."

Although Admiral Pashtani finished his admonition with a weak smile, Solomon read the statement as a warning. Further, while he believed it was intended for everyone, he felt it was particularly aimed at him. Whether that was because of his current frame of mind and *Mossad* operational instructions or not, was unclear. Yet, a psychologist would bet that the close relationship between his recent telegraphic conversations with Simon and the topic of the meeting had to be the main culprit. To top it off, there was the fact that he was the only civilian in the group at that time. Admiral Pashtani discussed the two incidents, as the hit in the south had been felt by the Revolutionary Guard while the torpedoes in the north affected the Iranian Navy:

"Let me preface this discussion with something even more top secret. We were the ones who shot down the Saudi plane; my colleague, Admiral Javad Shahani's Revolutionary Guards, executed the plan flawlessly."

Solomon swallowed very hard. In some ways, he had a hard time believing his ears. After all, this was, at least in his uneducated mind, an act of war. He was thinking: *"Why and how could Iran do that?"* He was brought back from his deep thoughts by Admiral Pashtani as he went on to explain that the guards used remote controlled underwater missile launching drones. More specifically, he made the point that there were two underwater launchers, each with two missiles, concluding:

"We fired a total of four missiles. Two hit the plane and the other two aimed at the escorting fighter jets missed."

His face became much more severe as he then made the point that the Iranian Government now knew that the Crown Prince was not on the plane. Looking at everyone in the room, though not stopping on anybody in particular, he added:

"This means that there must have been a leak somewhere. That's why I talked of a leak earlier: we can't have that! The guilty will be found out and summarily executed!"

His voice was rising as he finished his sentence. He noted the reaction around the table, which displayed both surprise and somewhat more fear than usual. His voice smoother, he calmed the atmosphere in the room by effectively arguing that it seemed to him that nobody who was in the room today could have been involved. As he put it:

"All this was planned in Tehran, with only two of us here in the loop. Even the officers who were on the submarine and those who were remotely controlling the firing of the missiles did not know the real target. They had been told it was a practice exercise. They expected a target, in the form of an aircraft, to fly on a certain vector. That was set given the orientation of the runway, but they did not know it. The missiles were heat-seeking and thus did not need to have precise coordinates for the target."

He added with a look of calm surprise on his face:

"The Saudi fighter pilots are really very well-trained. They avoided our fire with seemingly no effort. We need to learn to do better."

The room, which was already quite silent, became even tenser. Nobody dared ask any questions. The identity of the second person in the room that had prior knowledge remained unspoken, and thus unknown. Admiral Reza continued:

"At this point, though, as I said, we do not have any positive lead as to who is attacking us. But we must assume that we are seeing retaliatory actions by Saudi Arabia."

He argued that the problem was that Iran could not understand how Saudi Arabia was carrying out these attacks if they were indeed coming from them. He moved his arms in a wide circle and said that it would be even less understandable if the Saudis were not behind the activity. He went down to specifics which he rattled off:

204 | ANDREW B. LOUIS

"We know that they do not have any submarines. We know there was no Saudi ship anywhere in our vicinity, or in a place such that they could have launched the torpedoes which hit us near Baisadu. We have noticed no activity that could point to the Saudis placing mines off the southwestern tip of Qeshm."

He paused for effect, drank some of his hot tea, and continued:

"At this point, we still cannot imagine how it could have been done. And by the way, we're talking of two, possibly three separate hits. Torpedoes in Shahid Bahonar as confirmed by Solomon Barani here present. Mines **and** torpedoes in Qeshm. Anyone have any idea?"

Solomon initially waited for others to talk. His was the reasonable behavior as he would have expected military officers to speak first. Yet, as everybody remained silent, he ventured a couple of guesses:

"Any chance that the Americans are helping the Saudis? They would have submarines and underwater drones, we know that . . ."

Admiral Pashtani interrupted:

"Possible, Solomon. Possible. To be frank, this is one of our hypotheses. But even that does not explain everything. I'll grant you that it would explain what happened in Shahid Bahonar: you, yourself, made the point that there was no straight line which would have allowed the torpedoes to be launched. Do we know if anyone truly has GPS guided torpedoes?"

"As far as we know, Admiral, the only guidance system we are aware of for torpedoes are homing systems. That would not have worked on ships at anchor in the harbor. Someone may have developed something new, but I have not seen anything about that."

"Thank you again, Solomon. Just as I expected. Well, back to my earlier point: torpedoes are hard to explain and there would still be no explanation for the mines and the torpedoes in Qeshm."

Solomon replied, although he hesitated a few seconds. He did not want to seem to monopolize the conversation. On the other hand, he had been brought in as an expert and he had to earn his keep:

"I can see that. As far as the explosions at the southwestern tip of Qeshm, could those all be torpedoes as well, though you did say that we think that there may have been mines?"

Admiral Javad Shahani, ostensibly the senior member of the Revolutionary Guard team allowed himself a short smile and replied:

"Well, probably not, though I can't say it's a bad idea. One thing Admiral Pashtani has not mentioned is that the speedboat was hit by a water column. We have to believe it was a bubble jet effect, which, as you know, would most likely be caused by a mine exploding close to the hull of a ship. The other boats saw the water column as well . . . We can consider that a fact until proven otherwise. "

Admiral Pashtani asked:

"Admiral Shahani, what about the minesweepers?"

The reply came back like a flash:

"Had to be torpedoes, no doubt, torpedoes."

"From where?"

"That's the question. No other boat around, anywhere near. No sign of submarines on sonar. Beats me."

Solomon instinctively asked:

"Could there have been underwater drones positioned in the vicinity?"

"You're really on top of this, aren't you, Solomon. But that's why you're here, right? In answer to your question, none that we could see . . . But, as we know, they can operate from deep below the surface."

Solomon concluded that the facts pointed straight back to the Americans, with a submarine. He added:

"Any trace on any sonar?"

"Nope. You know there's always some background noise, but nothing which we picked up and could indicate the presence of a submarine. And there were clearly no boats within range of firing a torpedo."

Solomon kept asking:

"Any overhead flight? And that would be true for both Qeshm and Shahid Bahonar."

"Logical, but no trace. More importantly, we have printouts of air traffic control data and there is no trace anywhere below 20,000 feet."

Solomon paused in his questions, looking out of ideas. Yet, one last one came to mind:

"What if whoever was involved used sonar signals with transponders?"

Admiral Pashtani was surprised by Solomon's question, as if he had not considered it. He asked:

"Interesting. Very interesting! What do you have in mind?"

"As you know, Admiral, this is not my real area of specialty, but I'm wondering whether one could have a source send a sonar communication signal. That source could be far enough away that we would not normally consider it a likely aggressor."

He saw that Admiral Pashtani did not seem to follow, so he paused and added:

"I mean for communication rather than sonar detection purposes."

Admiral Pashtani signaled him to continue:

"That signal could then be bounced by some transponder located somewhere between the initial source and the eventual receptor."

Admiral Pashtani looked pensive for a few seconds and blurted out:

"That is a great idea, Solomon! I'm not sure how we can use it, but you may just have solved the riddle."

He paused and said:

"We need to figure that one out. Let's imagine how it might work and where the various emitters or receptors might be. Unfortunately, it doesn't make our life any easier. Who in the region could have that technology?"

Solomon blurted out:

"Israel?"

Admiral Pashtani looked totally puzzled by Solomon's reply. The idea clearly had not even crossed his mind. He was pondering it and started thinking out loud:

"Clearly, we don't know about their technology in depth. In fact, we really don't know enough as to what they have and what they don't have. You know, Solomon, I do not trust them one bit. They're capable of anything. They are incredibly tight-lipped. If anybody has the technology you're talking about, Israel probably does, maybe the Americans too. But aren't both of them, the Americans or the Israelis, way too far from here to carry out anything?"

He paused, as much to take a breath as to see whether anyone ventured a reply to his rhetorical question. Nobody spoke and he thus continued:

"Even if Israel has spy ships in the Persian Gulf, shouldn't they be visible? We have not seen any, though it is true that they could hide among the flotilla that's around Sir Abu Nu'Ayr, where the plane went down. All the small boats there are searching for clues. A spy vessel could slip into the fray provided it's not visibly a navy vessel, and we wouldn't know about it. So, granted, Solomon, you might have your emitter. But why would they be selling that to the Saudis? After all, the Saudis and the Israelis aren't even talking at the diplomatic level . . ."

He paused, in fact to make sure he had thought the whole thing through, and concluded:

"No. At this point, I don't see Israel in there, though they might take advantage of the mess to slip in and hit us. Everyone here: I want all posts to be on the lookout for any Israeli activity in the vicinity. In particular, let's focus all sonars on the shipping channel in the Gulf."

Solomon kept quiet. He could easily have continued the dialog and argued that it could be the theory that "the enemy of my enemy can be my friend." And, given Simon's brief words, he suspected that he was closer to the truth than others and should not be overeager. Yet, he really was not in the know and thus could not see any mileage in doing anything that could be seen as trying to shake Iranian self-confidence. At that point, he felt he had done his job: helping the admirals make a bit more sense of the situation.

■ ■ ■ ■ ■

The message from Solomon to Simon was short and sweet:

"Confused. Believe in American work for Saudis. Discount Israel totally at present. Watch for more sonar detection activity in shipping channel. They may look carefully at ships near Sir Abu Nu'Ayr."

Simon was delighted and simply replied:

"Excellent. Thank you. Stay as low as you can. Advance warnings welcome. But remain well-hidden. Let me know if extraction is needed."

Simon's last sentence suddenly brought Solomon back to reality. His work was dangerous; being a double agent is always dangerous, even if he was not a double agent, simply a government employee who spied for another government. His family was not involved, but who would believe it? He could never leave alone, not that he would have liked to, because his family meant too much to him. He kept thinking: *"why haven't I told them anything? Would they betray me?"* So, he needed to develop a plan for him and his family to leave Iran if things got too hot. And he would need to do that without telling the truth to his family; this was a risk he could not take. He began thinking of a long weekend trip to visit the hawksbill turtles nesting sites on Qeshm, or better yet on Hengam Island, just west of Qeshm, not more than a short boat ride away. The Island prided itself on not having any sealed roads. What better location to be picked up, near the shore, just off the main channel in the Persian Gulf?

With the Iranian Navy and the Revolutionary Guard fully occupied by happenings at the furthest end of Qeshm Island, *Mossad* elected to start the mining operations it had planned in the Bandar Abbas region. As was the case earlier, the *INS Dragon* submarine and two Orca underwater drones were in charge of the mission. They had planned to use the same procedure they had used at the other end of the island. Both Orcas would be dragging a chain of two-mine sets, one starting from near Larak Island, and the other seven miles further, just offshore Hormuz Island. They would both sail toward each other, effectively meeting at the deepest point in the channel. The submarine would be there to pick them up. The operation that began near Larak Island was working to perfection.

Unfortunately, the same was not true for the operation that was intended to start near Hormuz Island. In fact, things quickly heated up. The sonar of *INS Dragon,* which was trained toward Hormuz Island and to the channel between it and the Iranian coastline detected activity some distance away. The sonar technician called out:

"Captain Dayan, activity in the Hormuz channel."

"What kind of activity?"

"At this point, can't say. But it's definitely moving fast."

The captain called the officer in charge of the second ORCA, which was then near Hormuz:

"Don't care if the mines are not in the right spot. Full speed ahead and full depth as well."

He then called the other officer controlling the first ORCA:

"Where are you?"

"Almost finished."

"Dive as deep as you can and drop the mission."

Captain Elihu Dayan then focused on the *INS Dragon* itself and ordered:

"Maximum depth and vector 170 degrees. Maximum safe speed. Depth more important than forward speed. Dive. Dive."

Captain Dayan knew that the Orcas would be able to follow the *INS Dragon* as their remote pilots were remaining in full contact with them. Additionally, they were both much less likely to be spotted on sonar, being much smaller than the submarine, and made with considerably less sonic wave reflecting material.

The real surprise was that a couple of air-to-sea missiles were fired suddenly, seemingly from Larak Island, though Captain Dayan ostensibly did not know that, as his ship was deep below the surface. The crew of the *INS Dragon* could feel the impact of the explosions, as the waters became agitated and choppy. Captain Dayan was thankful that he had reacted early, thinking: *"a few hundred feet less deep and we could have sustained some damage."* He relayed to Captain Barack Decker on the *Charm of the Seas* the incident, using sonar communications. Barack immediately called David Heller, who patched Simon in. David remarked:

"We didn't even know they had any silkworm sites on Larak Island. We thought they were concentrated on Abu Musa, Qeshm and Siri."

"Well, that's one strike against our intelligence activity. However, before blaming ourselves too much, let's not assume that the missiles were launched from a permanent site. Could just as easily have been fired from mobile units. The question is why did they locate units there and why did they "see" *INS Dragon*? Or is it something totally different? Did they pick up one or the other Orca?"

Captain Decker hung up as he was no longer needed on the phone call after having asked for Captain Aaron to sail toward him to provide some additional help. David asked Simon:

"Do you think the mission is compromised?"

"Don't know, but I assume not. If Solomon had in any way been caught, he would have sent a signal. So, I prefer to assume that their analysis of their vulnerability in that area is the same as ours: the channel between Larak and Hormuz is crucial."

"What do you think we should do?"

Simon, displaying his solid managerial skills, surprised David asking:

"Tell you what, David. What would **you** do?"

David was surprised and took a few seconds to get his thoughts lined up before replying:

"Frankly, at this point, I would try to get as good a picture of the Larak landscape as I can and order a simple strike from the high altitude Kovesh bombs which Marvin discussed. We do have several of them without any Israeli markings, don't we?"

"Yes and yes. We can use them without risk that they'd be traced back to us. By the way, my friend, congrats, you passed the test. Your recommendation is exactly what I would have done. While I think of it, can we see where the mines ended up between Larak and Hormuz? Will they be usable? Should they all be brought up closer to the surface?"

David was ostensibly taking notes, saying:

"Should be able to, sir. They have GPS signals. I'll ask Captain Decker or Captain Aaron."

Simon was delighted that his protégé, and deputy, was so seemingly well on the ball. He knew that there was no better test than reactions under the pressure of the current action. He added:

"By the way, Marvin has even further improved these Kovesh bomb babies. They are now designed to explode in a way such that any fragment that might be recovered is less than a cubic inch in volume."

David hung up after having thanked his boss. He knew that they already had decent images based on satellite and Eitan drone surveillance. He asked for anything that showed Larak Island. In particular, he requested images from a time period which coincided with the time the missiles were shot. He was not really surprised that Simon's intuition had proven quite correct. The missiles did not seem to have been fired from Larak proper, but from an Iranian Navy vessel that was cruising along its southern coast. He thought to himself: *Well, this is going to make a strike a bit more complex. We need to track the vessel and get a bomb to hit it.*

Simon called Marvin:

"Any laser guidance available for the new Kovesh high altitude bombs?"

"Why are you asking?"

David summarized the situation for him. Marvin immediately replied:

"Can be done, but we need to program it into the bomb's systems."

"How long does it take?"

"Minutes. Tell you what, I'll call Khafji and get them to organize this. In the meantime, can you redirect the Eitan toward the island?"

"No problem."

The Kovesh loaded the two bombs under its wings after Marvin had entered the coordinates of the expected hit. Marvin knew that these would need to be amended as the Kovesh got closer to its target, because, at this moment, the Iranian navy vessel was still sailing parallel to the coastline. It would take about 45 minutes for the Kovesh to cover the 400-odd nautical mile distance between Khafji and Larak Island, assuming a flight plan that avoided Iranian airspace except at the very end, and thus approaching the island from the south.

The captain of the Iranian vessel which had fired the missiles did not have much time to be surprised. Less than two hours after she had fired a couple of missiles toward a suspected submarine, two bombs exploded, one on either side of his ship. The damage to the ship was severe enough that it sank, though it was close enough to shore that most of the crew could be rescued.

Solomon sent a cryptic message to Simon:

"Confusion even greater now. Cannot understand what happened to the missile launching ship."

Simon replied:

"Don't understand it myself."

CHAPTER.24

PERSIAN GULF, TEL AVIV, ISRAEL, AND KHAFJI, SAUDI ARABIA

Though it formally was part of the Sharjah Emirate, one of the seven Emirates of the United Arab Emirates—just like Sir Abu Nu'Ayr Island—Abu Musa was forcibly seized by Iran, together with a couple of other islands in the early 1970s. Iran initially agreed to some form of joint sovereignty with Sharjah, but effectively asserted full control in 1992 and stationed Islamic Revolutionary Guard Corps soldiers on Abu Musa in 1994 and 1995. Iran has since further consolidated its presence and made the island a strong link in its military chain.

Simon and David briefly conferred with Ariel Landau, the head of *Mossad*. With his blessing, they decided to impose serious damage on Abu Musa, though focusing specifically on the two harbors, located almost directly at each end of the runway which crosses the island almost perfectly from east to west and pretty much covers the full width of the island. Each harbor, partially protected by curvilinear sea walls, serves as moorings for the speedboats and larger ships of the Islamic Revolutionary Guard. Recent satellite pictures revealed a surprisingly large count of vessels. On the eastern side of the island, they were able to count as many as a dozen speedboats and four larger boats. Simon and David remarked that the presence of the larger boats was logical as they were probably meant to access more quickly the Strait of Hormuz and thus the entrance to the Persian Gulf. On the western side of the island, there were about three dozen speedboats, moored at times as many as four side by side on either side of the jetty. David remarked that the current armada seemed quite large. A couple of phone calls later, his intuition was confirmed. The earlier pictures they requested indeed showed about half to two thirds as many speedboats, which were most likely designed to harass ships already in the Gulf or to sail toward nearby islands, such as Siri, almost due west. Simon agreed that the larger ship count was quite potentially in response to the hostilities which Iran had experienced.

With only two Kovesh high altitude bomber drones currently available, the plan was designed around the use of twelve bombs, two per drone with three different waves of two Koveshes. The first wave had the drones take off from Khafji and fly almost straight in a southeasterly direction. The drone pilots knew that they would have to fly over Siri Island about thirty miles before hitting Abu Musa. The two drones hit the western harbor, the one with the largest contingent of speedboats and closer to the Khafji Base from which the drones operated—though their pilots remained in total safety at Palmachim Air Base about twenty miles south of Tel Aviv, on the Mediterranean Sea coast. The Islamic Revolutionary Guard was as surprised by the attack as in earlier instances: their radars had indeed not picked up the drones which dropped the bombs from nearly 50,000 feet, their ceiling; they were probably flying too high. After having dropped the bombs, the drones made a wide half circle flying south of the island and nearer the United Arab Emirates airspace. They were not able to take pictures of the western harbor at that time to check on the damage actually inflicted, but they knew they would soon have another opportunity.

David directed the second strike at the Silkworm missile sites on Siri Island, thirty miles due west of Abu Musa. The strike had two primary motives. The first was to attack a couple of known missile sites there. This would hurt the Iranians, at the very least disturbing their plans, and, at the margin, would make navigation in the Gulf safer. However, equally important was the second motive: lead Iran to believe that the enemy, whoever it was, was "done" with Abu Musa. After having dropped their bombs on Siri Island, the Kovesh bombers parted company. One was flown straight back to Khafji to prepare for the final wave, after having done a wide U-turn. The other continued on its trajectory to fly over Abu Musa Island and take pictures of the impact of the first wave. David was happy when told that damage on the western harbor had been significant but not lethal. He quietly muttered:

"Couldn't have expected much more."

The third strike went back to Abu Musa, though, this time, the two Koveshes did not carry the same kinds of bombs. One Kovesh dropped the same fragmentation bombs as earlier on the eastern harbor, with the goal to inflict as much damage as possible to the ships anchored in the port. Fragmentation bombs, which are designed to explode with a multitude of small fragments, would do the trick; as earlier, the explosion would be triggered by an altitude sensor: the bomb would explode about ten feet above the water surface. Fragments would hit the various vessels in the vicinity and inflict some more or less serious damage depending upon where they were anchored. The other Kovesh was using a totally different type of weapon: high blast concentrated damage bombs. These were aimed squarely at the runway, each about one third of the way from either end. These would explode on impact rather than above the runway. While David did not expect such a small strike to neutralize the runway totally, it would make its utilization far more difficult: a shorter "clean runway" between the strikes or the need to maneuver around the caters.

■ ■ ■ ■ ■

As could be expected, this time, Iran felt it had to react. However, it still had not figured out who was behind the assault. It was still, and Solomon confirmed it, discounting direct Israeli involvement. So, it elected to strike back at Saudi Arabia.

More specifically, they organized for two ship-to-air missiles to hit Khafji Air Base. Iran's surveillance had indeed observed what they believed was unusual activity in and around the base; they thought that a strike might slow the hostilities, if they actually originated there. Iran's decision surprised Simon. He and his team had been very careful not to project activity out of the ordinary in Khafji. When mines were loaded onto the submarine, most of the action had taken place underwater precisely to avoid detection. He assumed that the unusual activity had to have been due to the various takeoffs and landings, though he made a note of the fact that it had to mean that, somehow, Iran was capable of "seeing" stealth drone operations. He asked Abdul to check whether there was a count of takeoffs from and landings in Khafji in normal times and how that compared to the more recent activity. He was thinking: *"Dammit, it would be a serious issue if our drones are not as stealthy as we thought."*

Before agreeing to allow Israel the use of the base, though, Abdul had negotiated with the U.S. for a handful of anti-missile batteries, equipped with sensors able to detect incoming missiles from far enough away to have an opportunity to shoot them down: a much-reduced version of Israel's Iron Dome. The small size of the effort still made sense given two important contingencies. First, there was virtually no practical way that Iran could launch a missile attack from anywhere to the south or west of Khafji: this was Saudi Arabian territory and yet was too far from Iranian allies such as Yemen to hit. The second was Camp Arifjan, an Army installation that included elements of four of the five U.S. services: Air Force, Navy, Marine

Corps and Coast Guard. It was located around forty miles northwest from Khafji, in Kuwait. It offered important surveillance capabilities, which pretty much precluded any action on the part of Iran from the North and East of Khafji, unless using missiles shot from missile cutters or even a destroyer from near its Persian Gulf coastline. Yet, so far at least, there had been no indication of any activity in that direction. In short, there was only a limited triangular zone from which Iran could hit: it had to be southeast of Khafji and from the Gulf, though a contingency was prepared for the unlikely use of ship-based land attack missiles. Equally important was the fact that Iran would probably never want to be seen as directly responsible for the attack; this would have been an act of war. Coming on top of the shooting down of the Crown Prince's plane, it would have seen like courting disaster. However, allies here or there could always shoot missiles from "small boats" which could be easily "lost" in the Gulf's waters.

Though the anti-missile batteries did their job and exploded the incoming missiles before they could hit anything of substance, Saudi Arabia dutifully protested, directly accusing Iran, linking the strike to the other equally unprovoked attack on the Saudi Royal plane. Iran denied all responsibility and, for the first time, also formally denied it had anything to do with the attack on the Royal aircraft.

■ ■ ■ ■ ■

Inside Iran's navy command, in Bandar Abbas, the temperature and tempers were definitely rising. Admiral Pashtani and Admiral Shahani wanted better intelligence. They could not understand how so many enemy strikes could be successful without anyone knowing who was responsible. Lieutenant Rastafani, of the Iranian Navy, observed:

"We have recovered fragments of the various bombs that hit Abu Musa and Siri. They all seem to be similar, at least in terms of the metal of which they're made, except for the ones that hit Abu Musa's runway."

Admiral Pashtani asked:

"Any identification?"

"No, sir. None. In fact, given the number of fragments, we were surprised. One detail, though: they seem to have been designed to explode into smaller fragments than usual."

"And?"

"This means we're dealing with fragmentation bombs, which are designed to explode into a mass of small, fast-moving metal fragments that are lethal against personnel. It's unusual for such a type to be used against equipment."

"I see, anything else, Lieutenant?"

"Unfortunately, no, sir. We know that the bomb case consists of wire wound around an explosive charge. But we also know that these bombs are quite common. Anyone in the region could and probably in fact does have them."

"Thank you."

Admiral Pashtani turned again to the group and asked:

"Why is it that we cannot trace where they come from or how they're launched?"

Lieutenant Omanabad replied:

"We have come to the conclusion that they must be launched from the air. The problem is we have no trace of any aircraft on radar at around the time of the attacks."

"How can that be?"

"Well, sir, the only explanation has to be that the airplane is flying at an altitude that we do not monitor."

Admiral Pashtani virtually exploded:

"What? Wait! We don't monitor all altitudes?"

Lieutenant Omanabad hesitated but still nodded a weak yes. Admiral Pashtani came right back with a frown which told a lot about his frame of mind if the tone of his voice had not already communicated the message:

"Why aren't we?"

"They're probably flying too high. We've been monitoring activity up to flight level 420, but nothing above."

Lieutenant Omanabad was using a common aeronautical convention. Flight level 420 meant 42,000 feet, just as flight level 200 would mean 20,000 or flight level 500 would mean 50,000 feet.

"Why?"

"Most bombers fly lower . . ."

"How many bombers fly higher?

"Few bombers typically fly much higher, though a couple go up to flight level 500. I believe that only the Tupolev 160 reaches flight level 520."

"Is high altitude bombing a new strategy?"

"No, sir. It is common, but usually is seen as considerably less accurate."

"But they hit small targets, didn't they? I'm thinking of the ship which fired the missiles off Larak Island for instance."

"Sir, the bombs could be laser guided, but then that would give us two targets to look for, the bomber and the guiding plane. And the guiding plane usually would have to fly lower; much lower in fact."

Admiral Pashtani paused deep in thought and suddenly exclaimed:

"Damn it. Could we be talking of drones?"

Laser-guided bombs are typically dropped from a bomber while another aircraft shines a laser beam onto the target. The guidance system of the bombs locks onto the laser beam and follows it to the target. While laser guidance is commonly done from manned as well as unmanned aircraft, Admiral Pashtani had for the first time brought two points together: bombers that cannot be "seen" on any radar **and** bombs with accurate targeting. He did not think that it was realistic to assume that two planes would simultaneously be evading detection, though one or the other not being detected could be imagined. One simply had to assume that one of the two was flying at an unusually high altitude. However, laser guidance is usually not provided by manned aircraft flying at a very high altitude. On the other hand, if one assumed that one was talking of drones, the feat became not only feasible, but in fact more likely than any alternative. He asked:

"But, if we are talking of drones, who has equipment capable of that type of work?"

Lieutenant Rastafani was the first to reply:

"Other than the U.S., Israel, and a couple of countries in Europe, say the U.K. and France, and Turkey which is known to be a large exporter. Any other country that has drones would be expected to be our friends, Russia and China in particular."

"Thank you, Lieutenant, we may need to rethink this one completely. Solomon Bandari, congratulations, you were the first to mention Israel. You might have been right all along. But how would they do this?"

Solomon smiled and simply replied that he could only think of one possibility, and it appeared crazy to him. Seeing the encouragement in the eyes of Admiral Pashtani, he went a bit further and offered:

"What if there was some sort of alliance between Saudi Arabia and Israel?"

"You had implied that could be the case a while back, didn't you."

He paused but did not give Solomon the time to reply. He immediately continued:

"I agreed with you then that it seemed crazy. But now we've got to think again. But what brings you to that conclusion?"

Solomon was on the spot. He knew that he really had no firm data on which to rely, other than the broad earlier statement by Simon when he had said: "we may or may not be involved." That could mean many things, including nothing. He did not want to lose the credibility he had and on which he had even considerably built up in the recent past. So, he allowed his mind to speculate as he replied to Admiral Pashtani's question:

"Well, sir, you would have to assume that Saudi Arabia has asked for Israel's help. They might do it believing that Israel has strong stealth capabilities. In fact, did we not read somewhere that the attack on our uranium enrichment capacity had to have taken advantage of some stealthiness?"

Admiral Pashtani's reaction was still one of total disbelief. He kept going back to the issue of distance. He could not see how Israel could be acting against Iran from that far away. Solomon brought back the issue of the unusual activity which Iran had picked up on Khafji. Admiral Pashtani surprised him. He replied that none of that activity had involved any aircraft, adding:

"We had noticed quite a bit more loading and unloading in the harbor. Yet, we certainly did not see any drone being unloaded from a transport plane, taking off or landing for that matter."

He stopped dead in his tracks and continued:

"Damn it again. Khafji is a small base, and far from the rest of the Saudi installations. That could be a perfect hideaway. And the two missiles we shot with Yemen's help were destroyed before hitting their targets. Again, only two countries can do that among those who are not our friends: the U.S. and Israel."

He repeated his earlier congratulations to Solomon whose persistence in his words had formed a plausible explanation. He added for the benefit of the whole group:

"Let me take this to Tehran, because this involves more than the Navy. At this point, the only change in our stance is that I want all altitudes monitored, even as high as 52,000 feet. Consider that order approved by General Arbijan . . ."

General Arbijan headed up the Iranian Air Force.

■ ■ ■ ■ ■

A simple message went to Simon:

"Still confused. More seriously considering Israel and U.S. Should get out."

CHAPTER.25

SINGAPORE, DUBLIN, IRELAND, TEL AVIV, ISRAEL, AND KHAFJI, SAUDI ARABIA

Nikolai and Hock Chai were beginning to plan and execute their second attack on the cryptocurrency market. They knew that this would be wave two of a three-wave strategy, and they wanted it to be as successful as the first. As they were chatting, they were surprised to discover that two highly proficient computer and cyber experts would share so many views on the adverse effects which technology may have had on society over time. Nikolai, who, since he left CryptNotes, was probably the most cynical of the two declared:

"To me, it all started with the invention of the transistor and later of Sony's Walkman."

"Sony's Walkman?"

"Yes, I think it started the move away from communal entertainment toward more of a solitary approach. My parents kept talking of listening to the radio together, or even of watching TV together. The transistor and then the Walkman promoted solitary listening to music."

"Indeed, now people can't seem to walk down the street without talking on their cell phone . . ."

"Or listening to music on their earbuds."

"Exactly. And much too loud, by the way. We should go into the hearing-aid business. Everyone will need them soon—busted eardrums by loud sounds."

Nikolai smiled and commented that they would be a very late entry in that business. Then, returning to the topic of technology leading people away from society and reality, he noted the current fashion of living in a parallel, virtual universe:

"Games came on in the 1970s and initially were meant as a way to replace old entertainment such as pinball machines and the like. Nothing wrong initially. A good idea in fact. But, again, they moved from a communal space at the pub to a more solitary environment. With improved graphics and faster computers, we've gone from 2D to 3D and now to virtual reality . . ."

Hai Chock had to add:

"I hear that in the so-called "meta universe" we now have people buying and selling, often with real money, imaginary real estate, imaginary cars, and at times even imaginary yachts or art . . ."

"It all goes in the same direction; making people increasingly isolated in the physical sense and yet connected through the internet to other people, whom they've never met and may not ever meet."

"That's where the room for mischief expands exponentially."

"Exactly. I may be going too far, but I feel that one does not have to look much further to find reasons behind increased violence, depression and even suicide. At any rate, that's what was on my mind when I decided to leave that space."

"Nikolai, what space do you mean?"

Nikolai first paused. He just realized that he had allowed himself to be carried away by the flow of the conversation. Now he only had two options. Come clean or as clean as possible or invent an answer that would not be true. The friendship he had been developing with Hai Chock made the decision easier, though not without hesitations and even trepidations. He would come clean but had to warn him. So he said:

"I'm gonna tell you something that's totally secret. Just between you and me, only the Countess knows. I'm one of the two creators of CryptNotes . . ."

Hai Chock's jaw dropped. He seemed momentarily at a loss for words. Finally, he mouthed:

"Hideo Kamatsuka? Wow! Now I get it."

Nikolai replied with a surprised smile:

"Get what?"

"You know . . . I felt that you knew the space inside out and wondered where you learned it. Two creators; hey, I've got to be one of the few to know that."

No, in fact, I can assure you that you are one of the four who know that."

"Four?"

"Yes: you, my partner, Countess Renate and me . . ."

"Anyway, thanks for the confidence. You don't have to worry about me. Wish I could share a secret too, but I don't have anything that qualifies."

Smiling as he was completing his sentence, he returned to the project at hand. They quickly decided not to hit CryptNotes at all in this, the second attempt. Rather they would focus on two other cryptocurrencies. They had two main reasons for this approach. First, they wanted the market to worry about the whole cryptocurrency sector rather than simply CryptNotes. The last time they carried out the same exercise, they focused on CryptNotes; they succeeded, though the whole sector paid the price. However, they thought that a second hit on CryptNotes might lead some to believe that it was the only place where there was a problem. Nikolai explained that it would be almost useless if they simply managed to sink CryptNotes, which might be viewed as the sole "unsafe" cryptocurrency. They needed to inject a large measure of uncertainty over all others. As he put it:

"Unless we discredit all cryptocurrencies, we would only succeed in having CryptNotes replaced by another."

He paused, and added:

"And, by the way, I'm not sure the others even have the same rail guards as CryptNotes do."

Hai Chock noted Nikolai's comment, but immediately seemed a bit disturbed by it. His rationale was simple. In his mind, the mandate was to do something which would make China lose a lot of money in the CryptNotes they had purchased. So, he asked:

"Nikolai, are we not expanding the mandate?"

Nikolai smiled a wry smile and replied:

"Yes and no."

He explained that, in his view, one could not achieve one goal without achieving the other. He readily admitted that his agenda was a bit broader than that of Countess Renate, but immediately added:

"But that's only on the surface."

He showed Hai Chock that the success of the operation and long-term success in the prevention against a cryptocurrency taking over a role of reserve currency had to involve throwing a discredit on the whole of that sector. He added:

"Remember, when I first decided to leave CryptNotes, I did it because I had gone from the belief that an unregulated and decentralized market would do a better job at maintaining a reserve currency than politicized central banks to the opposite thought: a decentralized and unregulated market was exposed to fraud, and probably more so than the alternative. You could adapt the famous Churchill quote on democracy to this situation: central bank control is the worst currency management alternative except all others."

He smiled again as he saw that Hai Chock was nodding in agreement. He continued:

"Now, assume that there are several, totally independent such markets, you could argue that they may be able to self-regulate because of competition. But so far, that argument has fallen flat on its face. It's generally the same generic players on the one side and the same hopeful but not fully informed so-called investors on the other."

His conclusion was inevitable:

"I'm not saying that there is no future in crypto. True diversity within that space could be the eventual answer. So, for all I know, crypto and blockchain may well be keys to the future. But the way these markets work or rather do not work today is dangerous. So, we need to discredit them all. But you know that there is a second reason for shooting at other cryptocurrencies beside CryptNotes . . ."

Nikolai repeated that instead of fighting a possible misunderstanding, they wanted to motivate all supporters and providers of cryptocurrency trading platforms to worry about cyber security. He was conceding that there already was an important distinction between the cold and hot wallets that were available. But there was somewhat of a divergence in the way in which the hot wallet providers took care of safety issues; certain providers were very sensitive to cyber security while others seemed more in it to make a quick buck. They both agreed that everyone should feel that cyber fraud was a real issue, and, if they were successful in their current effort that everyone should start questioning the very safety of the approach. Nikolai added:

"It's a bit like what we discussed earlier on games and other computer-based entertainment. At the very basis of the idea, there is positive stuff. But people jump on the bandwagon and effectively take it to a lunatic extreme without stopping to think of what could go wrong."

"Couldn't agree more."

Nikolai added:

"I call that "technology blindness": if it's new, it has to be good; if it is new, it's progress; the new must be better than the old. And so on . . . People confuse motion with progress."

Possibly because of his own history, Nikolai was initially comfortable with the general integrity of the CryptNotes platform. He had been both totally surprised and frankly somewhat disgusted when he found out that illegal activities were being carried out. It led him to question whether the system was as good as he thought. Yet, he did believe that the platform had been designed in a way that was pretty much as safe as could be. However, he did not hesitate telling Hai Chock that he suspected certain variants to be pure frauds. Now, he was not sure whether they were Ponzi schemes or some other variant of attempts to take money from unsuspecting investors. Nikolai fully understood that anything that exists can be transformed into some form of digital non-fungible asset.

He could not resist returning to his main worry, effectively showing Hai Chock how much he had evolved since he and his partner, whom he did not name, had thought up the idea of crypto-currencies. Their goal was to help preserve the integrity of the global monetary system which they feared was polluted by central banks that had abandoned their independence from politics. Now, he could see that his invention was but one of a number of innovations that might be going too far. He was quite concerned and thought about it both as a scientist and a father of two pre-teenagers, that a whole class of individuals could no longer distinguish between reality and fiction. These, to him, would be the prime targets for digital entrepreneurs delighted to take their money. And possibly more . . . When he was at his extreme of pessimism, he viewed the technological revolution as a 21st century version of P.T. Barnum signs that said: "This Way to the Egress." Many customers followed the signs probably looking for some unusual animal, not realizing that Egress was a fancy word for "Exit." They kept on looking for this strange new attraction, the "Egress." Many patrons in effect followed the signs right out the door!

His concluding question was frightening:

"How does society survive, let alone prosper, if everybody is playing in virtual reality? Who deals in the real world? How does that avoid leading to a blow up, followed by some form of dictatorship?"

■ ■ ■ ■ ■

Just as they had the previous time, Hai Chock and Nikolai hacked into hot storage platforms. Using the same approaches and tools as earlier, they began to take joint control over as many accounts as they could, though they ignored any holding of CryptNotes. They used the experience acquired in the prior round to get access to accounts and went back, when they could, to those they previously hacked, and which held other cryptocurrencies beside CryptNotes. Their two targets were secondary cryptocurrencies, which they worried were not as genuine as purported to be. In the end, when they took sole control over the various accounts, they accumulated almost twice what they had "stolen" the prior time.

Following the same game plan, they immediately broadcasted the fact that they had been able to steal a large amount of the two less well-known cryptocurrencies. They cited amounts and named names although they were careful to use a different website from which to make these announcements. As Hai Chock had said:

"You can't ever be too careful."

Yet, this time, they did not immediately promise to return the funds. Though they eventually planned to return the monies seized, they wanted account holders to "sweat it" somewhat for a while. They hoped that this would lead to even more press coverage. In fact, they felt that the more press coverage they received, the greater the fear they would instill. The greater the fear, the more prices would fall, which should take down the value of the reserves currently being built by China, if the fall in the cryptocurrency market extended to CryptNotes.

As expected, there were two events on which journalists could report. Of course, they were related, but they made it easier to construct a narrative that could counter the rush to the crypto space. First, the obvious theft by thieves which were suspected to be the same as earlier but still mysterious was a story that had its own legs. Second, there were hundreds if not thousands of sob stories of people who had lost the entirety of their savings. Nikolai and Hai Chock smiled even most broadly at a couple of well-publicized stories where the owners of the accounts had financed their crypto purchases with debt. Now, they did not have the cryptocurrencies and had loans, a few of which were equity lines of credit, that they eventually would have to repay. These people were looking for an easy fortune and found themselves totally broke, with, possibly, not even a roof over their heads. Hai Chock concluded:

"I feel really sorry for these poor blokes. Yet, their pain is necessary to avoid more pain for more people later, particularly if the Chinese scheme were to succeed."

A couple of days later, which seemed like an eternity to those whose accounts had been hacked, a message went out offering to those whose money had been stolen the same option as the first time: contacting an encrypted email account to get their money back. Though people were relieved that they were not totally out, they still had solid reasons to be furious: the price of the two targeted cryptocurrencies had fallen by 65%, even more than the prior time, while the quotes for CryptNotes fell more than 50%. People did not seem ready to abandon the ship altogether; but the rumblings were getting stronger, and there was even some measure of gloating on the part of those who had stayed on the side lines.

The big change, this time, was that a number of governments and government agencies in the developed world started asking serious questions about the safety of the crypto world. Everyone had gotten used to the volatility in the prices of crypto assets. Yet, no one had bothered to ask the obvious question: how can I trust a currency whose price keeps fluctuating so much? All currency markets experience fluctuations, but not on the scale observed in these last two events, which took place less than eight weeks apart. How would day-to-day commerce be feasible if the price of the goods or services fluctuated that much from one day to the next? Financial oversight agencies as well as politicians jumped on the band wagon seeking to impose some form of regulatory framework. Nikolai was smiling all along, as, in many ways, a government-regulated crypto world is almost antithetical to the idea behind his and Frank's creation.

■ ■ ■ ■ ■

The help promised in the discussions involving the Singapore authorities proved particularly useful. Though it did not affect the prior hit imposed on the crypto market, it allowed Hai Chock to get into the computer systems of the lead broker behind the Chinese trades. He was able both to penetrate the systems of the local Singaporean branch and, through it, to gain access to the main computer in Hong Kong. Now, his firm expectations were that this might allow him to learn more about the accounts used by the Chinese to store their crypto purchases. Even more important, it should make it possible for him to place orders on behalf of the Chinese without anyone figuring it out until it was too late.

There was always one major risk to his expectations: what if the agreement between the Chinese and the broker required oral confirmation of each order? This is not an unusual arrangement in the world of finance, and frequently involves something called "a call-back on a secure line." Each client is asked for a telephone number on which he or she can be reached when an account is opened. Then, when the client places an order for any form of transaction, above a certain threshold, the client expects to be called back and asked to confirm the order. Unless that oral call-back confirmation is obtained, the order is ignored.

Thankfully, the safety systems which had been put in place in a large majority of the developed world had not extended to the always free-wheeling Hong Kong market, or, more specifically, to the relation between the Hong Kong broker and his Chinese client. Yet, at the outset at least, Hai Chock did not attempt to place any transactions through the account, but he did learn a lot about the intermediaries that were being used and where the reserves were being kept. He said to Nikolai:

"I may not be able to play in the market on their behalf, but I know I can try to go in and take some of their loot. Reminds me of something we did a couple of years ago, with a similar type of account, in Aruba."

He paused and immediately added:

"And, as always, that loot is either paid back to the rightful owners or, if there are no rightful owners, given to charity. We will never ever benefit personally or collectively, speaking of the Shadow Experts, from monies that do not belong to us."

CHAPTER.26

"I need to find a way to talk to you."

Solomon was surprised by Simon's message. Solomon had said to him in his last communication that he was thinking of getting out. So, he obviously assumed that Simon's message was dealing with that. Yet, in his own head, the plan was so simple that he did not see why there was a need to talk. He had rehearsed it many times and had not been able to find any flaw. One morning, he would tell a story of woe to his family and argue that they had to escape as quickly and surreptitiously as possible. The story he had concocted was that he had made a mistake on an important issue and that this was surely going to cost him his head, figuratively and possibly literally. Further, as he knew a lot and his bosses would have assumed that some had been wittingly or inadvertently shared with his family, he would argue that their lives were also at risk. One thing was certain, he was not going to talk in any way of his work for *Mossad* and was planning on carrying out the escape all by himself, except for a late assist, at which point he did not worry that a member of his family would become suspicious.

The plan was to drive to the Island of Qeshm for the normal weekend holiday, although in an Islamic country, that did not start on Friday evening, but on Thursday evening. He would load the car with its passengers on the ferry that regularly crosses 1.5-mile-wide Clarence Strait. Once on the Island, he would drive in a southeasterly direction to reach one of the handful of towns which sit along the coast. There, a boat would be ready to take them. He had abandoned the idea of using Hengam Island as adding unnecessary complexity with little incremental benefit.

Ostensibly, Solomon's plan had incorporated a detailed analysis of the various options. The one thing that struck him was the fact that the coast of Qeshm was also the area where Iran has placed a number of their permanent silk missile firing sites. From Direstan, around the Shib Deraz Cape all the way to Messen or even Suza, there were at least five well-protected harbors. That could indeed be good. A well-protected harbor might allow a discrete pickup without alerting anyone. But it could also be very bad. A well-protected harbor could also mean a harbor where several Islamic Revolutionary Guard fast boats would be moored, alongside other commercial fishing boats or passenger boats taking tourists sightseeing, particularly during the height of dolphin season. This would create a challenge to anyone who simply wanted to execute the discreet operation which would be necessary to rescue Solomon and his family. The so-called Qeshm Dayrestan International Airport, on the way to the coast, would not be a possibility either, whether for an aircraft or a helicopter. The area was simply crawling with Iranian defenses. It might work if there was only one person to evacuate, one person that could swim some distance offshore, possibly even with diving equipment, though it begged the question—where would he get that? But, with an unsuspecting wife and two pre-teenagers, there was no way that option was available. Interestingly but unbeknownst to Solomon, Simon had also rehearsed virtually the same points with David.

Solomon still replied to Simon's message with a question:

"Why do we need to talk?"

Simon simply answered that David and he had given a lot of thought to his escape and that there was no simple solution in his view.

■ ■ ■ ■ ■

Simon, David and Marvin were in Simon's office in Tel Aviv ruminating on a possible way to evacuate Solomon without leaving any trace. Israel was no more interested in being identified now than it had been earlier. Simon was somewhat unhappy that he was going to have to help Solomon get out of Iran because that meant that one of his agents in Tehran, Farzad Ghasemi, the one who had recruited Solomon, would also need to be evacuated. Thankfully, he knew that the Iranian regime had been sufficiently unpopular with the Iranian people that *Mossad* had more than enough contacts that could eventually be "converted" into full-fledged agents. Yet, losing two important field agents in a short time was not a joyful prospect.

David asked the obvious first question:

"Do we really need to evacuate Solomon and his family?"

Simon looked at David with a smile and simply said:

"That's why we need to talk to him. Don't you think?"

He expanded on his initial thought, asking himself and the group what it was that made Solomon want out. David offered that, from his point of view, Solomon had provided some information in the recent past, but surely nothing that seemed to be particularly secret. Marvin who, as always was more interested in technology than in the reason for the need for technology ignored the question, jumping directly to a possible option to evacuate the family:

"We still have the Koveshes which we prepared to evacuate the team from Iran when we attacked their nuclear enrichment plants.

We could surely use them again, if there is a spot where they can land and take off without triggering all sorts of bells and whistles."

Simon thanked him but noted that the satellite pictures he had looked at showed two almost parallel runways and within four miles of each other on Qeshm, explaining:

"One is the sole runway of the international airport, and the other is four miles south but I have to assume it's for military use. It's by itself and appears to have been extended to the southwest in the recent past, requiring the road to be rebuilt around it. Can't imagine why you would want another runway, parallel to the one at the other airport and so close to it. Can't possibly be because of excess traffic at the airport!"

He paused with a short but good laugh and went on:

"Add to that the fact that the extension is quite wide. It makes me worry that this might be where the Iranians might park fighter jets from time to time . . . Not good."

He paused and indicated that in his view, the least impractical route involved the Iranian mainland, adding:

"If only because there has been no military activity there. I've got to assume that the Iranians will be particularly careful in the areas of Bandar Abbas extending all the way to Qeshm. If there's anywhere where they might be a bit relaxed, it's got to be away from the South of the country, in other words closer to Tehran."

David and Marvin could only agree but wondered how anything could be organized rapidly and with a good enough chance of success. Simon concurred and simply concluded:

"That's why I need to talk to Solomon. David, I am not asking you to do that because there may be the need for a very unpleasant decision to be made. I don't want to put that burden on you at this time."

David smiled his thanks.

∎ ∎ ∎ ∎ ∎

Marvin and David were about to leave Simon's office when Simon motioned to both of them that he had another important topic on his mind:

"We must decide what we do with all the mines we have positioned . . ."

He offered his view that, unless Abdul and Countess Renate required more "activity" as he put it, he felt that the goals of the Saudi Crown Prince had been reached. There had been some material damage, though he conceded that some may never be enough; nobody seemed to have figured out who did what to whom; and the equipment worked very well. He paused for a second and offered:

"To me, it's time to declare victory and move on."

David had to ask:

"Have you talked to The Countess?"

Simon replied that he had in fact had a conversation with her during which he had expressed his views. He reported that she seemed to be in agreement though she argued that she needed to talk to Abdul first, adding:

"She has to talk to her client. Understandable."

Simon then reiterated that he had made it clear that Israel was not at war with either Iran or China and thus did not want to go beyond a certain limit. She had been totally supportive of Simon's position, but still felt that she should invite and maybe even coax Abdul into making that decision rather than declaring it unilaterally. Simon concluded:

"I am waiting to hear from her."

Yet he added:

"Whatever we decide in the end, it does not change the issue with respect to the mines. Frankly, at this point, without Captain Decker or Captain Aaron near the action, they are pretty useless."

Marvin interrupted to make an important point:

"They may be useless operationally, but they are also a source of a potential technology leak. Given the technology involved, I'd argue that there's a risk of something pointing the finger at us, not because of markings, but because nobody else is known to have those types of mines."

Simon retorted:

"Indeed. That's exactly the thought behind my question. What are the options?"

Marvin's eyes lit up. He was relishing his opportunity to contribute and to talk technobabble, not necessarily in that order. He explained that the real secret in the technology is what governs the small torpedo engine that allows pairs of mines to be precisely positioned in a horizontal plane. He added:

"Depth is a totally different issue, although we can save on some of the mine's internal energy by having the torpedo engine moving the two mines it controls in a vertical plane as well."

Simon asked:

"Is there a way to retrieve the engines without touching the mines?"

Marvin cleared his throat. He made the point that it might be technically possible, but it would be both dangerous and possibly still ineffective. He explained:

"Remember, Simon, we planned for enough fuel to allow the engines to make small moves, but they certainly cannot now move by much more than a mile at most. So, given the distances between the various mines, remember both channels are about seven miles wide, we're talking of a very cumbersome operation. It would have to involve the Orcas and to have them move from each set of two miles to the next, to collect the engine and move to the next set."

Simon interrupted:

"I see. Massive risk of being "seen" and being identified."

"Exactly, sir."

Marvin suggested that there was an alternative which would be considerably easier and involve a lot less risk. He added that the incremental cost would be the loss of all the engines. Simon and David looked surprised and interested. After all, they knew that Saudi Arabia had agreed to underwrite all costs.

Marvin explained that each mine pair plus engine could be ordered to rise to a depth where the mines would catch anything that sailed around them. The torpedo engine certainly had enough fuel to allow that maneuver. The next step would be to trigger the two small electronic clips which tether the chain from each mine to the engine to break open. At that point, the mines would all become independent and thus very much like any hydrostatic mine in the world. He said that the next step would be to order all the torpedo engines to dive back down to the bottom and "kind of self-destruct" in his own words.

He could clearly see that he had just lost Simon and David with that last statement. He added: Each engine has a small container full of *aqua regia,* a mixture of hydrochloric acid and nitric acid. He stopped and reminded his two colleagues:

"We used it in Natanz to dissolve concrete and steel."

They nodded and he continued:

"This is super powerful stuff. Now, clearly when the acid mix breaks the outer skin of the engine, it gets diluted with sea water and doesn't do much anymore. However, before it gets to that, the acid mix should have dissolved the communication equipment, which is really the thing we don't want anyone to lay their hands on."

Simon let go of a small whistle and then asked what would happen to the mines. Marvin replied that there were two options. The first was that they could all be remotely triggered, adding:

"Wonderful waterworks within reach of the Iranian coastline."

"And the second?"

"Well, David, we could let them float at whatever depth we have set. If that's what we decide, then my recommendation would also be to trigger another small acid container to destroy the communication cell on the mines as well."

Simon and David were both quite impressed. Simon argued that he wanted to bring Ariel and, possibly, the War Cabinet in on that decision, explaining:

"Even if they cannot be traced to us, I still worry that there could be nasty things coming our way later on . . ."

Marvin nodded, but immediately said:

"I understand but remember that a lot of nations have these mines. They could all just as easily have been laid by Saudi Arabia."

Simon agreed:

"Fair point, once you have had all the secret stuff, the communication equipment, self-destruct."

CHAPTER.27

Hai Chock was delighted to report to Countess Renate that he had been able to "remove" in his words, all the cryptocurrency holdings he could find in the Chinese account into which he had managed to gain access. He cautioned against excessive optimism:

"I certainly did not find the tens or even hundreds of billions of dollars' worth that we could have expected."

He added:

"And this is even true if you valued these crypto holdings at the price at which they were before we started our work."

"How much did you get?"

"A couple of billion dollars, mostly in CryptNotes."

Mischievously, Countess Renate asked:

"Could we sell them in the marketplace? That could depress the price further . . ."

Nikolai replied:

"We could, but I'd worry that we would run an unacceptable risk of being discovered."

The Countess immediately agreed with Nikolai's objection, arguing that the operation had so far been so stealthy that it would be stupid to take the risk, adding:

"Plus, I would not feel comfortable using the money. So, depressing the price of CryptNotes is still very much the order of the day, but we have already wiped out over half of that value."

She paused for a second and asked her team:

"Well, gentlemen, what is our next step? We've managed to depress CryptNotes and other cryptocurrencies by about 50%. That's good but not sufficient. China had, we believed, not bought a sufficient exposure to feel the loss as devastating. At most, a mosquito bite. A big bite, but still a big mosquito bite!"

Richard was the first to reply, not because he knew the most about cryptocurrencies, but because he wanted the mandate clarified. He asked:

"Do we want to impose major financial pain on China, or do we want to prevent any move on their part to replace the dollar as a reserve currency with something out of the crypto world?"

Countess Renate saw the question as totally fair and replied:

"I believe we are more on the side of defending the role of the dollar as a reserve currency until it loses it out of natural evolution."

She paused for a minute and explained her thought process. Clearly, she was sure that Jack and the U.S. authorities would not mind China feeling some pinch, but they had to know that the Shadow Experts could not achieve that goal even before the operation started. The U.S. could not tolerate a massive increase in interest rates, nor could it accept a massive decline of the dollar. Had the Chinese chosen to implement their strategy, which she conditioned on their current conclusions being correct, in a gradual and non-aggressive nature, she argued that there would have been very little that could or should be done. After all, any country with reserve assets should be entitled to do with them exactly what it wants. Yet, because China was aggressive, some action was needed. However, the other side of the point had to be that China would be stopped but that she would indeed be stopped before they had accumulated enough CryptNotes or sold enough of its U.S. Treasury bond exposure for the financial losses to be really material.

Richard agreed and surprised the group suggesting:

"Well, if that is the case, should we not declare victory?"

Nikolai was the first to reply. He admitted that there was little or no way he could see to inflict massive financial losses on China. Yet, he believed that his initial concerns with the crypto world were only reinforced by what they were able to achieve. Waving at Hai Chock on the screen he added:

"I don't know if anyone has the skills that Hai Chock has, but there is one thing I have learned about computers over the last twenty years: everything seems to get simpler as time passes, because computers have become increasingly powerful."

Hai Chock concurred but still felt he needed to add:

"True enough, but what you're saying about computers is also true of cyber security. So, as time passes, cyber security becomes increasingly strong . . ."

Richard interrupted:

"Agreed, my friend. Yet, what you and I seem to be seeing is that crooks are just as smart as cyber security developers. So, my worry is that we should not allow systems that have no human controls to get to the point where the few that control them can in turn control the whole world."

Hai Chock joked:

"Artificial intelligence anyone?"

Richard laughed and said:

"I must admit that I am in Nikolai's camp here. I know that we cannot stop progress. It would take a lot more than what we have to do it . . ."

Nikolai interrupted:

". . . But we can ensure that whatever is developed is well-enough understood by a large enough number of people that reality rather than narratives-driven developments."

Countess Renate smiled and simply added:

"Well said. Now, where does that leave us?"

Nikolai argued that his recommendation would be to find a way to annihilate CryptNotes. He said that he had an idea of how that could be done but would need some more time to implement it. He made the simple point:

"I don't want to turn philosophical on any of you all, but we do know that people do not learn from other people's mistakes. Lessons from history last at best a single generation. It is still true that the ultimate form of insanity remains to keep doing the same thing and expect different outcomes . . ."

Hai Chock interrupted:

"But you **are** turning philosophical on us. What's the point, my friend?"

Nikolai conceded:

"Sorry—got carried away. My point is that showing to the world that something which was considered the best thing since sliced bread and the future for all is in fact exposed to complete destruction should cause a few talking heads to think again. In fact, a number of very smart people have refused to let themselves be taken by the new world. Creating a complete melt-down would likely shake enough people to ensure that cryptocurrencies, if they are the future, become the future with a hell of a lot more security and safeguards than they have now."

Hai Chock visibly applauded his friend adding:

"Couldn't have said it better."

Frank Thistle was sitting in his comfortable, double-fronted, London townhouse, in Mayfair. In fact, he was in his office, on the ground floor, just to the left of the front door as one entered the house. Opposite the office was the living room, which morphed into a family room, opening up onto a small terrace and garden as one walked toward the back of the house. The rest of ground floor was occupied by the formal dining room with the kitchen next to it. Upstairs, on the second floor, were the family bedrooms with en-suite bathrooms; there was an extra guest suite on the third floor with a gym next to it.

He had seen the substantial decline in the value of CryptNotes and was fuming. He knew darn well that his friend, Nikolai, had warned him that something was up, yet, he had only sold less than half of his holdings. While this would certainly suffice for him and his family to maintain their current lifestyle, he could not but hate the notion that his "CryptNotes cushion" was now reduced by three quarters, half through his sales and the other half by adverse price moves on what was left.

The real issue that kept going through his head was the question of what had happened. Surely, he had read everything that had been printed on the two major cryptocurrency thefts. He had somewhat mentally accepted the fact that someone could intrude into the crypto world. Yet, he was surprised that anyone could have managed to grab as much as the thieves allegedly had. More importantly, he did not understand why someone would steal money and then return it. Clearly, there was somebody somewhere who had a strong interest in killing the cryptocurrency market. He was initially tempted to blame some of it on his friend, Nikolai. After all, was he not the person who warned him? At the same time, he did not feel that Nikolai had grown to dislike their own joint creation so much that he would have wanted to kill it. Further, as he was thinking of the various ways in which the natural weaknesses of CryptNotes could be exploited, he thought that there had to be a better way.

All of a sudden, an idea crept into his consciousness:

"Wait a second, if someone could use the door I am thinking of to kill CryptNotes, there must be a way to use the same door to restore it to its prior grandeur . . ."

When the phone on Nikolai's desk rang, he was quietly thinking through his next move. In particular, he knew that there was one arrow in his quiver that had not been used yet. In fact, even Countess Renate ignored its existence. Truth be told, he was very hesitant using that last arrow for the simple reason that only two people, him being one of them, knew of the arrow and had control over it. He had thought: *"Frank will immediately know it's me if I use it."*

Nikolai's phone suddenly rang. He picked it up:

"Hi Nikolai, Frank here. It's been a while since we last talked. How are you?"

Nikolai was quite surprised. His last conversation with Frank was when he had told him that he should sell out of CryptNotes. He had told him that he had heard stories of unusual activity in the CryptNotes market, and that the activity was totally incomprehensible. He had added that he worried that this was another fraud, in one way or another, and was concerned this could depress prices a lot, perhaps permanently. Frank had replied that he had heard of some unusual activity but had actually come to the opposite conclusion. He understood that there was a major buyer who was seemingly virtually insensitive to price moves, adding:

"Best I can tell, the buyer is buying without any attention to the price he is paying."

Nikolai could obviously not tell Frank that he knew about that, though he could tell him that he had read about that as well.

Mentally, Nikolai had first gone back to their last prior conversation, when he had tried to warn Frank. He needed to remind himself of as much detail as he could to answer his friend's question.

He recalled that, then, he had said that he had heard that some hacker was trying to get into CryptNotes and do something quite destabilizing. Frank had seemed a bit shaken, but he was clearly not buying the full line. Nikolai added what he had thought would be the clincher:

"I am simply getting totally out. I don't need the headache. I have enough that I never have to worry about any money problems for Silvia and myself as well as for our kids. Why tempt the devil? You and I had a great idea. It worked, at least for a while. So, I'm out."

Frank had tried to argue, but Nikolai was determined not to engage in any further discussion. In the end, they agreed to disagree, with Nikolai saying:

"Frank, I sure hope I'm not right if you do not sell, but that is not going to change my mind."

"Well, Nikolai, thanks for the warning. I will probably sell a bit, just to be on the safe side."

Frank paused and then surprised Nikolai arguing:

"But, you know, Nikolai, there is so much more you and I can do to frustrate the efforts of whoever is trying to hurt CryptNotes . . ."

That is when Nikolai had "calmly blown up" and warned:

"Remember, Frank, that's the one tool we both agreed we would never use . . ."

■ ■ ■ ■ ■

Back to the present and the current phone call, Nikolai simply replied:

"Frank, what a surprise."

Nikolai actually meant this and was happy to hear his friend's voice. Yet, he was at a loss figuring out why his friend was calling. So, asked:

"What can I do for you?"

Frank replied first by congratulating Nikolai on his connections, saying:

"Got to give it to you. You saw it coming and I didn't."

"Hope you sold a lot."

"Well, a lot maybe, but not nearly enough."

Nikolai was briefly really concerned for his friend. He asked:

"You're safe . . . Moneywise . . . Aren't you?"

Frank immediately calmed Nikolai. He said that he had sold probably close to half of his original holdings. He had traded a little in between the massive drops and strong rebounds. So, in his words:

"I really have no reason to worry about my financial future . . ."

He let that sink in and then stunned Nikolai:

"But I am totally pissed off at whoever is doing this. CryptNotes is our baby. Somebody is trying to hurt it and I won't let this happen . . ."

Nikolai took in a deep breath. He knew exactly where he stood and therefore was fully aware that he and Frank, this time, were on exactly opposite sides. He suggested:

"Tell you what, Frank. This is not a conversation we should be having on the phone. I'm still a member at Brook's. Let's have lunch there. When would work for you?

"Is the day after tomorrow all right for you?"

"Sure. Done. I'll reserve a table."

Brook's is a gentlemen's club in St James's Street in London. It is one of the oldest and most exclusive such clubs in the world. It is proud of having the first official English ballot box on display, as well as one of Napoleon's death masks. On the latter, most people believe that the mask that is exhibited is a copy of the original Antommarchi mask, named after Napoleon's private doctor who was present on

St. Helena Island when he died. Though quite old and exclusive, Brook's allows women into the club, in marked contrast with White's, supposedly the oldest club in London, which will not, with a couple of exceptions, usually related to the Queen. Nikolai met Frank at the top of the stairs, inside the front door.

"Reminds us of old times, doesn't it, Nikolai?"

"Absolutely. Now, Frank, tell me what's really on your mind."

The two compères needed to be quite careful because most London clubs prohibit business being discussed within the premises, although the rules have frequently been stretched to allow most conversations, but not the conclusion of a deal. Yet, they knew that they had to talk of something which had an unquestionable business element.

CHAPTER.28

Solomon was happy, though a bit surprised, when he heard back from Simon. He offered to call Simon from a "safe phone" that he had kept in his locker at the gym. Simon was delighted to see that Solomon was thus following all the general safety rules which *Mossad* requires its imbedded agents to follow. He mechanically asked:

"Under the Meyers name?"

The reply came, literally in a flash:

"Absolutely."

At the appointed time, Solomon called Simon, who answered at the first ring. Simon had taken the usual precaution of recording the call, just to make sure he did not forget or misunderstand any of the instructions. He told Solomon of the recording with a totally matter-of-fact tone of voice. Solomon did not react. However, he immediately asked why the plan he had suggested in broad outline via the flashlight would not work. Simon replied that the plan was in some ways much too complicated. He offered a simple explanation:

"If you were by yourself, this might have worked, but not with your wife and the two boys."

Solomon asked what the options were. Simon replied that he could think of two. But before discussing them he asked whether Solomon could find a way to leave for a few days, without his family and without raising too many alarm bells. He said that it would be possible, since he had been on numerous such trips on his own, adding:

"As you know, whenever there is an issue involving a vessel or a harbor, I am usually the first to be asked to go check."

Simon then asked:

"Where would such a trip be most credible?"

"Anywhere there is a harbor, or Tehran."

Simon continued:

"Assume with me that you have been able to leave Bandar Abbas without attracting attention, how easy would it be for your family to get to an airport and leave officially on some holiday, preferably somewhere that is a short and direct flight from Bandar Abbas?"

Solomon was gradually figuring out in his own mind the plan Simon seemed to have concocted. Simon explained that he could arrange for him to go to one spot while his wife and family would go to an entirely different one. Solomon would be rescued around a harbor and his family picked up where they had landed. Solomon asked:

"This means that you want my family to fly to an overseas holiday location, correct?"

"Absolutely. Tell you what, Solomon. Ponder this for a day or so and let's talk again tomorrow. I don't want to stay on the line for too long for all the obvious reasons. OK?"

"Done deal."

■ ■ ■ ■ ■

Simon called David to plan for the evacuations of Solomon and his family, and to deal with the issue of the mines at both ends of

Qeshm Island. David asked him if he had discussed the reason why Solomon wanted so badly to leave Iran. Simon conceded he had not, adding:

"He was calling me; he seemed anxious. Yet, I have not forgotten that this is an important piece of information for us."

Simon summarized his conversation with Solomon for David, who looked a bit surprised. In particular, he asked whether it was normal for someone like Solomon to plan to leave with his family and quickly revert to a different plan where he and his family would be separated. Simon calmed David's anxiety arguing that it was common practice. In fact, he reminded him of a group of three Iranians who had been evacuated in three different waves from Iran in the relatively recent past. David seemed to be less uncomfortable, but added:

"They did not change plans though!"

Simon did not disagree. David was further surprised when Simon said:

"Don't get me wrong, David, I know that with people like Solomon there is always a risk that they are not playing straight. Yet, our job at this point is not to second guess him, but rather to plan the escape so that we are still OK even if he plays a dirty trick on us."

David smiled. They discussed the plan to evacuate Solomon and then turned straight to the issue of the mines. David told Simon that he had already asked Captain Decker and Captain Aaron each to take responsibility for either end of Qeshm Island. They each would have an Orca at their disposal, with the *INS Dragon* cruising as deep as she could in the shipping channel of the Persian Gulf, staying in between the two Israeli vessels. He added that Captain Decker would be sailing the *Sea Dragon*, the dark-green-hulled and Panama-registered boat, while Moshe Aaron would be on the *Sea Riches*, a red-hulled vessel also registered in Panama. They were both fully fueled. Moshe would work at the southwestern end of Qeshm, and Barack between Larak and Hormuz islands.

Simon looked totally satisfied, yet still asked:

"What are you doing with the mines when they are "freed-up" from their torpedo engines?"

David replied that, as planned, they would float about five to six feet deep on their current locations, with the hydrostatic mechanism taking care of fluctuations due to tides. He added that the system would also keep them in the same general location, though some drift, due to currents, was unavoidable. Seeing Simon frown, he added:

"Not to worry, they cannot drift as far as the central shipping channel. They would be remotely exploded, if necessary."

Simon again looked perplexed, so David explained:

"The secret communication stuff does not deal with the remote control of explosions, but to their positioning."

"I see. Thanks. How long will this operation take?"

"I assume you mean the "freeing of the mines," correct?"

Simon nodded. David continued:

"Should be completed by tomorrow morning. We are going to work at night to minimize the risk of detection. All the work can be done in the dark of the depth of the sea since we're using sonar."

■ ■ ■ ■ ■

Solomon's next call came exactly as expected. Simon judged that he seemed quite a bit calmer than the previous day. Simon started the conversation with the question he had refrained from asking earlier:

"Solomon, why are you so anxious to leave Iran? What happened?"

Solomon seemed surprised by the question, if only because he did not, as he customarily did, reply virtually instantly. He eventually explained that he was getting concerned by what he was seeing. Simon asked how different that was from what he had been seeing for so many years. He talked vaguely of the harshness with which commanding officers were communicating their messages. He recalled the initial briefing he had had when Admiral Pashtani effectively seemed to threaten everyone in the case a leak would develop. Simon was still not totally satisfied: he obviously could not react to the issue of the tone of the Admiral's words, as he was not there to hear them, but he thought it would have been normal practice for such a threat to be made.

Simon kept probing until Solomon admitted that he was very worried for his family. He recounted instances where spies had been caught and their families captured, tortured, and eventually executed. He thought that it was only a matter of time before that risk turned on him, and he preferred, he said, to leave early before the proverbial shit hit the fan. Simon who was himself a very dedicated family man understood the concern, but added:

"What if we simply stop using you except in extra special circumstances?"

"How would that help?"

Simon explained that Solomon could hide all his spy paraphernalia including his communication equipment somewhere and make contact once a month, directly or through his friend, Farzad Ghasemi, in Tehran. Simon could thus find a way to reach him if something vital happened, but the rest of the time Solomon could stay completely away from any connection to Israel. Solomon asked:

"Is this not the way we are currently operating, except that I don't talk to Farzad any longer."

He paused and then blurted out:

"And what if they discover my paraphernalia as you call it?"

"Why would they? Isn't there a place where you would be totally safe. I don't know, a locker at the airport or the train station?"

"Couldn't they find the key and be suspicious?"

Simon had to concede that there remained a risk but that it would be quite remote. Solomon explained that he did not want to take that risk and preferred to go back to his Jewish roots. Simon asked:

"Want to resettle in Israel?"

"That would be my preferred location."

"Does your family speak any Hebrew?"

"No, but they can learn."

"How would you convince them to leave?"

Solomon explained that he had thought about it the previous night, adding:

"Virtually didn't sleep a wink."

He said that he would not tell the family anything but offer them a one-week trip to Dubai as a holiday, adding that he would meet them there once he had completed his mission. Simon could not resist:

"Don't you have stuff, memorabilia, which you would not want to leave behind?"

"We do, but there's not much of it. And, after all, once we start a new life, it will not be hard to forget the past. Remember, I've had to go through that."

"I know, but the fact is that it was your choice, not someone else's."

"True. But we are a very close family and I'm sure it will be OK."

Simon had to agree and asked Solomon to call him the next day so that they could discuss the plan he, Solomon, would have formed by then. Simon's only instructions were that he would not consider any evacuation which required any Israeli vessel to enter Iranian territorial waters.

■ ■ ■ ■ ■

The mine removal effort went like clockwork. Each time the tether from two mines to the torpedo engine was severed, the operator could see the mines rising toward the surface, while the engine dropped to the bottom. After the first couple of instances where the remote Orca operators used the underwater camera to see that everything was functioning as expected, they were able to accelerate the process, simply giving the "break-up" signal every mile or so and assuming that mines and torpedo engines would end up where they were supposed to. Additionally, not using the cameras also made the use of the underwater light unnecessary, which removed a however remote risk of being discovered. Keeping the Orcas as close as possible to the bottom of the water prevented any form of detection, although Moshe did see a couple of speedboats approach the area where he was working but then returning to anchorage. *"Standard patrol activity"* he thought.

■ ■ ■ ■ ■

On this, the anticipated last call with Solomon, Simon listened to the plan which he had prepared. Solomon originally stuck to the plan he had rehearsed, except that, this time, it would only involve him, by himself, and not the whole family. He said to Simon that we would indeed drive from Bandar Abbas to Qeshm, using the ferry to cross the Clarence Strait. Once on the other side, he would stick to the main highway driving first to Bandar e Laft, then to Tonban, using the only road that bisected the peninsula that protrudes from Qeshm toward the mainland. Once in Tonban, he would go in the direction of the International Airport, and upon reaching it, veer back almost due south to reach the coast and drive to Shib Deraz.

Shib Deraz was a small, picturesque village with a well-protected harbor. Its long beach was known for the fact that hawksbill and green turtles lay their eggs between April and July, an event which attracts a lot of tourists, although villagers work in shift to protect the eggs from predators, which, in their minds, include tourists. The village also served as a base for those who wished to visit nearby Hengam Island, which could be reached by small passenger boats. These passenger boats crowded a harbor which was also full of small excursion boats taking tourists who wanted to go on dolphin-watching tours. One could also see a few speedboats, undoubtedly belonging to the Islamic Revolutionary Guard.

Solomon then simply said that he would rent one of the smaller crafts. Though there would be a captain along with him, he assured Simon that he would carry a gun to keep him quiet as they approached any vessel which Simon would send nearby. Simon granted that the plan was generally workable, though he still had two major qualms. The first related to the presence of a captain on the boat which Solomon would rent. He added:

"The last thing I want is for some eyewitness to be left behind, and I will not order someone killed just because it's convenient. Do you have a boating license?"

Solomon looked surprised by Simon's question. He replied that he certainly did, adding:

"I need one in my line of work . . ."

"Then why don't you rent a boat without a captain? If it's a question of cost, don't worry. Pay what you have to pay, and we'll take care of it later."

Solomon reluctantly agreed and asked what the other concern was. Simon replied that he wondered whether a less populated place might not be preferable. Solomon replied that the coastline from the Shib Deraz cape had three feasible harbors. He explained that he had chosen Shib Deraz because it was the one that was furthest away from Suza, the provincial capital, adding:

"That's where you have the highest concentration of Revolutionary Guard speedboats. Messen is a possibility, but it is still close to Suza. The only other option is a small village that is in between Messen and Shib Deraz. I'm not sure, but I believe it might also be another garrison: there is a harbor going deep inland and a runway stuck in the middle of nowhere . . ."

Simon made a mental note that Solomon's story seemed totally credible, at least to the extent that it fit with his own observations. He replied:

"Enough said. Shib Deraz it is. In the meantime, Solomon, do some more homework on that last village you mentioned. I wouldn't want it to be another place from which a flotilla of speed boats could attack a lone fishing boat, which is most likely what we would send to get you."

"A fishing boat?"

Simon smiled, although Solomon could not see it on the phone. He simply added:

"They're innocuous. They're all over the place in that area. Can you think of anything more common?"

CHAPTER.29

SINGAPORE, DUBLIN, IRELAND, LONDON, ENGLAND, AND SOMEWHERE IN THE AUSTRIAN ALPS

"Frank, you simply can't do that . . ."

Frank had explained to Nikolai why he was so upset at the virtual disintegration of the cryptocurrency markets. He had made it clear that he understood that markets will fluctuate, at times violently. Yet, he was sure that there was something more than normal fluctuations at work there. Nikolai interrupted:

"Frank, we know that. We know that there has been a very large buyer of CryptNotes. I certainly don't know who he or she is, but there's no question he's there. I've heard speculations that the Chinese might be behind it, but I haven't seen anything that proves it. We also know that there have been at least two intrusions which led to significant amounts of at least three cryptocurrencies being stolen. But, inexplicably to me at least, the money was returned."

Frank countered that he knew all that and that none of it made any sense to him either. He pointed to the big buyer first, saying that no intelligent buyer would broadcast their size, adding:

"Why pay more than you have to?"

Nikolai replied that there was one hypothesis under which the move might make sense. Frank looked surprised:

"Which one?"

"Well, what if their purpose was not to accumulate as much CryptNotes as they could, but to depress the value of the U.S. Dollar against the price of CryptNotes?"

Frank pondered the reply for a few seconds. He blurted out:

"Still makes no sense. You said earlier that there are rumors it might be the Chinese . . . They have to have many more U.S. dollar reserves than what they've sold so far. So why would they not wait until they had sold much more of their U.S. dollars?"

Nikolai granted to him that this was a weakness of the scenario. Yet, he said that one could speculate that their goal was not to replace all their U.S. dollar reserves, but just to send a signal to the U.S. that they had the power to do things which would cost the U.S. dearly. Frank countered:

"Doing that would force them to come clean officially and that could start a real economic war . . . Don't you see that?"

"Agreed up to a point. What if they simply said that the recent experience proved that it could be done, without ever admitting they were behind it?"

Frank could see that there was very little progress that could be made on that front. It was obvious to him that Nikolai had constructed a scenario in his head which, though he himself did not buy it, was sufficiently sensible that he would not be able to change his mind. He went to the other developments, the two intrusions. He asked:

"What do you make of them? Why would you expose yourself to the risk of being discovered and not keep the money you've stolen?"

Nikolai replied that he could not make a lot of sense of that unless he assumed that the developments were linked to the large purchases. Frank frowned and could not help asking:

"How and why?"

Nikolai replied that a scenario he had built in his own head involved a conspiracy and a response to that conspiracy. He could see that Frank was initially not following. He explained, starting with the idea that his scenario on China, or whoever the big buyer was, wanting to send a signal to the U.S. was the reason behind the big, clumsy purchases. Frank wanted to interrupt, but Nikolai did not let him, motioning that he should let him finish. Frank acquiesced. Nikolai then simply asked:

"What if the two thefts were a means to counter the Chinese or, as I just said, whoever is behind the big purchase? You know you could also assume that Saudi Arabia, Iran, Russia, and a few other countries would want to reduce their dependency on the U.S. Dollar . . ."

He paused and noted that Frank's facial expression had become quizzical. He continued:

"Now, put yourself in the position of the U.S. Do you reply visibly? You can't, right? Unless you know exactly who is selling. You couldn't take the risk of blaming someone when in fact that someone is totally innocent. So, a direct, visible response is impossible. However, what if you were to engineer something which doesn't point to you and yet shows to the big buyer that there are two ways you can affect prices: massive activity in markets or anything that shakes confidence?"

Frank was now clearly somewhat shaken. He was still not convinced, but he could see that his friend had at least one scenario where the whole thing could begin to make sense. He exclaimed:

"But damn it, these guys, whoever they are, are playing havoc with our baby. I don't mind losing a game fair and square, but I can't accept losing it to trickeries . . ."

Nikolai was now on the defensive. He knew he could not go any further in his story telling. He already had disclosed, albeit as a hypothesis, as much as he could without giving the whole thing away. He tried another tack. He reminded Frank of the conversation they had had when they decided to leave CryptNotes, and each go their own way. He pointed to the fact that they had worried that some of the activity taking place in the cryptocurrency marketplace was increasingly questionable; he also noted that so much speculative fever had developed that what they had hoped would be a stabilizing factor in the global economy could just as easily become a factor of instability. Frank nodded but was still unconvinced, saying:

"I agree, and I'm a bit like you. I'm not happy with the developments. But we still have people screwing around with our baby, and I can't accept that. I don't want history to recall that CryptNotes was a total failure."

Sarcastically, Nikolai could not refrain from adding:

"And you don't want to lose so much money . . ."

"True, but unfair comment my friend, wouldn't you say?"

Frank paused and then added:

"Anyway, I'm thinking that this warrants us using what we used to call the nuclear option . . ."

■ ■ ■ ■ ■

CryptNotes mining involved a sort of a game, based on luck. As we know, the miner must generate a number such that the block content and that number are numerically inferior to the network "difficulty target." That "difficulty target" is adjusted after a set number of blocks are created based on the time it took to find them. Thus, if the prior set number of blocks seems to have taken "too long" the difficulty is reduced, and vice versa. Conceptually, this is simple, though it might seem hard to understand. Given the large number of possible permutations using some or all of the twenty characters in the vigesimal base and comprising sixty-four digits, one can always find some number such that half of all numbers will be below, and the other half will be above. In that case, one could say that the difficulty target using that number is 50%. Adjusting that difficulty simply involves varying the number of combinations of digits that are below a set level versus the total number of possible combinations. From this it follows, for instance, that the maximum difficulty would be a sequence of sixty-four consecutive zeros: there is no sequence that could be inferior to that. Conversely, a sequence of sixty-four digits represented by the largest of the twenty characters would offer the lowest possible difficulty: all sequences would be inferior to that target.

The nuclear option to which Frank was referring and which he and Nikolai had agreed they would never use involved using their network key to affect the setting of the difficulty target. It would involve two steps. The first would be to set the difficulty target at some arbitrary level. A sufficiently high difficulty would increase the time needed to create blocks and thus increase the rarity of CryptNotes; this should serve to raise its value, as it would at the margin become scarcer. The second move would involve increasing the number of blocks that must be created before the difficulty target is changed. This would work in the same direction, effectively reducing the odds of the system quickly finding its equilibrium anew after the externally induced period of turmoil.

I I ■ I I

Nikolai simply replied:

"Frank, we cannot do that."

Frank looked at his friend across the lunch table and was quite surprised. Nikolai's face, which had up until then projected kindness, friendliness and even humor, became seemingly cold as ice. If pushed, Nikolai would have conceded that he had at one point considered that very nuclear option to put the final nail in the CryptNotes coffin. He had thought of setting the difficulty at such a low level and of making it so much harder to adjust upward the difficulty level that CryptNotes generation would have become so much easier. That would have flooded the market. That would have been by far the easiest way for him to help Countess Renate and her team to achieve the goals for which Shadow Experts had been hired. Yet, he had decided against it for two reasons. He liked to believe that the first reason was ethical; he had given his word to Frank and that was it. The second was practical; he knew that only two people could do it, as only two people had the network key which allowed them unlimited access into the algorithm; if it was not Frank, Frank would know it had to have been him. He feared being exposed.

This time, however, the tables were turned. Nikolai had made what he believed in his mind was the right decision, but he worried that Frank could make the wrong one and in fact looked like he was about to. He added:

"Frank, we have an agreement. We said we would hand over our cryptographic keys when we left. Yet, you and I then agreed that we would not hand the keys fully over; we would retain a narrow version of the keys, as we wanted to preserve an opportunity to intervene if things got crazy. We also agreed that neither of us would ever use his key without the full concurrence of the other. So, I must tell you that if you violate our agreement by using your network cryptographic key, you are releasing me from my commitment not to use mine, just as independently."

Frank looked stunned. He had by then clearly appreciated that he and Nikolai were not on the same page in the current situation. Yet, he still viewed Nikolai as a friend and read his latest comment as a plain threat. He asked:

"Nikolai, what are you saying?"

"Quite simply that I am prepared to play the same game as you, but in the opposite direction. I am stunned that you are considering the move. It would be against our agreement. You would not be doing it with my concurrence. Does that mean we're no longer friends?"

Frank did not know what to answer. One way of wiggling out, he knew, would be to argue that he would not do it if Nikolai objected.

Yet, deep down, he knew that is exactly what he wanted to do. So, he kept quiet and did not reply. Nikolai continued:

"I will not breach our promise not to disclose each other's names; so, I will not point to you openly for as long as you do not point to me. But I can manage the difficulty target and its resetting algorithm just as easily as you can. You know that we agreed that neither of us could invalidate the other's key and ensured that this is hardcoded into the program. So, there is nothing you can do to prevent me from getting into the system as soon as I find out you have and take the opposite action: you try to create scarcity and I flood the system . . ."

He paused for a second, took a sip of his ten-year-old Corton Charlemagne and added:

"Also, remember, flooding the market is a lot easier than creating scarcity. That was why we designed it that way. You have no way of affecting the body of outstanding CryptNotes; you can only slow the increase in that body. By flooding the market with new CryptNotes, I can bring the value of the outstanding notes down to near zero . . . And there is no way back from there."

Frank was totally aghast. First, he had been totally mistaken in terms of how his friend would react. He had never seen him as serious and determined. Second, he realized that he was near powerless. The asymmetry of the power inherent in varying new note creation rates was absolutely obvious, though he had simply never thought of it. Though the meal was not finished, he got up from the table, calmly bid goodbye to his friend and simply said:

"Today, I just lost a friend."

"So have I, Frank. My door remains open if you are prepared to respect our agreement."

Nikolai calmly finished his meal and returned home from where he immediately called Countess Renate. He took her through his disappointing misadventure. She asked:

"Is there anything Frank can do to hurt you?"

"If by this you mean relative to CryptNotes, frankly I don't think so. However, he has a number of potential weapons, the sneakiest of which has to do with my reputation . . ."

He went on to explain that he was really disappointed that his friend and compère had been ready to suggest something which they both had agreed was unacceptable. Having noted that he had given him advance warning, he felt that his friend was ostensibly putting money and wealth above friendship. More to the point, he added:

"He feels so paternalistic with respect to CryptNotes that I am no longer sure that he would be prepared to keep both his and my name secret."

"Do you fear for your safety or even your life?"

"Countess, I certainly have not thought this through that far. But, as scary as it might seem, you make me realize that everything is possible. Anyway, why are you asking?"

Countess Renate explained that she knew very well that Nikolai had built a fine life for himself in London, where he had friends, and where his small family was very happy, not to mention quite comfortable. Yet, she also explained that she knew that Simon and *Mossad* had ways to help relocate people giving them a new identity such that they could easily escape any possible threat in the future. She asked:

"Any family other than your wife and two children?"

"Unfortunately, not. They were all lost in the holocaust or to normal end of life circumstances."

"Well, my friend, the option is open. And I am sure it does not have to mean Israel . . . Let me know if you ever want to take this further."

She paused and added:

"I am not sure that there is any need to share this with either Richard or Hai Chock. At this point, it seems to me that we've agreed that we will wait for further market developments and see. The two intrusions into client accounts plus the removal of cryptocurrencies from the brokerage account should be enough to shake people's confidence."

"Unless Frank does something . . ."

"Unless he does indeed. Yet, at that point, my preference would be for you to act alone so that you and I are the only ones that know of that option. By the way, before doing that, I would strongly suggest you consider my offer to invite Simon into the loop . . ."

CHAPTER.30

Simon and Solomon had agreed on all details. It had been agreed that the boat which Solomon would rent would be a small cabin cruiser as Simon had insisted that the evacuation would have to take place by night. Simon had also arranged for an Eitan drone to take on a holding pattern centered on the position which Moshe Aaron's boat would hold in the Persian Gulf, outside of Iran territorial waters. Solomon would have to concoct a story to the effect that he was going to sail first to Hengam Island and spend the night at anchor somewhere around there to see the bottlenose dolphins which normally congregate there and can be seen frolicking around boats. Then he would say that he was going to sail quietly back to Shib Deraz to see a few of the cliffs which are found around beaches along the coast of Qeshm.

■ ■ ■ ■ ■

David barged into Simon's office:
"Simon?"
"What?"

"Did you see the news?"

"Which news?"

David immediately brought Simon up to date. The prior evening, a Chinese cargo ship had suffered major damage as it went through the channel between Larak and Hormuz Island. Its destination was the port of Bandar Abbas. David then could not resist a smile:

"You wouldn't believe the coincidence . . . It's the same ship that we know had unloaded the underwater launchers and the communication systems which Hezbollah was using against us."

"Yahweh works in mysterious ways . . ."

■ ■ ■ ■ ■

If there was one phone call which Simon was not expecting, it had to be the one from Farzad Ghasemi, the *Mossad* agent in Tehran who had recruited Solomon and had at least initially served as his controller.

"Farzad, what a surprise, what can I do for you?"

"A lot or maybe nothing, Simon."

Simon was surprised by the tone of Farzad's voice. He was used to an optimistic tone which nothing ever seemed to change. Now he was talking to someone who seemed dead tired and to a certain extent emotionally exhausted:

"Is everything all right?"

Farzad's first reply was nothing was all right. Then, prompted by Simon, he explained that he was at home working when he saw some unusual activity outside his windows. A few cars had closed in on the front door of the building of his apartment. He chose to be safe rather than sorry and immediately went to his hiding place. He had discreetly built a closet that was not visible from the outside. A real closet in his bedroom had a false back partition. That allowed Farzad both to hide himself and anything that could be seen as spy paraphernalia, if needed as was the case then. The back of the closet opened into a small room which he had "carved out" of the next-door bedroom. That room was properly ventilated, and even had a light. However, Farzad knew better; the light remained off.

His fears were well-warranted, as minutes after he had slipped into the closet he heard a loud knock on the front door of the apartment. Seconds later, he could hear the door being banged open and then the voices of what he was convinced were Iranian internal security agents. He could follow what they were saying but kept hoping against hope that they would not find him. They slid open the door to the closet, looked behind the hanging clothes and then moved on to the next room. Farzad breathed a first sigh of relief. He could not see, but he surely heard the agents pulling all drawers out and emptying everything on the floor. Eventually, all noise stopped. He assumed that they had left.

Farzad knew better than to come out of hiding right away. His experience of the internal security services taught him that one of the most elementary tricks in the book involves making a lot of noise while searching and exiting, only to leave one or two agents quietly hidden in the apartment. While he was in hiding, he kept rehearsing every step he had taken in the recent past and could not figure out where he had made a misstep. He thought: *"how could they know about my other activities?"*

He chose to spend the full night in the room taking from the provisions he had stored there: some tepid water to stay hydrated and a few munchies to quiet his stomach. He also had a small quantity of adult diapers which he chose to wear, as he knew he would not be able to keep from going to the toilet for the whole night. He kept listening as carefully as he could and did not hear anyone murmuring anything. More importantly, the motion detectors which he had in each of the three rooms of the apartment had remained totally quiet during the night; he had organized for them to switch on small red lights in the closet if they were triggered, even if the alarm system was not on. That had to mean that there was nobody in the apartment or that they knew how to remain perfectly motionless. After all, his enemies were subjected to the same laws of nature as he. They could not have avoided going to the bathroom for the fifteen hours he chose to spend hidden.

He carefully emerged from his secret lair, and with his handgun at the ready, swept the apartment to confirm his original conclusion. Clearly, he was correct and there was not a soul there. He did not believe himself totally out of the woods yet. It was always possible that some trap had been set somewhere in the building; there were plenty of possibilities: within the flat, say with a piece of thread across a hallway or between two pieces of furniture; once tripped, it would create noise which would attract security back in. It might even not create any noise within the flat but flash a signal outside telling the security forces to come back in. And such a trap could be located in the hallway in front of his door; in the hall of the building on the ground floor; or in the basement where there was a parking spot for each apartment. First, within the apartment, he moved as carefully as he could, avoiding the eyelet that allowed him to see in the outside hallway, but also allowing somebody outside to see, though much less clearly, in the flat—though the door was no longer totally closed shut, but rather partially ajar, the lock having been broken when the agents barged in.

Having confirmed that there did not seem to be anyone in front of his door, he decided that there was no real point looking in the other places in the building other than the stoop just beyond the front door to the building. He used a simple contraption to check the area just outside the main door to his building, a sort of a periscope which would allow him to see the outside of the building without having to show himself leaning out of a window. He was very cautious making sure that he avoided all windows, as there was always a risk that someone might be hiding in another building across the street. He kept crawling through the apartment to avoid that risk.

In the end, he went to the bathroom and used a couple of tools which most *Mossad* agents have. The first was a substance like Botox mixed with fat which allowed him to alter the shape of certain parts of his face, particularly cheekbones, lips or even jaws. The effect of the drug was intended gradually to fade, the speed of the fading depending upon how fast the body absorbed the fat. *Mossad* had packaged the drug in pre-filled syringes. He used two twenty-five milliliters subcutaneous injections, one each right on each cheekbone. Two smaller injections on either side of his mouth gave him fuller lips. He then replaced the syringe in his toiletry kit, packaged as it was to look like an insulin injector. Next, he turned to the shampoo which was also part of his special kit: it mixed bleach and coloring agents,. He used it on his hair and his beard and made it look quite a bit greyer than its normal dark brown color shade. He did not forget to apply some of that same shampoo to his eyebrows. To complete his transformation, he wore black framed rectangular glasses.

He walked straight out of the building and noticed one person he did not know on the side of the door and another one ostensibly waiting in a car. He had used clothing which was also hidden in his lair to make sure that no one could possibly have seen the suit before. He politely saluted the man to the right of the door and started walking, with his attaché-case in his left hand. The right hand was hidden in his pants pocket and was holding onto the handgun he would not hesitate to use if needed. He was delighted both to note that he was not being followed and that he had not needed the gun. A half a mile away from his building, he walked into a public garage. There he walked to a car, opened its door and drove away. For Simon's benefit, he added:

"The car that I have driven for the last twelve hours is not the car I normally drive. It is a second car I have maintained, precisely to deal with situations such as these."

"Where are you now?"

"I've been driving northeast from Tehran; it's a main road, but again, nobody knows my face or my car. Before I got to Tabriz, I veered right toward Ardebil, about fifty miles from Astara, in Azerbaijan. From there, I can stay on the coast road along the Caspian Sea until I reach Baku."

"That's quite a ways . . ."

"Yes, I know."

Farzad went on to explain that his sole goal was to drive as far and as fast as he could without being caught. He noted that he was really quite lucky: he was still a bachelor with no one to worry about. He laughed as he said:

"My last girlfriend left me two weeks ago. So, I don't even have to worry about somebody looking for me . . . Or for her."

Going back to the current trip, he noted that the risks were relatively minimal that he would be arrested. Everything about him and the car were perfectly in order. He had false papers made out to a different name and the face he just recreated. The car was registered to that person, as was the insurance. He confessed that he even had a bank account in that name, and the parking, insurance and registration fees were all paid from that account, adding:

"By the way, that's why I ask you for some cash a couple times a year. It goes straight into that account . . ."

Simon admiratively replied:

"I see. Come to think of it, I seem to recall your mentioning it at some point."

He added that he had driven initially to the main train station, where he retrieved a suitcase that he had placed in a locker there. It contained some more clothes, as well as a number of other things he could not keep at home. That is where he had some extra ammunition for the handgun. He would still need to stop here or there both to fuel up the car and to buy some food. Simon changed the topic completely after having wished Farzad good luck and told him to call from Baku as soon as he arrived, adding:

"We have ways to get you out and back from there."

"I thought our relations with Azerbaijan were not that good."

"Well, there's the official stuff and then there's the less official stuff. Trust me. I'll give you a name there then, but don't want to do it now. You understand."

"I'm afraid I do. You don't want me to risk disclosing if I was captured and drugged . . ."

Simon smiled, although Farzad could not see his face on the phone and said:

"Absolutely."

Simon then turned to the most important issue. He asked point blank whether Farzad had figured out who or what could have pointed to him. Farzad replied that he had absolutely no idea. He rattled off the names of all the people that could have known of him and could not find anyone that was in any way suspicious. Simon asked him how far back he had gone in that exercise. He replied that he had not thought about going beyond the recent past, rhetorically asking:

"Why go back too far? If they had known about me for a while, why wouldn't they have arrested me sooner."

Simon replied that he could think of at least one reason why things might have worked out that way. Cautioning Farzad that this was clearly only a hypothesis, he imagined a scenario where another *Mossad* agent is caught. For whatever reasons, that agent agrees to switch sides in exchange for his life. Simon added:

"Not a situation I would relish to find myself into by the way."

He could hear a short somewhat nervous laugh at Farzad's end of the line. Simon continued with the scenario arguing that the other agent agrees to become, in effect, a double agent. Taking his scenario further, Simon said that for things to work in the current case, you have to assume that the double agent would be asked about people he could denounce. So far, Farzad was following, but did not appear convinced. Then Simon mentioned something that immediately rang a bell in Farzad's head:

"From that list, the Iranians could choose either to arrest and eliminate the agent, or to allow them to continue operating but under surveillance. Am I making any sense?"

"Not only you are, but you might be a lot closer to the truth than you might have believed."

Farzad let go of a heavy sigh and went on to relate a situation which had taken place at least a couple of years earlier. He explained that he was surprised one evening to receive an unexpected visit from people who introduced themselves as agents of Internal Security. He noted that, in contrast with the most recent rash intrusion into his apartment, they had politely knocked on the door, asked for permission to enter and were in general quite cordial. They made the point that some unusual activity had been reported from within this or another building in the area and they wanted to do a quick sweep just to be on the safe side. Again, he said they had asked permission, which he felt he could not refuse. They seemed to conduct a careful survey of the apartment, though they did not go deep into closets, chests of drawers or other piece of furniture. They left with what looked like sincere thanks for him, only asking him to contact them if he ever saw anything unusual. Simon asked:

"Interesting. Did you check the apartment afterwards?'

"Sure did. Did not find anything obvious, you know, no bug in particular. However, a few weeks later, I noticed that my neighbor's apartment was occupied by someone else . . . Met him in the hallway and he greeted me saying he'd just bought it."

He paused and then:

"Oh, my God. Now I get it. That's why my old neighbor never said goodbye. I have been under surveillance all along. It still does not tell me why they didn't arrest me or question me more."

"Well, It's a good thing that you haven't had much of a reason to talk to us. They could have arrested you then. Anyway, safe drive and see you hopefully soon in Tel Aviv . . . In the meantime, think who could have outed you. It sure seems to me that someone did."

CHAPTER.31

Countess Renate called her team together to report on the current status of their operation. She had spoken at length with Jack Turnbull who was quite satisfied with the results so far. She reported that his main concern was that, at this point at least, the Chinese ostensibly had lost some money, but nothing that would make them change their behavior. She noted that the world of cryptocurrencies had suffered a serious blow but had to concede that the size of the market was still material, and that there was no way of knowing whether the loss of confidence would be a lasting impact, or something more transitory. Similarly, the U.S. Treasury bond market had stabilized, though the average level of interest rates had climbed by about 0.25% across all maturities. A final piece of information that she wanted to impart onto the group was that the Fed seemed to have managed to agree with a few additional countries that they should help with the management of a transition from the current excessively easy monetary environment to one that was somewhat tighter. She added:

"Despite all of this, gentlemen, the proof will be in the pudding. We still have the need for the U.S. and for that matter most of the developed world to transition from the misguided policies of the last ten years, and I for one do not see how it can be done without some pain here and there."

Richard was the first to talk, as the individual most in tune with financial markets. He totally agreed with Countess Renate's assessment, but in fact took it one step further:

"I cannot believe that the world can get out of this without some serious pain. And I do not believe that the pain that is necessary is acceptable to most politicians."

Nikolai asked:

"Richard, what do you see coming then?"

"Well, I would expect some material inflation lasting for a significant period. After all, the main issue is excess debt outstanding. Inflation eats away at that debt, as debt needs to be repaid in current dollars, which will have their real value partially eroded by inflation."

Nikolai was not through:

"Doesn't that mean that pensioners, retirees and people who have been careful managing their debt loads will be hurt?"

"Absolutely! Anybody who lives off fixed income will lose, while those who earn real dollars and have some sort of debt will do well. By the way, that's why economics textbooks tell us that inflation is bad. But, for politicians, this has got to be better than a recession, no, a depression which would cause massive unemployment. The press would report on unemployment because there are always victims to interview. The people who will be losing in my alternative scenario of higher inflation longer, will be losing gradually. That doesn't make for a good story, unless the losses have become unbearable."

Countess Renate was about to close the debate when Hai Chock interrupted:

"Just got a call from a friend of mine here in Singapore. Does anybody know why the price of CryptNotes is suddenly rising?"

Nikolai grabbed his head simply saying:

"Oh. No. Tell me he didn't do it."

"Richard had to ask:

"Who didn't do what?"

Nikolai hedged his reply, as he had no way at that time to be sure. He wanted first to find out what the market was saying to explain the price increases. He asked his compères:

"Anybody seen any news on CryptNotes ?"

Richard was looking at his iPhone; he was the first to respond:

"I see a news item here. It says that the difficulty level in CryptNotes had been changed. It says that nobody knows how, why and by whom, but it has been changed, in fact it has been substantially raised. What does that mean, Nikolai?"

"Simply that someone is trying to make the market believe that there will be scarcity in CryptNotes. Bulls are buying."

Richard asked whether it made any sense. Sadly, Nikolai replied that it did not because it brought out into the open a secret that nobody knew:

"There is a way to interfere with the CryptNotes algorithm from the outside."

He continued:

"To my knowledge there are only two people who can do this without hacking into the system."

He paused and added, even more sadly:

"Hai Chock has proven to me that there are very few things that cannot be hacked into. So, I'm now ready to believe that other people will find ways to hack and fiddle with the difficulty level."

"Which means?"

"Well, Countess, what it means is that CryptNotes is dead. Maybe not dead right now, but it is already well on its way to the ICU unit. It won't come out alive."

"Why would that be?"

"Simple. Why would you trust something as a store of value if you cannot tell how scarce or prevalent it really is? Now, with people eventually feeling that anybody with cyber skills and a powerful enough computer can tinker with it, why would they own it?"

The Zoom setup allowed the whole group to see Nikolai almost lose his countenance. He had just found out that his baby was dead. In a funny quip he added:

"No need to worry about anyone using CryptNotes to replace the U.S. Dollar as the world's reserve currency. Jack Turnbull owes you a lot, Countess."

■ ■ ■ ■ ■

Interestingly, the almost total demise of the original world of cryptocurrencies was only a phase in a longer-term movement which saw some new forms of cryptocurrencies emerge, though in a considerably more regulated manner. This did not allow for the dream formed by Nikolai and Frank to be realized: a totally independent currency system with no one in control. Their thought had one inescapable flaw; a lack of control is an invitation for criminals to come in and take advantage of the resulting anonymity. Paradoxically, the global banking system did not really suffer from the consequences of the "trap" as most of the major banks were more on the side of resisting to cryptocurrencies than in favor of adopting them. Specifically, most of the largest holders of cryptocurrencies were capitalists who were either mining the various currencies or convinced by the appeal of their key design features. Thus, cautiously warned by the Monetary Authority of Singapore as they were as soon as the decision was made to set up the trap, Roy Pierce and his colleagues did not suffer any pain. They simply allowed themselves to move to the sidelines, though it might be fair to say that Roy immediately guessed that any such action would likely boost the U.S. Dollar and put a cap on U.S. long-term interest rates, a couple of excellent trades.

CHAPTER.32

Simon was definitively shaken by the news from Farzad. However, David's reaction was even more dramatic: he was totally flabbergasted. He drew up a list of the *Mossad* people in the field who had a connection with or knew of Farzad. He focused initially on people who were now or had been in Iran for the prior two or three years. His primary concern was to make sure that the double agent, if there was indeed one, could rapidly be identified and neutralized. As usual in these cases, the list was not huge, but still contained quite a few names. David casually added:

"Note that Farzad had done a great job in Iran. There are at least five agents who are still active and whom he effectively recruited, though none in the last two years or so."

He paused a second and asked a question that initially looked crazy:

"What if Farzad was the double agent? Creating suspicion on any one he recruited in the last many years."

"David, you have a really crazy mind. But could it be that you are our next "Steel Trap?"

David laughed out loud, but only replied with a wide smile:

"There's a world of difference between Ariel and me. Any resemblance with anyone living or dead would be sheer coincidence . . ."

He then added:

"No possible confusion . . ."

Simon laughed as well, but regaining his seriousness he argued that there was only one way to see whether Farzad was genuine or not:

"If he is not genuine, he will disappear from the surface of the earth. By contrast, if he does contact me from Baku, there's got to be a good chance he isn't a double agent."

He paused and added:

"The ultimate cynic would correctly argue that my logic isn't foolproof, but it surely leans in the right direction."

David agreed though he did note that plots concocted by spies and double agents are rarely simple, concluding:

"I'd still keep an open mind."

Yet he immediately shifted to the next obvious point. He noted that one of the names on the list he had drawn up of agents who knew Farzad was Solomon Bandari. So, he asked Simon:

"If it's Solomon, what do we do?"

Simon conceded that this was exactly what he was currently concerned with:

"I'd even go a bit further. I've got to guess that the double agent is either Solomon or Farzad. The timing is just too coincidental."

He continued and argued that the so-called evacuation of Solomon might be a way to attract Israeli vessels into a trap. They could be attacked at any moment by forces that might have been set up just there, awaiting their arrivals. Simon added:

"I don't want to crucify Solomon quite yet, but we have to plan the evacuation as if it was a trap. And, by the way, it will be a trap, except it will be a trap that we set up for the Iranians, not one they set up for us."

Countess Renate called Abdul to report on the activity so far and seek his reaction to the campaign. Abdul told her that the Crown Prince was very grateful and would like to find a way to thank Simon or the Israeli Government directly, though at this point this was a bit difficult. Countess Renate suggested that Abdul should call Simon and see what could be done. Abdul then brought her up to date on the actions which the Kingdom expected to take. He did not go into an immense amount of detail, rather staying quite generic. Countess said she understood the need for discretion and did not ask additional questions. She added:

"At this point, Abdul, is it fair to say that we should wind up the activities?"

"Absolutely Countess. I will arrange for your compensation. I will also call David Heller or Simon Rabinowitz directly to find out our monetary liability and to organize any of the moves which will have to take place out of Khafji. You must remember that there are overflight issues which I will need to clear up ahead of time. There should be absolutely no problem, trust me."

He paused and almost out of the blue asked:

"And what about any vessel currently in the Persian Gulf?"

Countess Renate replied that she was not aware of the Israeli plans and that would also be something that Abdul should discuss directly with David or Simon.

Simon had asked Captain Decker and Captain Aaron both to use a radio frequency on which he could also listen to the action. David Heller was in Simon's office as well. The operation started precisely at midnight, as had been organized.

The plan was that Solomon would approach Moshe's ship, the red-hulled *Sea Riches*, and would only approach from due north, which was the obvious vector since he would be leaving from the vicinity of Hengam Island. Moshe had brought along one extra sailor whose sole duty would be to use a 40x60 infrared outdoor monocular, which could "see" as far as six miles. Even at full speed, it would take Solomon about 10 minutes to cover the six miles separating it from the *Sea Riches* once the cabin cruiser had been detected. Moshe was relying on his infrared binoculars, which could not see quite as far but were reputed to have such high resolution that he could see a golf ball a mile away. David had asked Captain Decker to position his vessel, the *Sea Dragon*, right behind Moshe's boat, but he was to keep all navigations and anchor lights off. While everyone recognized that this was somewhat dangerous as the boat would be without lights, the consensus was that the risk could be managed as both ships were sufficiently far away from the center of the shipping channel. Additionally, with the *Sea Riches* having her navigation lights on, one would have to assume that any vessel sailing in the vicinity would at least see her and thus give her a wide berth.

Both vessels had very sophisticated electronic surveillance equipment onboard. The technicians operating them were instructed to maintain a very careful Sonar coverage of the whole vicinity, both in front and on the side of each boat, and even below the surface. They knew they would see the *INS Dragon*, the Israeli submarine which had taken position close to the middle of the shipping channel, remaining submerged at maximum depth, to ensure full clearance for any kind of ship above her, and minimum risk that any such ship would detect it on their own sonar. However, David and Simon had worried that Iran might also call on one or two of their submarines if this was a trap. It was therefore absolutely crucial that any such submarine presence be identified before it could launch a torpedo, for instance.

The two Orcas had also been brought, via the submarine, to the area. Each would be stationed at most a couple of miles upstream and downstream of the *Sea Riches* relative to the tide in the Persian Gulf. Initially, they were released from the *INS Dragon* with a full set of buoyant mines that they set around the front and the side of the *Sea Riches* about a mile away in the direction from which Solomon should be coming. They did leave a small channel through which a boat, presumably Solomon's boat if he was legit, would be able to sail and reach Moshe's ship. However, the channel was also small enough that no other boat could come close enough.

Overhead surveillance was provided by an Eitan drone equipped with infrared vision capabilities. This would allow it to "see" any approaching vessel, as there was very little that one could do to hide the heat generated by the engines of speedboats. The Eitan was flying a figure-8 pattern centered on Moshe's boat, as the team had anticipated that Iranian speedboats, if there were going to be any, could literally attack from virtually any direction, except from behind The *Sea Dragon*. The mines which had been left at both ends of Qeshm Island, and which had trapped a Chinese cargo ship would probably ensure that no big Iranian navy vessel would be on the spot. However, with the number of harbors along the southern coast of Qeshm, and potentially also hidden behind Hengam Island, a great deal of care was an absolute necessity.

The first indication that something was not the way it was supposed to be came from the Eitan. It reported small flotillas of speedboats coming out of Messen and Suza from the starboard side of Moshe's ship and from the tip of Hengam on the port side. Simon swore under his breath:

"Solomon, you bastard. Glad we thought of that. Hope Farzad will make it safely to Baku."

The man with the monocular signaled that he could see a speedboat approaching from general direction of the stern of the *Sea Riches*.

David muttered:

"Action in less than ten minutes."

Then, on his radio, he barked:

"Everyone ready. It looks as if it is what we feared. Except we know they set up a trap for us, but they don't know we set one for them."

Captain Elihu Dayan instructed all the torpedoes on the *INS Dragon* to be armed and ready to fire. His sailors would turn on the power of the torpedo. At the same time, immediately prior to launch, the tube containing the torpedo would be flooded with seawater. Its pressure would be equalized with the outside sea pressure and the muzzle door opened. At the point of firing, water would be injected into the tube at high pressure, propelling the torpedo outside. Captain Dayan knew that he could fire up to four torpedoes at once, with a couple of minutes at most to reload new torpedoes into the tubes.

The *INS Dragon* sonar operator yelled:

"Submarine to starboard; distance 5 miles."

Captain Dayan, replied:

"Fire tubes 1 and 2."

A couple of minutes later, the sonar operator announced:

"Hit confirmed."

Simon looked at David and said:

"Hope there is no other one, but so far so good. They surely could not have expected this kind of fireworks."

The next call came from David who was receiving the live feed from the Eitan:

"Fast boats closing in from both sides, as well as in front. Hold a minute; I see the Iranian submarine surfacing . . . And a good part of the Suza flotilla is no longer coming our way. They're going to rescue the submariners. Yet, watch out for speedboats, still coming. "

Simon asked:

"Where is Solomon?"

"Still coming our way . . ."

Simon was pondering whether Solomon who he was now convinced had turned double agent would now try to turn back to Israel, effectively betraying the Iranians. He asked an assistant to check the passenger lists on any plane going from Bandar Abbas to Dubai:

"Any trace of the Bandari family?"

He knew it was going to take him a couple of minutes to get that information, but still hoped he would get it before having to make the decision to shoot or not to shoot at Solomon. His attention was captured for a short minute when his cell phone rang. He immediately picked it up and breathed a sigh of relief. Farzad was calling from Baku. Simon gave him the phone number he should call next, it belonged to Merv Stringer, *Mossad*'s station head in Baku, Azerbaijan. The story seemed increasingly, but quite sadly clear. He would still wait for his assistant to provide him with the answer to his question on the Bandari family. However, deep down, he felt he knew what the answer would be and what his decision had to be too.

In the meantime, the two Orcas had moved slightly forward and released two buoyant sets of mines each. These were expected to stop or at least slow down the flotillas, as their detonators were geared to the frequency of the underwater sound of speedboat engines. The flotillas were still at least four miles away, but that was about where the Orcas were. A number of mines exploded at ounce, sending boats as well as bits of boats high in the air. What was left of the flotillas slowed down but kept coming at a very slow pace. They chose to shoot from where they were. The speedboats did not carry missile launchers; however, they still had heavy machine guns and rocket launchers.

Simon decided that he had had enough of the whole thing. He had earlier ordered two Koveshes equipped with high altitude torpedo-bombs fly from Khafji in the direction of where he expected the action to be. He instructed the pilots to drop these bombs in the middle of the two flotillas. He never expected any of these bombs to score a direct hit, as the speedboats were relatively small and moving fast, but he was convinced that, as a group, both flotillas presented a large enough target that material damage would be inflicted. The first two bombs surprised the speedboats, which immediately stopped all forward progress. Though they remained on the scene, they were ostensibly awaiting further instructions. The second set of bombs hit closer to the targets. The Iranians should have thought of staying as far away from one another as possible. Rather, congregating as they did in a more compact group meant that more damage was inflicted. From afar, the sailor with the monocular was able to inform Moshe that all the small boats were now busy rescuing their comrades and thus no longer moving forward.

Simon received the information he had asked from his assistant. Sadly, but deliberately, he ordered:

"Sink Solomon's boat."

EPILOGUE

Previous such books have been written by my boss and mentor, Ariel. Ostensibly, he was too far removed from the action here to be able to do it this time. I must confess that he pushed me as hard as he has ever pushed me to write this. He knows that I hate to put myself forward and that, to me, teamwork is the word. Yet, in the end, Ariel convinced me. The clincher? This was a way to celebrate the exceptional work and dedication by so many members of my team. I should add that I take a real pleasure in observing how unlikely regional alliances can bring about significant change. I am surely not naïve enough to believe that all the various enmities that existed prior to the onset of this adventure have been put to rest. They have not, if only because no one wanted to win an absolute overwhelming victory. Such a victory would have disclosed high and low who the players were and that was exactly the opposite of the goal we all had going in.

Yet, some welcome change has taken place. Let me take the example of the Arab Israeli relationships. Clearly, no one has publicized who did what to whom and for what reason. Yet, once it became abundantly clear that Iran was behind the attempt to shoot down the Crown Prince's plane, Saudi Arabia lodged a formal complaint at the United Nations. The Security Council, surely, was not going to touch this one with a ten-foot pole. Everyone expected at least two vetoes, one from China and the other from the Russian

Federation and feared that only the U.S. would vote in favor among the other three permanent members. Well, we did see the expected Chinese and Russian vetoes, but everyone else voted against Iran. Whether this will or will not lead the country to change its behavior is clearly much too early to tell. Yet, one can hope. It could play a very important role if it chose to.

Interestingly, it never came out that our agent in Teheran, Farzad Ghasemi, was the one who had picked up the Iranian intentions to shoot down the Crown Prince's plane. Admiral Reza Pashtani and his colleague Admiral Javad Shahani of the Revolutionary Guards casually alluded to it riding together in Tehran in a car whose military driver happened to be one of Farzad's contacts. As to Farzad, I am happy to report that he is now on another assignment in the region, after having safely returned to Tel Aviv thanks to the help from Merv Stringer in Baku.

Similarly, Iran retaliated against Israel, using both regional missiles fired from Lebanon and Gaza, but also with ballistic missiles coming straight out of Iran itself. As anyone would expect none of them escaped the vigilance of the Iron Dome. A few fragments fell here or there and caused minimal damage; however, thank God, no loss of life or serious injury. Israel lodged a complaint at the UN. Again, we were not able to escape the obvious two vetoes, but we were immensely gratified to see a number of Arab countries, under the leadership of Saudi Arabia and the United Arab Emirates vote in favor of Israel. If that is not something historic, I wonder what we will have to see for something to be called historic. I am now absolutely sure that I shall see the day when the Arab world will consider Israel as a valid partner. We have so much to contribute to these countries and so much to learn from them.

I understand that there were some direct conversations between the U.S. and China. I am as surprised as anyone that nothing has leaked so far. Yet, I suspect that China has learned an important lesson. Superpowers do play their games around the margins of the zones of interest of their competitors. They should not attempt anything as obvious as what China seemed to have tried: someone was bound to respond, and no matter who is in the White House at the time, the risk of any miscalculation is simply too high.

Ostensibly, the great disappointment to me had to be the confirmation that Solomon had betrayed us. Unfortunately, we will never know why he did it as he probably sunk with his ship, though it is still remotely possible that, somehow, he survived and might even have been picked up by one of the Iranian boats. Thus, I can only speculate about why he would have become a double agent. Yet, I can make an educated guess thinking of a scenario which I have seen twice before and of which I have heard from others as well. The whole process would have started with Solomon being identified as a spy by the Iranians. I am convinced that he did not start as a double agent because some of the information he provided in his very early days working for us, right after he was recruited by Farzad, was simply too good to have been some form of bait for us. Of course, I cannot even guess at how he was picked out as a *Mossad* agent, as there are so many ways that anyone can slip up. Whether it was because he said at home something he should not have said and that led his wife to denounce him, or because he was actually pointed out by some Iranian spy of whom we and he ignored the identity, the next steps are unfortunately obvious. He must have been confronted and, probably because he was perceived to be a valuable plant, might have been offered to spy for Iran in exchange for his life or that of his family. Similarly, whether he retained some residual form of loyalty to Israel or not must remain unknown, as only he knew. One thing is for sure, he certainly was serving his Iranian masters well and what saved our sailors that were supposed to collect him at sea was the phone call from Farzad.

With respect to the financial market developments, or rather the way in which discussions had to be had between the various states that had been fighting in the shadows, I am afraid that most everything that actually happened took place behind closed doors. Indeed, everybody could see that the crypto world had lost quite a bit of credibility. Who knows, something good and productive might still come out of the disaster; the blockchain approach is still quite promising.

I know from Countess Renate that Nikolai had to use his influence at least once to put the market in its place. Interestingly, Nikolai and his family, after some hesitation, elected to relocate to Israel. I do not believe that his life was in any danger, but I share his view that the risk was serious that someone was going to "out him" as one of the creators of CryptNotes and, possibly, as one of those who orchestrated its demise. I am sure he will miss Brook's and the clubby atmosphere of London, as well as its world-famous entertainment scene. On the other hand, he probably will appreciate the climate in Israel and the fact that his children will be able to learn as much as they desire about their Jewish Faith. Finally, who knows? He might still relocate elsewhere, maybe even under a different identity . . .

As Ariel used to do, before concluding, I want to thank each and every one of the people whom I consulted as I wrote this story. Clearly, there were numerous circumstances where I was not in a meeting or missing in action somewhere. Particular thanks go to Countess Renate who agreed, for the purpose of the writing of this story, to take me a bit behind the scenes to cover the conversations she had with members of her team. I must, however, say that neither do I know where "somewhere in the Austrian Alps" is, nor do I know anything more than disclosed about the Shadow Experts. Beyond my thanks to her, I want to congratulate Countess Renate for the fabulous network she has created and for the incredibly high quality and dedication her teams bring to each crisis they accept to address.

I also want to thank all the *Mossad* members who participated in the various operations that took place, as well as the Israeli Defense Forces with whom they worked. Not only did they perform exceptionally well during the action which has been related here, but they also had to be discreet in the "clean up" actions that took place afterwards. They felt a responsibility to ensure that all navigation channels were open and safe without revealing their presence as they deactivated or exploded mines that had been left behind.

Finally, let me conclude by announcing the formal retirement of my predecessor, boss, mentor and friend, Ariel Landau. I am sure—and he has promised—that he will be available as an external, unpaid advisor if I need him. I surely do not believe him when he says that his advice will be worth every penny which I pay him. My successor as the Head of Disruption will be David Heller, although, as previously agreed, I will maintain a bit more of a focus on these activities. The name of my Chief Administrative Officer will be announced after he or she has formally accepted the position.

Signed: S.R.